BEN
and
BEATRIZ

BEN
and
BEATRIZ

KATALINA GAMARRA

GRAYDON
HOUSE

Recycling programs
for this product may
not exist in your area.

ISBN-13: 978-1-525-89995-9

Ben and Beatriz

Graydon House
22 Adelaide St. West, 41st Floor
Toronto, Ontario M5H 4E3, Canada
www.GraydonHouseBooks.com
www.BookClubbish.com

Printed in U.S.A.

For my grandfather—for being the only one of them to see me.

BEN

and

BEATRIZ

"Happy are they that hear their detractions and can put them to mending."

—William Shakespeare,
Much Ado About Nothing

"Ignorance is no protection from the consequences of inaction."

—Isabel Wilkerson,
Caste: The Origins of Our Discontents

MARCH 2017

1

BEN

"What makes you think the subway is a good place to flip through nudes?"

I look up to see Beatriz staring down at my phone. I start to say, "What the hell," but then she says, "Alexis from the philosophy department, Morgan from Alphi Phi *and* the girl who's been Hula-Hooping on the quad. How *do* you keep track of them all?"

"I have a bulletin board with red string connecting everyone, like on *Homeland*. Why do you care?"

Beatriz grits her teeth. "Because I heard Alexis crying about how you told her you liked her then never texted her back. And Morgan's been posting about how her new boyfriend actually wants to *be* her boyfriend. And right around the time you stopped publicly making out with her every goddamn day, Hula-Hoop Girl started an Instagram page on why final clubs should be abolished."

I blink. "You sure *you* don't have a bulletin board charting all my hookups? And aren't you snowflakes above slut-shaming?"

"I don't care how many people you sleep with, I care that you ghost them the second you've come. Keeping track of guys who treat women like they're disposable isn't hard. Especially when you have a sparkling reputation as Harvard's hottest misogynist."

Beatriz Herrera is the bane of my existence. She's got this way of looking at you that feels like she's about to cancel you for sneezing too loud, and she is so fucking hot that I wish I didn't care.

She's sitting next to me on the subway, her cousin Hero on her other side, while I'm next to Claudio—the whole reason I'm stuck next to Beatriz in the first place.

Claudio's been my roommate since freshman year. A streak he didn't want to break even though we're seniors and could totally have gotten singles.

"How many people are still bros with their first-year roommate?" He'd said when we got our housing forms last year. "That's fucking fate, man."

"Cool," I said, not letting on how psyched I was. We're in different majors, and I was worried we'd stop being friends if we didn't live together. Claudio's the only dude I talk to about shit I usually pretend not to feel—and I hate how much I need that.

But this year, Claudio wanted to bring Hero home with us for spring break since he finally made her his girlfriend after years of pining. But Hero wanted Beatriz along in case Claudio and I turn out to be serial rapists or something.

To be honest, I wasn't really listening because Claudio ran

all this by me last night just as a girl I recently ghosted strode toward us across the dining hall. So I mumbled, "Sure," then bolted. By the time I understood what I'd gotten myself into, we were rolling our suitcases to the Harvard Square T stop and it was too late.

"Are you intending to use the colloquial interpretation of *misogyny*—meaning 'lack of respect for women'—or the real definition, meaning 'hatred of women'? Because *hate* is not the word I'd use to describe how I feel about what women have to offer." I raise an eyebrow at Beatriz, but she turns away and takes out her phone.

But I spot an opening. "So you think I'm hot, huh?"

"Your head sure is."

"How long ago did you designate me one of Harvard's most bang-able?"

She snorts. "The fact that *that's* your takeaway makes the misogyny title oh-so well deserved."

"I'm just saying. In Latin last year, you called me a misogynistic twat, but this time you went with 'hot.' You trying to tell me something?"

"Fuck off, capitalist." She turns away to say something to Hero in Spanish. Hero smiles, tucking her blond hair behind her ears, and mumbles quietly back.

I've never met someone as shy as (or with a name as weird as) Hero. Every time she talks to me—which is not often—I feel like I need hearing aids.

Beatriz shoots me a final look of disgust before pulling a book out of her backpack. Only once has Beatriz acted like I don't repulse her, and that was our first night on campus.

When we had sex.

Beatriz is the last person I thought I'd attracted to—she's not skinny, her head's shaved, she has more attitude than my brother when a waiter takes over three minutes to take his order, and she—well—let's just say my family wouldn't approve. And it's just easier not to get on their bad side.

But I couldn't *not* notice Beatriz. She was wearing a shirt that said, "Fuck the Beats, Read Austen," and was the only girl at the orientation party who wasn't all over me when they heard who my dad was. I walked over to her and said, "If you'd actually read *On the Road*, you would find—"

She cut me off saying, "If you quote Jack Kerouac, I swear to god I will dump my beer over your head. At least go for Ginsburg, he was less of a twat." She walked away and I thought my groin would explode.

Later, we ended up near each other on the dance floor. Alcohol had dulled her rage, and when she looked at me, I could tell I wasn't the only one who felt something. I put my hands on her hips, and when she brushed her lips against my neck, all I could think about was getting her alone. The next thing I remember was being in my room, her mouth all over me, my body on fire, our lust pushing us together with an intensity I'd never experienced. And haven't since. Afterward, I vaguely remember cuddling—which I *never* do—and talking, but who knows what about.

Then I woke up to find Beatriz gone. Which was surprising because usually I have to make up an excuse to get girls to leave.

I saw her a week later, looking at her phone while a bunch of students waited in front of a locked classroom door. I glanced over my shoulder to make sure no one I knew was around and walked up to her.

"Hey."

And Beatriz looked at me with more disgust than I thought eyes were capable of emoting. The few times we've crossed paths over the three years since, she's made it clear that whatever was said between us could only result in bad blood.

And it drives me absolutely insane that I was too drunk to remember what it was.

My phone buzzes as we pull into our stop.

John: im here asshole

My stomach seizes. "He's here," I mumble to Claudio. He nods and leans around me to Hero.

"Ben's brother is here."

"Perfect timing." Hero seems to sink into herself as she smiles, her shoulders rising like they're mimicking the corners of her mouth.

Claudio blows her a kiss, and I try not to roll my eyes. I'm honestly surprised Claudio and I are as tight as we are. We couldn't be more different. He smiles all the time, except for when he cries at commercials about puppies finding a forever home.

Whereas I…don't. Crying is for war widows and smiling makes my jaw hurt.

I text John back as everyone exits the carriage and heads to the escalator. Where are you? In the station?

John: why do u text like your writing an essay

I clench my teeth. I don't. I text with proper grammar.

John: ppl r gonna think your uptight imagine that

Ben: Dude, just tell me where you are.

John: not until u—

I almost fall onto Beatriz. I'd been so caught up reading John's message that I didn't realize the escalator had ended.

"Jesus, have you never used one of these before?" Beatriz

asks, smirking. "Or are you used to a driver giving you door-to-door service?"

"You know, it says a lot about a person who, when someone else falls, chooses to be a dick instead of asking if they're okay." I stalk over to the next set of escalators before looking back at John's text.

John: not until u ask nicely

My jaw starts to hurt. Will you please fucking tell me where the fuck you are?

John: no

"Jesus Christ."

"What?" asks Claudio as he gets on behind me.

I hold my phone over my shoulder and Claudio takes it. "Bollocks," he says quietly. "Any idea where he might be?" When people first meet Claudio, they're confused to learn he's from Italy since he speaks with an English accent. But if you stop to think about it, it would be kind of weird if European countries taught their kids non-European English. The fact that he lives abroad is why he stays with me most major vacations.

"John fucking loves to do this." I shove my phone into my pocket, my stomach contracting when it vibrates again.

But it's not my brother.

Meg: T-MINUS TWO HOURS UNTIL I GET TO ANNOY THE SHIT OUT OF YOU

The corners of my lips twitch. Meg has been my closest friend since we were four.

But the idea of seeing her is just as stressful as it is exciting.

She often falls to pieces in ways that only I can pick up—and I've had to pick them up more times than I'd like to count.

"So, where's your brother?" Beatriz asks as we step off the escalator.

I check my phone but it's blank. Claudio saves my ass by saying, "He's not here yet."

"Didn't you say that he was when we were on the T?" Beatriz asks, turning to me. "What, you have a 4.0 but can't read a text?"

"Suck a dick, Beatriz!" My hands are shaking so much I almost drop my phone. "Can you not be a bitch to me for, like, five fucking seconds?"

"HEY."

It wasn't Beatriz who spoke, but Hero. She plants herself between me and her cousin, her voice loud enough to stop a train in its tracks. "Don't call her that."

I'm in such shock to hear something from Hero that doesn't require lip reading that all I can manage is, "I—I'm sorry."

Hero nods, her voice returning to three decibels. "So…is your brother here?"

I'm about to answer when someone's phone rings.

"It's me," says Claudio, fishing his phone out of his pocket.

My fists clench as I read the caller ID: John Montgomery.

"Hey, man," Claudio answers, glancing helplessly at me.

I walk away, depositing myself by a trash can. I unzip my backpack to see if I've got any pencils. When John winds me up like this, the only thing that can calm me down is snapping a shit-ton of pencils before locking myself in my room with *Pride and Prejudice*.

I would rather die than let anyone find out *that's* my favorite book instead of, say, *The Wolf of Wall Street*. But it's not my fault Jane Austen throws nineteenth-century shade that's too savage to ignore.

"We're, uh, at the station," I hear Claudio say. "Uh-huh. Alright. Laters."

I turn around as Hero and Beatriz head toward the elevators at the end of the platform.

"He said he always picks you up at the curb." Claudio starts rolling his suitcase after them. I give him a look and he sighs. "He also called you an Ivy League pussy."

"That's rich coming from a twenty-eight-year-old free-loading off his parents."

The elevator is packed, meaning that Beatriz crowds close enough to me that I can smell her. My body feels hot, and I can already tell it's going to be a long nine days.

BEATRIZ

So the thing about Ben Montgomery is that he's legitimately the most attractive person I've ever seen. He's exactly what you picture when you think, "hot, rich Harvard guy." He's tall, blond, ripped as a rower, I've seen him wear three different Rolexes on three different occasions, and he looks so good in maroon cashmere that I understand why some people marry rich.

But Jesus fucking Christ, I hate him so much.

He's obnoxious, he's pretentious, he's just plain wrong about most things, and every time I look at him, I'm reminded of the horrible, *shameful* fact that I've had sex with him. I was eighteen and dumb, but still. I don't usually want to bone dudes whose complicity secured Trump's win.

Not even Hero knows, which is why she didn't understand why I all of a sudden decided to hate the roommate of the guy she's been into since sophomore year. But she backed off when I told her it's because Ben's a dirty capitalist who represents everything wrong with this country. That shut her up.

BEN AND BEATRIZ

The first thing I see when the elevators slide open is a sleek black Tesla double-parked with its hazards on, blocking an entire lane of traffic.

"Asshole," I mutter. I've lived in Boston long enough to know that when an expensive car is inconveniently parked with its hazards on, there's a 1 percent chance it's stopped for an actual emergency, and a 99 percent chance it's because an entitled, rich asshole feels like finding an actual space is beneath them.

So it shouldn't surprise me when a tall, attractive guy jumps out of the car, yelling, "Little bro!" and jogs over to Ben. Ben looks uncomfortable as his brother pulls him into a one-armed hug, squeezing him so hard that the little body fat on his face is all scrunched up. His brother ruffles his hair as he lets go. Ben starts straightening it immediately.

Ben's six feet tall, but his brother towers over him, with dark brown hair that has a slight curl. He's not as ripped as Ben, but he clearly goes to the gym. I wonder if he's flexing his bicep on purpose as he says, "Sup, Claudio?" and daps him. Then he turns to Hero, raising his eyebrows. "Well, *hi*." *Gross.*

"Hi," she says politely.

"John," he says, holding out his hand. "You Ben's girl-friend?"

"Um, no," says Hero, looking taken aback.

She glances quickly at Claudio, who steps forward. "She's, um, mine."

"Nice one, dude," John says, thumping Claudio on the back. I hear him whisper, "Let me know if you wanna share."

Please die, I think as my jaw tightens, preparing to introduce myself next. But before I can say anything, John turns his back on me to lean against the car, asking Claudio how much he's been bench-pressing lately.

Hero and I exchange a look.

Cars behind us honk. John is blocking an entire lane of

traffic, but he's brushing lint off his crisp button-down as if the cars are nothing but gnats he has to ignore.

"Why the fuck did you park here?" Ben asks, waving apologetically at the angry drivers and opening the car trunk at top speed before throwing in his suitcase.

"Wanted it to be convenient for my little man's homecoming," says John, winking at Hero as he lazily tosses her suitcase in after Ben's. Hero gives him a tight-lipped smile before opening the back door and climbing in.

"I'll take that, man," John says, reaching for Claudio's roller bag and tossing it in.

But as I make to chuck mine in, too, John shuts the trunk without looking at me and walks back to the driver's seat.

I narrow my eyes. This has been my life since moving to Cambridge—wealthy white people acting like I'm not here.

Hero and I are both mixed. My mom and her brother, my Uncle Leo, both partnered Latinx people, but Hero's mom, who died when she was a baby, was Puerto Rican, and my dad's from Panama. At least, that's what Uncle Leo says. I've never actually met my dad.

Uncle Leo's white skin combined with light-skinned Puerto Rican genes means that Hero was born with sharp blue eyes and blond hair that never darkened. We're only fluent in Spanish because Leo has had us in bilingual schools since pre-K, so we "wouldn't forget our roots."

But my dad's dark, Indigenous skin made me unmistakably brown. And I was only four when I learned that that's all some people can see.

I'm about to open the trunk again when someone beats me to it. I look up to see Ben's fingers pressing the Tesla logo, and the trunk eases open.

"Sorry," he says, his eyes surprisingly kind. "He's just—he can be—"

For a second, I'm reminded of the Ben who kissed me freshman year. Who pulled me into a shitty twin bed, gasping that he'd never wanted anyone so much. For a second, I'm the Beatriz who pulled him to my chest as we—

"I can take that." Ben slowly reaches for the handle of my suitcase, lingering before he takes it so I have a chance to refuse. And I'm so shocked by this consideration that I don't.

Ben closes the trunk, gives me an awkward smile, then opens the back passenger door, waiting for me to go in first.

"The middle? Seriously?" I say, raising an eyebrow at him.

"I just figured you'd prefer being between Hero and me instead of trapped beside a dirty capitalist," he says coldly, the earnestness of mere seconds ago already gone. "So you can have girl talk or whatever."

This is why I don't hook up with cis white guys. "I'll sit in the middle," Hero says from inside the car. "Bea, ven por este lado."

I glare at Ben before walking around to the other side of the car and sitting next to Hero.

"Everyone cozy enough back there?" John asks as he starts the car. "I'd tell you to put your seat belts on, but I don't give a fuck."

A Top 40 radio station blasts through the speakers as we finally unclog the lane. In the distance, the skyline looks so pretty at dusk that I look out the window for a few minutes before my phone goes off. Hero's texting me in Spanish— we're too densely packed to be sure of a private conversation.

Hero: Did John ask Claudio if he wanted to share...me?

Beatriz: yeah i almost castrated him on the spot

Hero: Did you hear what Claudio said back?

Beatriz: no. do i need to castrate him too?

Hero: I didn't hear either. I was asking

Beatriz: ah

Hero: I wish I could ask Claudio about it

Beatriz: i mean u could

Hero: I feel like he wouldn't like that. I mean, he didn't say it TO me, so it's not really any of my business

This kind of shit is why Claudio has yet to earn my seal of approval—I just don't get the vibe that Hero feels safe with him. Which is saying a lot because they've been tight for a *while*. They met sophomore year when Hero needed tutoring for her Italian class, and now it's March of our senior year. For *years*, Claudio has been all Hero could talk about.

"Claudio's actually from Italy! How cool is that?"

"Claudio just spent five hours watching *Gilmore Girls* with me, and he really likes it! I've never met a guy who would admit that!"

It could not have been clearer that Hero was *so* into him, but it took Claudio almost two years to ask her out.

And the fact that Hero's a virgin and doesn't do casual sex is the only reason I can think of as to why.

Beatriz: so? dont couples share everything with each other?

Hero: This already isn't going how I hoped it would

Beatriz: we'll be fine ♥

I glance up at Hero and see Ben peeking down at her phone. I roll my eyes and start a new message.

Beatriz: unless ur suddenly fluent in spanish u wont be able to read that

Ben: I'm blindly assuming this is Beatriz. How the hell do you have my number?

Beatriz: u gave it to me

Ben: When?

Beatriz: when the fuck do u think?

Ben goes red. His thumb hovers over the keyboard.

Ben: If you kept my number in the hopes of getting in my pants, get in line. Your bulletin board knows how many girls got there first.

I grit my teeth and shove my phone into my pocket. A misogynist indeed. I just wish I could forget about the "hot" part.

2

BEN

After an hour that feels like forever, we're finally home. My muscles relax as we drive through the streets of Chatham on Cape Cod, and I remember that my parents are out of town for a few weeks. Maybe I'll actually get to relax without Dad around to breathe down my neck.

I see my huge beachfront house looming in the distance and remember how close I am to my own bed. College beds fucking suck. I usually end up going down on girls on the floor.

"Alright, alright, alright." John channels Matthew McConaughey as he parks the car in the garage, like he's not already enough of a poser. I open the car door and stretch.

I look up to see John winking at Hero and hoisting her bag over his shoulder like it weighs nothing. Claudio narrows his eyes.

I walk up the garage stairs and into the kitchen. Where I'm

instantly tackled by a tiny person dressed completely in black with a face of eyeliner-heavy makeup.

"YOU'RE HOOOOOOOME!"

"Jesus, Meg!" I say, breathing heavily as I look down. Meg's grinning up at me. Her short hair—that has never been its natural black since we were twelve and she forced me to dye it neon blue—is streaked with pink and pulled into a ponytail. "Why do you do that?"

"Why do you think, mate?" Meg says, letting go and punching me on the shoulder. No part of Meg is British, but she's so obsessed with movies and TV from across the pond that she regularly sneaks British slang into conversation. She fucking *loves* Claudio.

Beatriz introduces herself and extends her hand, which Meg takes. "And this is my cousin, Hero," Beatriz adds.

"Hero? As in super?" Meg asks. "I've never heard that one before."

"It's a family name," Hero mumbles.

"Cool!" Meg grins before starting to jump up and down. "I'm so excited! I didn't know there'd be the possibility of girl time! I thought I'd be stuck with just this one for a week," she says, elbowing me.

"Ow." I glance at Beatriz, but she's staring at her phone.

Meg rolls her eyes. "You guys want a tour?" she asks Hero and Beatriz.

I run my hand over my face. "Meg, you don't even live here." But she's leading Hero and Beatriz into the foyer before I finish talking.

I turn to see that Meg's brother, Peter, is here too. It's not surprising I didn't notice him. He's so reserved he makes Hero look like Miss Bates from *Emma*.

As Peter daps John up, I watch money slide from his palm to my brother's.

I turn to follow Meg, Beatriz and Hero. Plausible deni-ability.

"Okay, so that was the kitchen," Meg is saying as she skips down the hall with Beatriz and Hero in tow.

I glance over my shoulder to see Claudio rolling his suitcase toward the room he stays in whenever he's here.

"That's the living room," Meg says, pointing into the cav-ernous family room no one uses.

"Fancy," Beatriz mumbles. Our eyes lock, and guilt over our text exchange in the car punches me in the stomach. I lied. She can skip the line of girls banging down my door anytime she wants. Too bad it's clearly the last thing she wants to do.

"But the place we all hang out is on the second floor," says Meg, bounding up the spiral staircase and into the den. "Here!"

"Whoa." Beatriz's mouth falls open.

I look away from her and try to see the den with fresh eyes. It's less a room and more an entire floor dedicated to recreation. Two sectionals make a square in the middle of the room, with a coffee table between them and a pool table on the left. The right side is flanked by a bar—not a minibar, but a well-stocked dry bar with full-size liquor bottles on display like in a restaurant. A two-lane bowling alley occupies the long corridor by the wall of windows, and a huge flat-screen TV where Claudio and I play video games is mounted on the wall across from them.

"And down at this end…" Meg runs to the back of the den, opening the door of the home theater.

"Hoooly shit," Beatriz says softly. "You…you can have this in your *home*?" She stares around the room, her eyes stopping when they land on me.

I leave with a shrug, walking through the den and down the hall to my room. I unzip my bag, pushing clothes aside until I get to the books hidden at the bottom. Books college seniors aren't supposed to still read—Percy Jackson, The Heroes of Olympus and The Kane Chronicles.

After I've unpacked, I head back to the hall. I'm about to check my email when a voice behind me says, "Well, this explains why you dress like Jared Kushner."

I whip around and Beatriz is leaning against the wall by my room.

"Uh…" I look behind her but Hero's not there "…you looking for something?" I ask, flicking my eyes between Beatriz and my bedroom door.

She rolls her eyes. "Don't be gross. Turns out Meg wants a back tattoo. And Hero's starting an apprenticeship at a tattoo parlor next year, so they're vibing like crazy."

I'm shocked. "Hero wants to be a tattoo artist?"

"Yeah," Beatriz says, like it's obvious. "Why?"

"Just doesn't seem like she'd have time, what with trying to get Claudio whipped."

Beatriz's eyes go dark, and her eyebrows narrow. "See, this is exactly why I'm here," she says, coming closer. "Of course you would think an attractive, quiet woman could only have ambitions tied to a man. How could she ever have ambitions of her own?"

"I mean—" I *don't* think that, but when Beatriz is mad at me her chest starts heaving and her eyes do this thing that is equally scary and sexy. It's probably why I provoke her so much.

"Watch it, asshole," she breathes. "If Claudio hangs out with *you*, no fucking way is he good enough for my prima."

Annnnd this is why provoking her ends up pissing *me* off. She always finds a way to make it clear I'm a problem that doesn't deserve a solution. "Whatever."

I start to climb the staircase to the third floor, but I stop when Beatriz leans against the railing and says, "So is it we-came-over-on-the-*Mayflower* money, or daddy's-the-vice-president-of-Amazon? You live on West Egg or East?"

Wait, did she just reference *The Great Gatsby*?

I look down at her. Her sweatshirt is snug, and I have to make a conscious effort to not stare at the way it hugs her curves. It's also pretty sexy that she casually sneaks in references to classic literature when she's roasting me.

"Go hang out with your cousin if I'm such a shithead," I say, swallowing and willing my eyes to stay on hers.

"I would, but shockingly I'd rather put up with your arrogant bullshit than hear Hero explain the difference between stick-and-poke and line art to your booty call."

"Wha-a-t?" My mouth forgets what words are. "Meg's not— Dude, she's like my *sister*."

Beatriz just raises an eyebrow at me.

"She is! Do you not believe me?"

"Not really."

"Why not?"

"Because you seem like exactly the kind of guy who would have girls in every port. I mean...you certainly lost no time freshman year."

My stomach lurches. It's the first time she's acknowledged out loud that we've had sex. Sure, she alluded to it in the car, but there's something about hearing the words cloaked in her sharp voice that makes my mind spin.

Does that mean she gets drunk and replays it over and over in her head like I do?

And if so, does she...want to do it again?

She's infuriating, but hate sex is not something I'm opposed to.

I open my mouth, but before I can say anything, Hero's

voice calls from down the hall: "Trizita! We're gonna order food!"

Without another word, Beatriz walks back to the den. I watch her go, unable to ignore how perfect her ass is.

God. I need a drink.

BEATRIZ

I almost regret being the only person sober. Hero and I had a celebratory Midterms Are Over happy hour last night, and while Hero stopped herself after a respectable three glasses of white wine, I downed a liter of vodka. I'm pretty sure my body will murder me if I put any booze in it tonight.

But Jesus Christ, drunk people are annoying.

"Beatriiiiiiiz, why aren't you drinking?" Meg asks. She's on her fourth drink, and given that she's maybe five foot one, she's toasted.

"Just don't feel like it." I bite into a dumpling. John ordered Chinese food, not failing to mock Hero and me for only ordering the "American Chinese food." We got fried rice and dumplings. It's our take-out order every Friday at home when we hunker down with Uncle Leo in the living room to watch rom-coms, like we have ever since I was nine and moved in with them. It's mostly ninety minutes of Hero and Leo being all *aww, love* and me going, *ugh, this is gross* but secretly enjoying the family time.

The closest thing I got to family time with my mom was cleaning the kitchen by myself after she made dinner because "I cooked, so you do dishes." Which was nuts because I was six and had no idea what qualified as dishes being "clean." I think I even got sick from eating off a germy plate, which made my mother yell at me for not being smart enough to clean all the grease off.

I'll take cringey rom-coms any day.

Everyone else ordered what John called "authentic Chinese cuisine," like he was the authority on the subject, as opposed to the actual Chinese people in the room. That was an hour and two margarita pitchers ago. The second pitcher was drunk entirely by Ben and John, the latter of whom is at the counter making a third. Hero and Claudio are just buzzed enough to be staring adoringly at each other and laughing at jokes no one else gets. Peter's just started slurring, and Meg is *sloshed*. I've never seen someone so red. Her whole face, chest and shoulders are the color of an overripe tomato.

"Is she okay?" I ask the table in general. I look up to see Ben's eyes dart away from me. Again.

Ben keeps looking at me in a way I don't like. And I know he's not just staring into space, because every time I meet his eye, he looks away hurriedly, like a middle schooler caught staring at something shameful.

"Sh-she'ss *fine*," Ben slurs, his tone making it clear it's a stupid question.

I clench my fists under the table. I turn toward Hero, but she's playing hangman on a take-out napkin with Claudio and doesn't notice me.

I look around the room, the loneliness I'd been dreading finally settling in. Everyone here has somebody—Hero has Claudio, Ben has Meg (jury's still out on if they're fucking), and John's got Peter. I realize that I've pretty much agreed to spend nine days shut up in a strange house with no one but myself for company. It makes me feel so shitty, I could cry.

If I was the kind of person who cried.

Instead, I get up and leave the kitchen, Ben's eyes on my back. Once in my room, I text Uncle Leo.

BEN AND BEATRIZ

Beatriz: sup

Leo: Trizita! How are you, mija?

I smile. Even though Leo's white as hell, he's always used Spanish names of endearment.

Beatriz: fine. Heros good too

Leo: Awesome! How are the digs?

I look around at the twin bed that creaks whenever I move, the slanted ceiling I've already hit my head on three times, and my backpack, which I've thrown all the way across the room but can still reach without getting up.

John insisted on "being a good host" and taking everyone's luggage to their rooms for them. Which was how I ended up in what I'm pretty sure is a storage closet barely converted into a guest room.

Hero, on the other hand, is staying in a master bedroom with an attached bathroom and Jacuzzi. Wonder how that happened.

Beatriz: its fine

Leo: Glad to hear it. I miss you, honey ♥

Beatriz: miss u too

Leo: Call me any time, okay?

I won't, but it's still nice to be reminded.

Beatriz: okay

Leo: I love you ♥

Beatriz: love u too

I pull out some textbooks and start reading the first assignment for the day we go back. I'm halfway through when my phone goes off.

Hero: Where are you?

Beatriz: studying

Hero: Nerd ♥

Beatriz: more like bored

Hero: Come back then!

Beatriz: nah, im good

Hero: Want me to come to you? We can watch something, I'll even let you choose something scary

I smile as warmth spreads through me. But this room barely fits one person, let alone two.

Beatriz: no its ok i'll come down

Hero: You sure?

Beatriz: yeah

I close the textbook and stretch before heading down the stairs. I'm just passing the den when I hear a soft, "Hi."

I look around and see Hero sitting by herself on one of the couches.

"Where is everyone?" I asked, hoping it might just be the two of us.

"They're in the theater. I came out so you wouldn't go all the way back downstairs." Hero smiles and squeezes my hand. "They're watching *Iron Man…2*? *3*?"

I laugh. "Dude, you haven't seen, like, any Marvel movies, how do you know it's an *Iron Man* one?"

"I texted Claudio as it was starting. He told me."

I look at her quizzically. "Why did you text him instead of just asking?"

Hero blushes.

"Oh my god, what?"

"We…we just got into the habit of texting during movies."

I frown. "Even when you're next to each other?"

"Yes."

"Why?"

Hero looks at the floor. Man, she's really embarrassed.

"I…I have an easier time flirting if I don't have to say it out loud," she mumbles.

It takes all my willpower not to burst out laughing.

"Don't laugh!" says Hero, pushing my shoulder.

"I'm not!"

"But you want to."

"That's just the cutest thing I've ever heard." Even though Hero's twenty-two, Claudio is her first boyfriend. Honestly, I wouldn't be surprised if he's her first kiss. So it's no shock that, even though they're together, she's still shy about flirting with him.

I've only been in one relationship and quickly learned that all they accomplish is complicating what would otherwise be great sex. So why bother.

"Yeah, yeah." Hero's phone buzzes. She pulls it out of her pocket and smiles.

"Alright, let's get in there so you can pretend you don't know your knee is touching Claudio's for the rest of the movie."

3

BEN

"What?" says Claudio.

I tear my eyes away from Beatriz as she and Hero enter the theater. Claudio's looking at me like I did something bizarre.

"Huh?"

"You just inhaled, like, really sharply," he says as Hero sits beside him, Beatriz next to her.

"I did?"

"Yep."

"Headache," I say quickly.

When *Iron Man 2* is done, I put in the third one while John goes downstairs to get more drinks. I feel the start of an actual headache. As soon as John goes to bed, I'm switching to water. I'd do it now, but I don't want to deal with John calling me a pussy.

Hero and Claudio leave about halfway through, their hands

bumping against each other. Peter slouched out hours ago, and I look around the theater to realize that it's just Meg, Beatriz and me. Must have missed John leaving.

Or maybe John left with Peter and I blocked it out because I know what they get up to when my parents leave for a few weeks. And I don't want anyone else to find out.

I grab my water bottle—which had started the evening full of gin—and head down to the kitchen. I hold out my arms and sock surf down the hardwood floors because no one is around to make fun of me for it.

I've always loved my house at night. When no one else is up, I feel—calm, I guess, in a way I never do during the day. I can munch on popcorn while reading *The Lightning Thief* at the island without worrying Dad will walk by, saying, "That girl who left this morning—she'll fatten up our genes." When the girl in question was a size three.

I rinse the last of the gin from my water bottle before filling it all the way up.

I'm halfway back up the stairs when I hear pounding feet above, like someone's sprinting down the hall. I walk faster, taking the stairs two at a time, and almost collide with Beatriz.

"Hey—what's wrong with you?"

Her eyes are wide, and she's pulling at her fingers like she's trying to yank them from the sockets.

"Meg's not okay." Beatriz's voice is high, and if she wasn't her, I'd think she was close to tears.

I take the stairs more quickly. "She's still in the theater?"

"Yeah."

"When you say she's not okay, I assume you mean she's passed out and covered in puke?"

"Yeah." Beatriz sounds surprised. "She threw up in her sleep, like right after you left. How did you—"

"I've got it." I run through the den, yank the theater doors open and flip on the lights.

I can smell it before even entering the room. "Christ." I pull my shirt over my nose and walk down the first row to the last seat, where Meg is passed out. "Meg," I say, kneeling down so my face is level with hers.

Her hair is splayed everywhere, makeup sweated off, her black tank top covered in vomit. I look at the floor and see multiple piles of puke, as well as clear liquid she must have thrown up when she'd emptied her stomach.

"Shit, shit, shit, SHIT. Meg. You need to fucking wake up." Meg doesn't move.

"MEG!" I yell, gently tapping her face with my fingers.

She's still. I place my thumb against the back of her wrist. Her pulse is still going, thank god.

"Is she—"

I jump and look around. Beatriz is still here.

"She's okay, but I need to take her to the ER, like *now*."

I hoist Meg from the chair gently but quickly, sliding my arms behind her back and knees—just like I've done every year since we were fifteen. Meg somehow manages to keep it together when I'm at school, but it's like the minute I come home she becomes the person I hoped she was done being.

Vomit starts to soak into my shirt, and I know I'll be mouth breathing for the rest of the night.

"At least get the door if you're gonna gawk at us," I say to Beatriz, slowly getting to my feet.

Beatriz mutters something undoubtedly snarky but gets the door. "You're not driving, are you?" she says at a normal volume.

"Of course I am. She needs to go to the hospital."

"Dude, you've been drinking all night!" Beatriz follows me down the stairs.

"I'm fine! I've done this multiple times a year since I learned to drive."

Beatriz doesn't say anything but keeps following me.

"Fuck, where are my keys?" I look at the spot on the kitchen counter where I always toss them, but they're not there.

"These them?"

I turn as much as I can while still holding Meg and see Beatriz holding the Porsche keys.

"Yes, thank god, give 'em here."

Beatriz doesn't move.

"BEATRI—"

"I'm driving."

Beatriz pushes past me and through the garage door so fast, she's all the way to the bottom of the stairs before I even start to follow.

"The fuck you are," I say, adjusting my grip on Meg as I reach the last stair. But Beatriz is already sitting in the driver's seat with the car started.

"Jesus fuck." I walk to the back door, and Beatriz opens it from the front.

"You should sit with her," she says, as I buckle Meg in. "Just tell me where to go."

"Fine." I slam the door and get in on the other side. "Turn right out of the driveway."

I expect Beatriz to say something bitchy about how crazy it is that I'd drive after drinking, but she's quiet the whole way. I also thought I'd have to tell her to go faster, but Beatriz goes at least ten miles over the speed limit the entire drive, speeding up at yellow lights and even running a few red ones.

We get to the hospital faster than I've ever gotten us here.

"I'll park and meet you inside," Beatriz says as she pulls up to the emergency room doors.

Beatriz drives off the second Meg's in my arms, and I head for the automatic doors.

"God, again?" says the receptionist as I approach the desk. Before I can respond, he waves his hand toward the seating area. It's empty, which isn't that surprising, given that it's almost three in the morning during the Cape's off-season.

A few nurses come out pushing a stretcher. It's not until I've set Meg down and she's wheeled out of sight that the panic starts.

Yeah, Meg does this a lot. But every time, I'm worried it's going to be the day she doesn't wake up. Even though she assures me that she's not an alcoholic, she just likes to party. A lot. Starting when we were, like, fourteen.

I try deep breathing, but all that does is fill my nose with the smell of bile. I look around to make sure I'm alone because I can feel it starting—the pain in my chest that I can't control, that's going to end in something humiliating.

The receptionist is gone, the waiting room empty. I sit down and start to cry. Gross, snotty crying that clogs my nose and makes my eyes hurt—crying that leaves my head throbbing because my alcohol-ridden body is already dehydrated.

I don't know how long I'm sitting there being a weak-ass motherfucker, but next thing I know, someone says, "Um, hey."

I jump and look around. Beatriz is standing there, holding a plastic shopping bag in one hand.

Perfect. Fan-fucking-tastic. Now she can add "cries in public" to the list of things about me that repulse her.

"Oh, hey." I look away. "I think I'm allergic to…linoleum."

"Okay," Beatriz says in a clipped voice. It makes me feel even worse.

I hear the plastic bag rustle and turn around. Beatriz is holding out a Kleenex packet. I just stare.

"I came in earlier and you seemed…" She trails off, and I look away. "Well, I got a couple of these at the 7-Eleven across the street. Thought they might be helpful."

I nod. Beatriz puts the bag at my feet before taking out her phone. I look down and realize it's not empty. In addition to tissues, there's also a packet of Cheetos and a bottle of Mountain Dew. I snort. Beatriz could not have picked more stereotypically "guy" snacks. She'd have given me so much shit if I'd picked these out for myself.

I open my mouth to point this out, but she stiffens before I can say anything, and I pause. She *did* get these out of the goodness of her heart, or whatever. It'd be pretty shitty to make her feel bad for it.

"Thanks." I blow my nose before taking out the Mountain Dew. "Want some?"

She hesitates, then says, "Sure."

I screw the cap back on when Beatriz is done and offer her the bag of Cheetos. She takes a couple before going back to her phone.

I don't know how long we sit there, scrolling through different social media feeds, but eventually Beatriz yawns. "Tired?" I ask.

"No, I'm yawning because I'm wide—" She stops. "Um—yeah, a bit."

"You could take a nap." I check my phone. "Christ, it's late."

"I'm fine." Beatriz stands up to stretch. Her sweatshirt rides up, exposing her stomach. I see curved marks on her skin, but she lowers her arms before I can figure out what they are.

"You really do this all the time?" Beatriz digs her palms into her eyes. "Sounds exhausting."

Her tone pisses me off. "Only a couple times a year."

42

"Oh, sor*ry*," Beatriz says, her voice dropping sarcastically. "What a huge difference."

"If you're going to be a bitch, just go."

"Seriously, how do you get so much action?" Beatriz's hands rest aggressively on her hips. "Or do you only fuck sorority girls?"

"I don't remember *you* complaining much," I shoot back.

Her nostrils flare. She opens her mouth but doesn't say anything.

And for once, I want her to.

"I'd love to fuck off," she finally says. "But I drove us here. And your dumb ass is drunk."

"Am not."

"Whatever. I'm not leaving." Beatriz sits down angrily, as if to prove the point.

I make a noise I hope comes off like contempt, but probably sounds more like a sniffle. As Beatriz plays what sounds like an Instagram story, I realize this is the first time I'm not alone in an ER waiting room, wondering if Meg is dead or alive.

The last time it happened—the last night of Thanksgiving break—Claudio had been asleep. I didn't want him to think Meg's some kind of deranged alcoholic, so I didn't wake him.

But Beatriz came looking for me the second something was wrong, and she insisted on getting us here safely. And now, when I'm purposefully being a little bitch, she's sticking around.

My face heats up. "Sorry," I mumble to her shoes.

Beatriz looks up, surprised but unfazed. "Thanks."

I glance at her. She's slouched in her chair, her legs spread out, one hand cradling the back of her head while the other holds her phone.

As I watch her scroll, a weird thought pops into my head—I *want* to talk. Maybe it's because it's nearly four in the morning.

Or maybe it's because she's already seen me bawling my eyes out, so the chances of her thinking I've got my shit together are already shot. Or maybe it's because being alone with Beatriz in a room away from gossip and exams and stress, makes the idea of talking to her less unappealing.

Or maybe I'm just drunk.

"It…does happen a lot," I say, turning to face her.

She closes whatever she was watching and looks at me. "Yeah?"

I nod.

"Since you guys were in high school?"

I frown. "How did you know that?"

"Back at the house, you said something about doing this since you could drive."

"Oh. Yeah. I guess I forgot."

"I mean, a lot of stressful shit has happened in the last hour."

"I guess." I hug my knees to my chest, resting my chin on them. If John were here, he'd tell me to stop sitting like a girl.

"You alright?" Beatriz asks.

"No," I say quietly.

Beatriz doesn't say anything for a second.

"I don't know what to do in situations like this," she bursts. "Usually I would just not say anything and hope you wouldn't bring it up again, but my therapist says that can make people feel like their feelings aren't important—and that I should just be honest about why I'm uncomfortable and shit. So…I guess I wish I was equipped to do more, and I'm sorry I'm not."

I sit up. "You're in therapy?"

"Yeah, why?" Beatriz says, instantly defensive.

"I just…would've pegged you as someone who doesn't believe in therapy."

"That excuse runs out real fast when you have a shit childhood." Beatriz's eyes glaze over as she looks at the ground.

"You seem fine," I say, trying and failing to keep scorn from my voice. Beatriz glares at me. "I'm not trying to be insensitive or whatever, I genuinely don't get it."

"Just because people act happy doesn't mean they are," says Beatriz. "I mean, look at you."

I let that wash over me. I suddenly realize that this is the most real conversation I've ever had—not just with Beatriz, but with anyone—which was the last place I thought this evening would go.

"So," I say because I don't want her to know that what she just said resonated. "What do you have lined up for next year?"

Beatriz narrows her eyes. "Nothing. Yet, I mean."

"What?" I'm shocked. "But—you're smart."

She rolls her eyes. "Gee, thanks. All my academic work has been in the hopes you would realize Latinx women are indeed intelligent."

My chest seizes. "What? I didn't—I don't think—"

But Beatriz is smirking at me. "Fuck you," I say, trying not to smile. "It just doesn't make sense that you wouldn't have gotten a job offer," I say, so she doesn't notice.

The mirth in her eyes is gone. "The hell is that supposed to mean?"

"Just… I've had classes with you and—" I hope I'm not blushing "—you, uh—always have smart-ish things to say, so—"

"Wow, fuck you, asshole," she says.

"I mean—" Shit. "Just—"

"Do you have any idea how hard it is to get a job right now?" she bursts, sitting up. "If everyone who was 'smart-ish'—" she puts air quotes around the words "—got a job immediately after college, we wouldn't be wrecked with student loans for ten-plus years." She looks disgusted with me again. "You probably got a job handed to you, right?"

A six-figure position at my dad's firm in the financial district in Boston. And a penthouse apartment that the firm pays for. But I feel like I should keep that to myself.

I shrug.

Beatriz rolls her eyes and checks her phone. "Hand me the Dew, would you?"

I toss it to her, and she takes a swig. I drain the bottle when she hands it back. We're on our phones for the next few hours, my eyelids slowly growing heavier and heavier. The next thing I know, a female voice is saying, "Mr. Montgomery?"

I jerk awake and see a doctor standing in front of me, the pink light of early morning floating through the windows. I try to sit up, then realize something feels off.

Beatriz is asleep, her head on my shoulder.

Something warm spreads through my stomach, and I wonder if I have to pee.

"Yes?" I say to the doctor.

"Margaret Xie can go home now."

"She's okay?" I ask, realizing too late that it's a redundant question. But the doctor seems unfazed.

"Yep. But it was close this time," she says seriously. "I gave her some information about Alcoholics Anonymous. I strongly suggest she look into it."

I nod. "Right, okay. Thanks."

"She'll be out in a second."

The doctor disappears, and I feel Beatriz yawn. I want to say "hi" or "hey" or something, but I'm 99 percent sure that the second Beatriz wakes up, she'll take her head off my shoulder. And my shoulder is cold.

Beatriz moves groggily, her eyes slowly blinking open. "Why am I sideways?" she says, her voice heavy. I smile to myself as Beatriz raises her head. "Sorry," she says quickly. "I guess I passed out. Also, you *reek*."

I look down. My clothes are puke stained.

"No one asked you to sleep on me," I say, even though the sight of her, all sleepy and confused, makes my heart beat faster. "Meg's gonna be out soon," I say before Beatriz can snark back.

"Oh good. She's okay?"

I snort. "Obviously."

"Well, I don't know, dude! For all I know, they could be releasing her just for us to take her to rehab."

"She doesn't need rehab!"

"I didn't say she did."

"Well, you were implying—"

"I was implying that your booty call almost died last night, and asking if—"

"God, I'm *not* sleeping with her! Why do you keep saying that?"

Beatriz scoffs. "No, you're right, she's not your type."

"And what *is* my type?" I ask, crossing my arms.

"Morgan, and Alexis, and Hula-Hoop Girl, and—"

"So my type is girls I've fucked?"

"Your type is whi—" But she stops. My heart thuds in my chest because I think I know what she was about to say and I want to tell her it's not true. Beatriz just stares at me. I'm about to tell her how wrong she is when she says, "I'm getting a drink of water." Beatriz leaves her chair so aggressively it thuds a little against the floor. Right after she turns the corner, Meg comes out from the other direction. She's dressed in hospital-issued garb and clutching a bag full of her soiled clothes.

She's crying before she even reaches me.

"I'm so sorry, Benny," she wails, covering her face with her free hand. "This is the last time. It's been seven fucking years. I *hate* doing this to you, I—"

"It's okay." What Beatriz said is still ringing through my head, but I push it away. Focus on Meg. I squeeze her shoulders, which shake with sobs. This is as much a part of the routine as getting her here. Every time, she hates doing this to me, and every time is the last time.

"I'm trying to stop." Meg's voice cracks. "But every time I think I've got it, I just—"

Beatriz reappears but stops walking when she sees Meg. The anger on her face slips and she looks at me questioningly.

I jerk my head over my shoulder, indicating that she should come over.

"Hey, Beatriz is here," I whisper to Meg, who stops talking and starts frantically wiping her tears. "She drove us."

Meg turns as Beatriz reaches us.

"You good?" Beatriz says, nodding at Meg.

"Yeah. Thanks for getting me here." Meg smiles like she wasn't in the middle of spilling her guts to me. She hugs Beatriz, and I have to bite my lip to keep from laughing because Beatriz looks like someone's just dumped a bucket of water over her head while she's fully clothed.

She mouths, *Shut up*, over Meg's head at me. I look away so she doesn't see I'm smiling.

Meg finally releases Beatriz, who looks relieved, and we head home.

Everyone's still asleep as we trudge through the kitchen and up the stairs.

"Well, night," says Meg, collapsing onto a couch in the den.

"Night." Beatriz walks with me down the hall, and I pause outside my room. "Well, I'm gonna fall straight into bed and sleep until dinner."

"Uh, you might want to change first," Beatriz says, looking me up and down. "You're still covered in puke."

God, right. The stench has been on me so long I've gotten used to it.

"Oh god. I should probably wash it now." I groan and let my head fall back so I'm facing the ceiling. "I'm so tired—"

"Ugh, I'll help you."

"What?" I open my eyes to stare at Beatriz, shocked. "You don't have to do that."

"Well, if I don't, you'll probably end up bleaching your shirt."

"I know how to do laundry, Beatriz. It's not the 1950s anymore. I can do basic household tasks."

"I'm not saying you can't do laundry, I'm saying you're tired." Beatriz crosses her arms. "Just show me where the laundry room is."

"Uh…" I wrack my brain, but nothing comes to mind. I think harder, and then it hits me—I have no idea where the laundry room is because I've never done laundry at my house. Mom or a maid always has.

"Oh fuck, do you not *know*? No wonder rich white dudes are defacing the working class—they were never taught what actual work is," Beatriz says.

"Look, I didn't choose to have money!" I say, the words garbled because I'm gritting my teeth. "The way I grew up was just different from you. I bet you know tons of cultural stuff I have no idea about."

Beatriz's eyes burn. "Are you actually comparing your spoiled-ass life to my *cultural heritage*?" She gestures angrily and I see she's wearing a bracelet of the Panama flag.

"It's an apt comparison."

"It is not, you fucking ass—"

"The laundry room is off the kitchen."

Beatriz and I look up to see Meg's head poking sleepily out

from the den. "I used to help Dad," she says in response to my questioning look.

My stomach twists. I don't like being reminded that I'd never have met my best friend if her dad hadn't been our housekeeper. I'm pretty sure the only reason my parents didn't discourage our friendship was that Meg's dad has some sort of advanced degree from abroad that took a while to transfer to the US.

"Well, good night." I push past Beatriz toward the stairs. I'm halfway down before I hear footsteps and realize she's following me. "What the f—"

"Shut up. I still hate you."

We find the laundry room, and I pull off my shirt, tossing it into the washing machine. Beatriz's eyes linger on my chest and my pulse races.

"You might want to do your pants too," Beatriz says. I look down and realize they're stained yellow. "I'll turn around," she says quickly.

"You don't *have* to," I say because her eyes are just one of Beatriz's body parts that I want on my chest. "I mean—it's not like you haven't—"

Beatriz turns around.

I pull my phone from the pocket of my chinos before throwing them in the washer. I look quickly down to make sure my boxer flap is buttoned as Beatriz turns around. She doesn't seem to have any reaction to me standing pretty much naked in front of her.

"Alright, where's your detergent?" she asks, scanning the shelves above the washer and dryer. I open the detergent compartment as Beatriz spots it on the ledge of the washbasin. She unscrews the cap and fills it all the way to the top.

"Wow. Way to conserve for the environment and shit."

Beatriz gives me a look. "Want your clothes permanently smelling like barf?"

"I'm just saying." I take the cap and start pouring it into one of the compartments. "What would Greta Thunberg say?"

"That you're the one percent and it's six in the morning. Also, that's for fabric softener."

"What?" I stop pouring and look down. Now that I'm looking, I see words etched behind each compartment. "Oh. I thought they could just go in any of them."

"I rest my case."

Let me just say that Beatriz is the only girl I've slept with that's never been into the fact that I didn't have to learn any of this shit. And I hate that it makes my pelvis ache.

I pour the rest of the detergent into the correct compartment and start the machine.

"Oh my god, it's so late," I say, looking at my phone as we climb the stairs.

"Or early." Beatriz yawns.

"Well—you did okay," I say, as we reach my room. I try to put my hands in my pockets as I lean against the wall, then remember I'm just in my underwear.

Beatriz frowns. "Huh?"

"I mean, you're not bad at wifely chores for someone with a Tax the Rich sweatshirt." I watch her eyes.

Beatriz shoves my shoulder and I laugh. She turns to walk away but I stop her. "Hey."

"What now, asshole?"

"Thanks."

Beatriz's eyes soften. "No big deal."

I stare at her, not looking away for the first time all evening because she's staring back.

We stand there, looking at each other. Me in my underwear. Outside my bedroom. I can't tell if she's lingering because she's tired, or wants to yell at me again…or if she's remembering the same thing I am.

"I still think about it," I blurt out. Beatriz's eyes widen. And I know she knows what I mean.

"It was three years ago," she says softly.

"I know."

Beatriz opens her mouth but nothing comes out. Then, so quietly she sounds like Hero, "I do too."

I step closer.

"We shouldn't," Beatriz says as my hand lifts to her face. Shit. My hand falls. "I mean, yeah, I just meant—"

"I'll see you tomorrow."

"Oka—"

But she's gone before I even finish. I walk into my room and lean against the closed door, hoping to god neither of us remember what I just did in the morning.

BEATRIZ

Given that I've been up all night, I should have fallen asleep the second I got in bed. Instead, I lie awake for an hour, thinking, *Ben still wants me, Ben still wants me, Ben still wants me.*

I try one of the lucid dreaming techniques my therapist, Lorna, and I talked about in our last session, but all my brain wants to do is think about how good Ben looked leaning against the wall in his underwear, and how much I liked feeling the curve of his neck against my head as we slept at the hospital.

"Fuck you, libido," I mumble into my pillow. "Assholes shouldn't be allowed to be hot."

But it's not just visuals of Ben that keep me up. I can't get over how…vulnerable he seemed at the hospital. There's really no better way to humanize the enemy than watching them ugly cry. I might never forgive him for what he said the night we hooked up, but my loathing for Ben Montgomery is less black-and-white now. And I'm not sure how I feel about it.

I must have fallen asleep eventually though, because the next thing I know, Hero's bouncing into the room saying, "Trizita, ya son las tres, vamo—"

I open my eyes to see Hero looking around my room.

"¿Por qué tás durmiendo aquí?"

"Huh?" I'm still half-asleep.

"There are four unoccupied guest rooms downstairs. Why are you in this maldito closet?" There's bite to her tone. I sit up and see Hero staring around at the slanted ceiling above my head and the lamp on the floor.

"It's fine," I say quietly, lying back down and rolling over so I'm not facing her.

"This is where John put you?" The anger in Hero's voice grows more intense, and I open my eyes to see her kneeling in front of me.

"Jesus! You're too close."

"Por qué no me dijiste." It isn't a question.

I close my eyes and pull the comforter over my head. "Quiero dormir, Hero."

"This isn't okay!" The covers are yanked off me.

"Hero!" I see her balling up my blankets and dropping them on the floor before pulling clothes out of my suitcase. "The fuck are you doing!" I jump out of bed and try to take my bra out of her hands.

"Get dressed. We're gonna go fucking talk to John."

Wow. She must be really pissed because usually the idea of talking to someone she doesn't really know gives Hero panic sweats. She doesn't meet my eyes, and I know it's because if she does, she'll start bawling. I've never met someone who cries so much when they're angry.

"Come on, I'm fine."

"I know you are." Hero shoves a shirt and jeans into my hands. "I'm not."

Jesus Christ. I pull my sleep shirt over my head and pull on the yellow bralette Hero's holding. "Are you seriously making this about you right now?"

"You just said you were fine!" Hero crosses her arms and blocks the door. She's so timid that I forget she can be kind of scary when she's mad. Her eyes do this thing that makes her look like Cruella de Vil.

"I *am* fine," I shoot back, matching Hero's tone as I pull on my favorite denim jacket. "But that doesn't mean it's not shitty."

"Why do you think I'm trying to fix it?" Hero's voice cracks and tears fill her eyes.

"It's not worth it, okay?" I button my jeans and zip the fly. "Pick your battles, and all that. Let's just leave this, okay?"

"No."

I whip around, accidentally stomping my foot on the floor. "What the fuck is your problem today?"

"My *problem*—" Hero says, angrily enunciating as the tears start rolling "—is that someone isn't treating my prima fairly, and I'm going to fix it."

"You don't get it, Hero," I say quietly, walking toward the door. But she doesn't move.

"What don't I get?"

"Dude, I don't want to do this right now."

"*What* don't I get?"

"Let me out."

"Then tell me what—"

"You can pass!" I yell, anger flooding out of me. "You fucking look white, Hero. You'll never understand what this is like—because you look like one of *them*. So just let me fucking handle it y deja de tratar de salvarme."

Tears stream down Hero's face. "¿Crees que me gusta?" she chokes out.

"Why the hell wouldn't you?"

"Because people are *constantly* whitewashing me, even you!" Hero's voice breaks as she shoves her hands across her face, pushing at her tears. "You have no idea how shitty it feels to tell people I'm Puerto Rican and have them laugh because they think I'm joking. I *wish* I was darker, then maybe people would stop telling me I'm not a fucking person of color."

"Oh, boo-hoo."

"Fuck. You." Hero's voice cracks as she slams the door behind her.

I'm breathing heavily, but despite how angry I am, I also feel a little guilty. I hate fighting with Hero. It doesn't happen all that often, but when it does it's *bad*—like Amy-burning-Jo's-manuscript bad.

I climb back into bed and pull out schoolwork. But I keep thinking about the sound of the door slamming as Hero stormed out, and it makes my eyes hurt. I pull out my phone and text my therapist.

Beatriz: fought with Hero

Lorna: Oh no! What about?

Beatriz: the dude whos house were staying at put me in this tiny guest room even though there are tons of bigger ones, and Hero found out and got pissed

Lorna: Well that's shitty of him. Any idea why he might do that?

Beatriz: theyve got mega white Gatsby money and I look like someone who would be their servant

Lorna: Oh Bea ♥ Fuck that noise. How did this end in a fight with Hero?

Beatriz: she wanted to go confront him about it, and I didnt and she kept pushing it, and it ended up in a fight over how she can pass and I cant

Lorna: Ah. That's a really loaded issue, huh? Is it the first time you guys have talked about it?

Beatriz: maybe? not sure

Lorna: Okay ♥ This is a much bigger issue than we can discuss over text, but I'll say this for now—Hero is still your ally, and you're hers. Of course, that doesn't mean you're not allowed to be angry with her. You most certainly are! But one fight won't change what you two mean to each other. It's natural for sisters to fight, and in terms of familial relationships, you guys are more like siblings than cousins. Do you feel like you could talk to her about it? I'd just hate for you to go through the rest of spring break feeling like Hero's not in your corner, especially if you're in an environment where micro aggressions seem more likely. And we can talk about all this in more detail in our next session

Beatriz: okay

Lorna: You are an amazing person, Beatriz, who is entitled to her emotions. ALL OF THEM. Even the ones that make life hard. Keep me updated, and please reach out if you need me. And don't forget to lean on Leo if you need him too

Beatriz: okay. thanks

Lorna: Any time ♥

I go back to my schoolwork, which is a little easier after talking to Lorna. When my brain starts to hurt, I head downstairs.

Everyone's in the den—Ben doing schoolwork with Meg curled up beside him, while John's playing an extremely violent video game. Claudio has his arm around Hero while they're both reading the same book.

I sit on Meg's other side, taking out my phone. Ben looks up and goes pink before looking back at the book in his lap. He picks up a water bottle I saw him carrying last night and hands it to Meg, who takes it gingerly. Like she's not sure she wants to.

Hero glances at me but quickly looks away. I wish I wasn't fighting with her. But I'm also not going to apologize.

"You ready to go?" she asks Claudio as he slides a bookmark onto the page.

"Sure!" He beams at her. "We're off for a walk," Claudio says, putting the book on the coffee table and taking her hand as he gets up.

Ben nods, Meg says, "Use protection," and John pauses his game.

"You know, I've never seen someone so thin have an ass that great," he says to Hero, like it should make her day.

"Oh. That's nice of you to say," she mumbles to the ground. I've been trying for years to get Hero to stand up to people when they treat her like that, but she always says, "It's just easier if I don't."

Claudio's eyes narrow at John. "Maybe next time keep it to yourself."

"Chill, bro," John says, clapping Claudio on the back. "You've got dibs."

Hero and Claudio leave, and for a crazy second, I want to go with them. I really don't want to be alone with two women-haters and a budding alcoholic who might be fucking one of them.

"So, Beatriz, you're not doing any homework?"

My chest tightens as John speaks to me. "Uh, no."

"How come?"

"Because we're on break?" I have no idea why he's talking to me, especially since he acted like I didn't exist yesterday.

"You're the only one who hasn't done any work so far," he says, like it's impossible that I would get anything done without him around to witness it.

"What's it to you?"

"I figured you'd have a specific GPA you have to meet."

"Why?"

But I know John's not going to respond, even before he resumes his game. My white grandma used to pull shit like this on me all the time.

The summer before Hero and I started preschool, the white side of our family gathered for a gee-look-how-fast-they're-growing-up dinner. I remember Grandma popping her head into the room and saying, "Beatriz, dear, put your blocks away. You're making a mess," before smiling widely at Hero and leaving the room.

"Does Hero have to put her blocks away?" I called after her.

"No."

"Why?"

No answer.

"WHY?"

But Grandma ignored me until I eventually pushed my castle down and left the blocks scattered on the floor.

I asked my mom about it, but she just waved me away saying, "Jesus, I don't know. Maybe you should play more like

Hero, nice and quiet." That's one of the nicer interactions I remember having with my mother before Uncle Leo got custody of me.

It wasn't until Leo found me crying in the bathroom that I finally got an explanation. I remember his face bursting with anger as he said, "Firstly, and most importantly, you *do not* have to be more like Hero, you are wonderful just being YOU," and taking me in his arms and rubbing my back as I cried.

"W-why did Mami say that?"

"I don't know, sweetie. Sometimes when people are upset, they say things that don't make sense. And secondly, what your grandma did was not fair."

"Then why did she do it?"

Uncle Leo hesitated. "This is not *ever* okay to do, and I'm going to talk to her about it, but…she did it because you and Hero…look different." I didn't get it. I kept badgering Leo with questions until he finally said, "Your grandma treats you and Hero differently because—because Hero's skin is lighter."

Hero's block tower stayed in the living room for three days. And every time I walked past it, I felt like someone had punched me.

Now here I am again, fifteen years later—facing passive-aggressive racism that I can't call out because it's subtle enough to be passed off as me being "too sensitive."

But I know what John's "not" saying. Of course, someone that looks like me could *only* be at Harvard on scholarships, and would therefore need to maintain a specific GPA.

I do have scholarships, but so does Hero. And he didn't assume that about her.

I open my mouth to tell John to go fuck himself, but Ben's book slams shut before I can.

He glowers at his brother. "Fucking leave her alone, dickwad. You wouldn't know what it's like being at an Ivy League. You don't even know what it's like to finish high school."

John zeroes in on Ben. "Aww, Benny," he says mockingly as he glances between us. "You must be desperate."

I feel like I've been punched. I look at Ben, wanting him to stick up for me again and hating it—but he doesn't. He just turns red and looks away.

"Yo, Meg, where's your brother at?" John asks, smirking.

"You know better than to ask me questions at hangover o'clock," Meg snaps, one hand shielding her eyes.

I expect John to shoot her down, but he doesn't. Instead, he laughs, says, "Alright, kid," and leaves. His eyes lingering on Meg's a second too long.

I glance at Ben and he's scowling. Meg's phone goes off and she gets up.

"Where are you—" But Meg walks out of the den before Ben finishes his question. Leaving his water bottle on the floor by his feet.

As Meg's footsteps fade, I wonder if she knows Ben tried to sleep with me last night. She was sitting so close to him earlier, but I honestly couldn't tell if it was a sisterly closeness, or a we've-shared-one-body closeness. Suddenly, the idea of Ben hooking up with Meg makes me queasy, and I have to leave too.

Back in my room, I pull out the homework I started yesterday and read until my brain hurts. I have no idea how long I've been sitting there, but I jump when there's a knock at the door.

"Fuck off, Hero."

"It's Meg."

Why the hell is Meg knocking on my door? Did she find out Ben tried to sleep with me again and wants to reenact some *Friends*-era catfight? I open the door to Meg, who is clutching a metal tin.

"Um, hi?"

"Can I come in?" she asks.

"I guess." I step aside.

"Why are you in the kids' guest room?" she asks, looking around for a place to sit and realizing there's none.

"Why do you fucking think?"

"You like enclosed spaces?" When I don't respond, Meg's face changes. "Ohhh. John put everyone's crap in their rooms for them?"

"Bingo."

"Well, that's bullshit. The room next to Ben's is empty, come on."

"I really—" I don't know what to say. I don't want John to find out that I've moved rooms.

It's just easier that way.

"If John asks you about it, tell him I came up here to smoke weed and moved all your shit. I'm weird enough that he'll buy it." Meg picks up my backpack, looking so determined that I feel a little more okay playing along.

She leads me downstairs and into the room beside Ben's. He comes out of his room holding a weird-looking deck of cards that he quickly puts behind his back when he sees us.

"What are you—"

"John put her in the kids' guest room," says Meg, opening the door and marching into the empty room.

"Are you fucking serious?" Ben follows us, his jaw tight.

"Yep. If he asks about it, though, tell him that that's my weed den and I kicked Beatriz out."

Ben snorts. "Yeah, okay." He shuffles from foot to foot in my doorway. "Meg, are you—"

"Fuck off, it's girl time!" Meg says jovially, smiling like this was the plan all along. She kisses Ben on the cheek and gently shoves him out of my room as she closes the door.

Meg sets my backpack down in front of an armchair before settling on the floor next to it.

"I just wanted to thank you for last night," she says, holding out the tin she's been carrying this whole time. I'm greeted by the scent of freshly baked snickerdoodles when I open it. Now that I think about it, an amazing smell had been wafting through the house while I worked earlier.

"Thanks." I take a bite. They're almost as good as Uncle Leo's. Meg doesn't say anything else, so I keep chomping on cookies. I realize I haven't eaten all day.

"I—I'm sorry you had to see me like that last night. It must have been scary."

I finish my third cookie. "It's fine. Just glad you're okay."

"Are *you* okay?"

"Yeah, why?" I don't look at Meg as I break a cookie in half.

"You were MIA for hours. I think Ben was low-key worried you'd killed yourself or something."

"Ben wouldn't worry about me. He hates me. It's a mutual thing."

"I wouldn't be so sure. He's a worrier. He worries about *everyone*, even people he doesn't like. He'd never admit it, though."

I raise my eyebrows. "Really?"

"Oh yeah." Meg nods vigorously. "Is that surprising?"

"He just…" I try to find the words to describe Ben's particular brand of pretentious aloofness. "He doesn't seem like the kind of guy who would worry about anyone he can't get something from."

Meg frowns. "Really? He must be different at school."

"I mean, isn't that where you met him? I assumed you guys went to high school together."

"Nah. If we had, I would've slept around way less."

My stomach clenches. "How come?"

"Ben's protective," Meg says, shrugging.

"In what way?"

Meg raises her eyebrows. "Why do you wanna know?"

"You just said we were having girl time or whatever, and I thought all girl time mandated guy talk," I say, snapping a little.

But Meg laughs. "I wouldn't know. I've never had a lot of female friends, or any friends, for that matter."

"What?" I say, my voice jumping an octave. "But…you seem cool."

"Thanks, babe." Meg smiles at me. "But being the only Chinese girl in an all-white school doesn't exactly help you fit in."

I nod, thinking of how many classes I'd taken at Harvard where I'd been the only brown person in the room.

"Eh, it's fine." Meg brushes it off in a way I recognize. "At least I got good sex out of it. You wouldn't believe how many people still think the whole cute-Asian-girl stereotype is like, hot. Like a fetish or something. Playing that up got me more action than Ben."

I frown. "But like—does that do it for you?"

Meg blinks. "I don't follow."

"I mean, isn't the point of hooking up wanting someone who clearly wants you? I can't imagine sex being good if you're wanted for being…not you."

Meg snorts. "As if anyone would want Dumpster Fire Meg Xie. But the kinds of people who want an anime character come to life are a dime a dozen. And before you try to be nice and say I'm not a dumpster fire—" she wags her finger playfully "—trust me, I am. I graduated high school by the skin of my teeth, I work at a fast-food restaurant and still live with my parents, I like drinking more than I like people, and the only friend I have is leaving to be an investment banker."

Of *course* Ben got a job as an investment banker.

God, will *I* ever find a job? Will employers assume I've lied about graduating from Harvard because I don't look like I've ever set foot in a country club?

My first week on campus, I overheard an upperclassman bragging about how little work he had to do to get in. And it just made me think about how I went to tutoring every day after school, working my ass off to have enough extracurriculars, putting in four hours of study for every subject to combat my learning disability when everyone else was done after one.

I have to work twice as hard to get half as far, not just because I'm brown, but because I'm neurodivergent too. So why the fuck am I spending my spring break at a rich white boy's mansion instead of firing off every job application possible in hopes someone will take pity on me?

"Wait," I say, because I need to get out of the spiral in my brain. "How'd you and Ben meet if not through school?"

"My dad used to be their housekeeper."

"Oh." Meg might understand how John made me feel earlier in a way no one else could, not even Hero. Especially if Meg was so dehumanized in high school. "Has John ever—" I trail off. I have no idea how to phrase this.

"Been an asshole?" Meg suggests.

"Not just that." Part of me wants to confide in Meg because no matter how much I deny it, I'm desperate for someone to get me. But I also don't want to confide in anyone ever, even if they've just confided in me.

"I honestly don't know John super well. Most of the times I'm here, I chill with Ben. And he and John don't vibe that much," she says, not meeting my eye.

I wonder what kind of "chilling" she means.

"Yeah, but it seems…it just seems like John's like this all the time." I don't know what I mean by "this," but I hope Meg does, because I don't want to say it out loud.

But Meg looks blank. I sigh. "Does John—does he ever—does he ever treat you differently because you're—"

But I can't say it. Not here, not to someone I don't know, not when I'm feeling so vulnerable and isolated, and not when part of me—the tiniest part of me—wonders if we're imagining everything.

"Never mind. Thanks for the cookies."

4

BEN

"Hulk out, bitch!"

I hold my breath and push. Meg is spotting me in the home gym while I bench-press. I do eight reps, then drop the bar back on the pins.

"Nice!" Meg moves from behind the rack to dance around the gym. The Ed Sheeran song that's playing literally everywhere I go is blasting from the speakers. She seems a lot better than she was this morning. But she still won't finish what she started to say at the hospital.

"Do we have to listen to this on repeat?" I ask, breathing heavily as I rest between sets.

"If I have to look at you shirtless without barfing, then you can deal with listening to a low-key sexy bop."

I sigh. "You know, you're the only girl who's ever objected to seeing me shirtless."

"That's because I saw you shirtless when we were four and it was not hot."

"Ready to go again?"

"*Shape of youuu!*" Meg sings along before taking her place behind the squat rack again. I'm almost done with my next set when Meg asks me something that nearly makes me drop the bar.

"So you've hooked up with Beatriz, right?"

The bar slams back onto the pins. "What—how—Meg!"

"So that's a yes."

"When have we ever talked about my sex life?" I push myself off the bench and grab a towel, wiping my face.

"She's just got that scorned woman energy going, and I wanted to see if my hunch was right."

I drain my water bottle and want this conversation to end. "Yeah, I did, now shut up about it."

"So, what'd you do to make her hate you?"

I put my water bottle down. "Nothing."

Meg sighs, like *I'm* the frustrating one. "I love you, man, but you've been a player since we were in high school, and every girl was begging me for your number." My phone goes off and Meg checks it. "The defense rests," she says, holding it out. I see five texts from four different girls—a mix of pictures and messages that are supposed to be sexy but just come off as clingy.

Meg lies down on one of the floor pads, starfishing. "Beatriz is cool. I think you might regret fucking her over."

She needs to let this go. I lie down across from her and start doing sit-ups. Meg is staring at me when I'm done—her raised eyebrows making it clear that my not responding is all the response she needs.

"Dude, what?" I ask, walking over to the treadmill to do a cool-down run.

"Do you *like* her, Benny?" Meg asks, like we're in fourth grade.

"No."

Meg's eyebrows rise again.

"I don't!"

"You're being awfully vocal about it."

"Shut up."

"Look, I know she's not...what Mr. and Mrs. M would want." Meg and I don't look at each other as she skirts around a truth about my parents we've never spoken aloud. A truth that Beatriz alluded to last night without even meeting them. "But I think if you stop being a womanizing douche for two seconds, you'd see that she's maybe something *you* could want. And you're already doing enough for them."

"Whatever." I'm amped up enough that this is quickly switching from a cool-down run to an anger run, so I hop off the treadmill. Meg's never acted like this before.

And apparently, she's not done. "Look, dude. You're about to graduate from fucking Harvard with a business degree. You're starting at Mr. M's firm the day after graduation. You know about the taxes on this house—and the Zurich one. *And* you have your boating license so you can host the pontoon parties if your parents are in Europe."

"What the fuck is your point?" I sit on a bench on the other side of the room.

"Just...don't get so caught up in continuing the Montgomery legacy that your WASP persona becomes your personality. Because I've known you since we were four, Benny, and that's not who you are."

"I'm fine."

"But, dude—"

"Meg, shut up!" I jump to my feet. "If I listened to anything

68

you have to say, I'd be a dropout frequenting the hospital so much that the receptionist knows my name."

Meg's shoulders slump.

God, I'm such an asshole.

"Fuck, I'm sorry," I say, sitting down next to her. "I just… don't like this conversation."

"I noticed." Meg gets up. "I'm gonna get high, then bake some cookies. Wanna come?"

"Nah, I have to cool down."

Meg nods and heads for the door.

"Hey, Megasaurus?"

She stops and looks at me. "It's been a while since I've heard that one."

"We okay?"

"We'll always be okay, Benny." She smiles and leaves.

Beatriz doesn't reappear until after dinner. Not that I'm looking for her. John was just an asshole, and I feel like I should apologize. I try to push my conversation with Meg out of my mind because she's wrong—if I ever had an aneurism and actually wanted a girlfriend, Beatriz would be the worst possible choice.

She wanders into the den close to ten o'clock. Claudio and I are playing *Super Smash Bros.* while everyone else watches a movie. She's wearing a bralette and a sleeveless shirt that says Latina AF. Her jean jacket is covered with pins of vaginas that say things like Smash the Patriarchy, and Defend Roe V. Wade where the *V* is a woman's spread legs.

Yeah. This nightmare socialist is *definitely* the girl for me.

"I assume you guys have already eaten?" Beatriz says.

I nod, trying to catch her eye. Claudio beats me by knocking me off the edge of the map.

"Yeaaaah!" Claudio drops the controller and pumps his fists

in the air. "Babe, I did it!" he calls, running into the theater toward Hero's laughter. Leaving Beatriz alone with me.

"So…" I slide my hands into my pockets as I stand up. "Um…are you hungry? It's like nine thirty, right?"

"Nine *forty-five*," says Beatriz, like I should feel bad for not guessing the exact time.

Usually, I would fire something back, but Beatriz looks… so disheveled. Like she spent all day looking out a foggy window for someone who'll never come. It's a look I recognize.

"Well, is there food anywhere?" Beatriz asks, starting toward the stairs. "Or if you give me the name of some takeout places, I can order something."

"I could make you some food," I say, following her.

She turns and looks at me in surprise. "You cook?"

"You sound shocked."

"I mean, you didn't know where the laundry room was in your own house."

"Look, it's not my fault my parents never made me do laundry," I snap, unable to stop myself. "What kind of person *asks* their parents for extra chores?"

Beatriz doesn't say anything, and it makes me uneasy. We're not friends, so our banter is the only barometer I have to indicate that she's okay. I don't care that much if she is or not, but after everything she did for Meg and me last night, I feel like I owe her.

"Have nothing to say?"

"I'm just hungry." Beatriz sounds so defeated that I instantly feel bad.

Neither of us says anything else until we reach the kitchen.

"What are you in the mood for?" I ask, opening the fridge and scanning the interior.

Beatriz sits at the marble island, pulling at her fingers the same way she did last night when telling me about Meg.

70

"Whatever," she says. "I don't really know what you can make."

"I could make you mac and cheese." I open the cheese drawer to make sure there's enough.

"I mean, I can make a box of Annie's," says Beatriz derisively. "That's not really cooking."

I let out a breath I didn't realize I'd been holding—the snark is back.

"No, like from scratch." I take out the cheddar, pecorino, Havarti and gruyere.

Beatriz is quiet. I turn to see her gaping at me.

"Seriously?"

"Yeah." I pull a cookbook out from under the counter, opening it to the well-worn mac and cheese recipe. "You wanna help?"

There's a pause. "Sure."

She slides off her stool and drags her feet across the floor as she walks toward me.

"Why aren't you being an asshole?" she asks, still tugging at her fingers.

I pull the cheese grater from a cupboard and shrug. "You helped me out last night. Plus, my brother was a dick to you, and people need food."

"You think John was a dick to me?"

"I mean, yeah," I say, unwrapping the cheddar. "It was pretty obvious, wasn't it?" Part of me is asking because if another person had noticed, it would mean I didn't make it up. Whenever I've called my family out on shit like this, they've made it clear that I'm "imagining things," or "being uptight," or "not getting the joke." And since Trump's win, certain things have become uncomfortably clear.

"It was obvious to me," Beatriz says quietly. "I just didn't know you..." She doesn't finish her sentence.

"I did," I mumble. Our gazes meet. Beatriz's eyes are so deep, I could drown. I'm torn between wanting to kiss her and ask her more questions. But before I can decide, she looks away.

"So you wanted my help?"

"Um, yeah." I shake my head slightly, not knowing if I'm relieved or disappointed that the moment's gone. "I'll get the ingredients out, and you can measure them." I take some mixing bowls down from the cupboard, while I point to the drawer with the teaspoon measurements and pinch bowls.

"You don't just go?" Beatriz asks, sounding surprised as she opens the drawer. "My uncle just starts the recipe and gets things as he goes."

"No, I use the mise en place method." I hoist myself onto the counter to reach a box of pasta that someone (John) has put in the space between the cupboards and the ceiling, where no one could reach it. I hop back down to find Beatriz looking expectedly at me. "What?"

"What the hell is mizon plus?"

"Mise *en* place." I roll my eyes. "It's French for 'everything in its place.'" I set the pasta next to Beatriz and open the fridge.

"Christ, can you not be pretentious for like five minutes?"

I look up, surprised. "How is that pretentious? You asked what it meant, and I told you."

"Because you're spewing French cooking terms at me and correcting the way I say them when I have literally never taken French in my life and acting like I should just know what they mean."

"Well, s*orry*, I was answering your question like a decent human being." I grate the cheese a little harder than necessary while Beatriz shoves garlic into a garlic press.

"If you wanted to act like a decent human being, you wouldn't correct my pronunciation of a term I've literally never heard in a language I don't speak," Beatriz mutters. "I just can't deal with anyone else making me feel like shit today."

I almost drop the grater. "Did that make you feel bad?"

"I mean, wasn't that your goal?" she asks, not looking at me.

"No!" I turn to face her, and she just stares disbelievingly at me. "Alright, sometimes I do try to piss you off, but not just then. I was just trying to answer your question." I thought I was filling a gap in her education, so the next time she hears the term, she doesn't come off as uninformed.

"Well, you didn't have to treat me like an uncultured noob. Nobody likes it when someone else makes them feel inferior."

What the fuck is she talking about? "That made you feel inferior?" When Beatriz responds by glaring at me, I hold up my hands. "I'm genuinely asking! It's just always what my parents did—they said it was important to respect foreign customs, and to correct other people if they were misinformed."

Beatriz snorts. "Sure."

"It's *true*."

"I believe you," says Beatriz, her tone making it clear there's a catch. "But I bet it was only important to respect the customs of people your parents actually respected."

"Like?"

"Like making sure I'm informed about a *French* cooking term. But if I walked around saying that Molas are native to Argentina instead of Panama they wouldn't give a shit."

"I have no idea what those are."

"Exactly." But the passionate frustration I'm used to hearing in her voice when we argue is gone.

I watch Beatriz make a roux per the recipe's instructions. I think about what she said and want her to be wrong—I *hate* feeling like someone's gotten the best of me. It takes me back to being eleven and John is forcing me to do his calculus homework. "Come on, you skipped a grade, kid genius. How is this hard for you?"

But now that I think about it… Beatriz might be right. I think about how my parents never shut up about the differences between Metropolitan French and Aostan French, but every year for Meg's birthday, they give her a kimono. Even though she's Chinese. And every single year I've told them that (a) you'd have to be blind to think that metal AF Meg would be caught dead in a kimono, and (b) kimonos are Japanese. And every year, they say, "Oh, like there's a difference."

"You wanna listen to some music?" I ask as Beatriz pours milk into the pot.

"Sure."

We don't really talk after that. Beatriz mumbles, "Thanks," when I hand her a bowl, but she's on her phone the whole time we eat. So I'm on mine too.

When she gruffly says good-night to me outside my room, I figured I wouldn't see her again until the next day.

But I wake up abruptly hours later. At first, I have no idea why but then I hear a faint, muffled scream from next door—like someone screeching into a pillow.

"The fuck?" I sit up in bed, straining my ears to see if I can hear anything else. Silence.

Huh. Must have imagined it. I lie back down, but then I hear it again.

I look across the dark room to the wall I share with Beatriz. There's nowhere else it could be coming from. I start to get out of bed but stop myself—if Beatriz is upset, I'm the last person she'll want to see. Better to let Hero handle it.

But when I hear her scream twice more, I can't just lie here. I slide out of bed, pulling a T-shirt on so I don't show up at her door in just my underwear. After unplugging my phone from the wall, I turn on the flashlight and head next door.

No one answers when I knock. But Beatriz screams again. I slowly open the door and am greeted with a pitch-black room. I hold up my phone and see Beatriz in bed—thrashing around like someone is trying to strangle her.

I rush over and turn on the lamp on the bedside table. She's alone, but her face is scrunched up and she's rolling around like she's being chased.

"Hey," I say quietly. Beatriz keeps thrashing.

"Beatriz."

Nothing.

"Beatriz!"

She jolts awake, her eyes widening when she sees me. "What the fuck are you—" She can't finish, she's breathing too heavily. Sweat is beaded across her forehead. I've never seen someone look so terrified.

"Are you okay?" I ask quietly.

"I'm fine, fuck off."

I hesitate.

"What?" she yells at me.

"Dude, you're freaking me out!" I say in a hushed voice. "Like…do you need something?"

Beatriz stares at me with such loathing I think she's going to scream at me again. Then her eyes slacken, and she does the last thing I expect.

She bursts into tears.

It's intense—her shoulders shaking, her voice cracking. She's breaking down with as much vigor as I'm sure I did at the hospital.

I tiptoe to the door and shut it so no one else wakes up. When I turn back to Beatriz, she's sitting up—her back against the wall, hunched over like she's trying to make herself as small as possible.

I just stand there. I have no fucking clue what to do. Beatriz strikes me as someone who *never* cries. The only person I've seen break down is Meg, and I can only comfort her because I know the alternative is losing her.

So I just stand there, watching Beatriz cover her eyes, like she's ashamed.

Then I remember something she said at the hospital last night—that just letting someone break down while saying nothing is worse than straight up admitting your ineptitude.

"Fuck. I…wish I knew what to say." I take a step toward her so she can hear me through her crying. "But—I don't know how to—I don't know what you ne—" But I can't finish. Vulnerability makes my throat close up.

Beatriz looks out from behind her hands. Her eyes are swollen, snot running down her face. I spot a box of Kleenex on the dresser and toss it to her. She nods in thanks and blows her nose.

"I guess this is fair," she says, her nose still clogged. "Now we've both seen each other ugly cry."

"Ha ha, yeah, I guess."

Beatriz raises her eyebrows at me. "Did you actually just say, 'ha ha'?"

"Did you actually just cry out all the water from your body?"

"Yeah, I'm copying you, asshole." Beatriz blows her nose again. She wipes her eyes and pulls her knees up to her chest, resting her chin on them.

I hesitate before sitting next to her on the bed—close enough so that she knows I'm here, but far enough away so she doesn't feel like I'm trying to hook up with her. Especially since I did last night.

God, what is wrong with me? We slept together once, three *years* ago, and the first time I'm truly alone with her since,

I try to get in her pants. I want to bolt from the room more than anything. But I can't just leave her like this.

"Do you wanna—talk—" I have to practically choke the word out "—about it or something?"

She shakes her head. "I think if I tried to talk about it, I would cry even harder. And no offense, but you're the absolute last person I want to lose my shit in front of."

I don't say anything. I suspected as much, but it still sucks to have someone say, *I would rather be miserable than trust you.*

"Fuck, are you upset now?" Beatriz asks, sounding somewhere between concerned and annoyed.

"No, I'm fine," I say automatically.

"Your stony silence begs to differ."

"Well, how do you expect me to—" I stop. I'm pissed, but Beatriz has a point. I've given her absolutely no reason to feel comfortable showing weakness in front of me. She has every right to tell me to fuck off when she wakes up from a nightmare to find me staring down at her. For all she knows, I'm only here to throw it back in her face the next time we fight. "I'm sorry."

Beatriz's mouth falls open.

"What?" I say defensively.

"I'm just shocked you know what an apology is."

"Yeah, well, you're upset I'm consoling you."

For the first time since we've arrived at my house, Beatriz laughs.

"Shhh." I make shushing motions with my hands, smiling a little. "It's like four in the morning."

"Is it?" Beatriz grabs her phone. "Oh fuck. I should go to bed."

"Yeah, me too."

I don't get up, though. She meets my eyes. "What?"

"Will you… I mean, will you be able to go back to sleep?"

I expect her to scoff at me, but she shrugs. "Don't know. Maybe. I get nightmares a lot, though. Don't worry about it."

I want to not worry about it, but that's not really how I'm wired. I think about the air mattress stashed under my bed for the times Meg's not quite drunk enough for the ER but isn't sober enough to sleep by herself.

"If you want—I don't know if it'd help—I have an air mattress, you can crash in my room if that—if you'd feel better."

I swear Beatriz gets as close to blushing as her dark skin allows. "Thanks, but I'm fine."

"Are you—"

"I'm *fine*."

"Okay."

I walk into the hall. I'm about to shut her door when she says, "Hey."

I poke my head back into her room. "Yeah?"

"Thanks for…coming to make sure I wasn't dead or whatever."

"I mean, having the cops turn my house into a crime scene wouldn't have been the relaxing spring break I had in mind. Plus, everyone would probably think I'd murdered you for your irrational adoration of Marx."

Beatriz rolls her eyes. "Night, asshole."

I smile a little as I close the door. "Good night."

BEATRIZ

I've just finished my shower when someone knocks "Shave and a Haircut" on my door. Hero.

"Hi," I call from the bathroom.

"Hey," she says, leaning against a door frame. We've reached a tacit stalemate, like we always do after our fights. I know

Lorna encouraged me to talk it out, but it's too hard. Hero and I have never really talked through a disagreement before and I'm scared of what she'll say—will she be mad at me? Will she hate me forever? Will she regret the role she played in getting Leo custody of me?

"Which one was it?" Hero asks as she walks into the room.

I look at her questioningly, and she nods at my arm, which is covered in scratches. Just like it always is after my nightmares.

"I'm sorry I couldn't stop it," Hero says before I can respond, biting her fingernail.

"I mean, you don't stop them anyway."

"Yeah, but… I could have made it better." Whenever I have nightmares at school, Hero climbs into bed with me. We both opted out of singles senior year for that reason. Sometimes I don't even realize I've had a nightmare until I wake up with her arms around me. At home, we keep the doors to our rooms open at night so that all Hero has to do is pad across the hall to comfort me.

This is actually the first time I've slept alone in years. Which is probably why I had the nightmare about my mom.

"The one where she was chasing me," I say quietly, turning off the bathroom light and walking back into my room to start getting dressed. It seems like every room in Ben's house has a private bathroom.

"Hmm." Hero takes a notebook out of her purse and opens it. "Any new details this time?"

I shake my head. "No."

Hero nods but starts sketching.

Her biggest dream is to be a tattoo artist, specializing in cover-up tattoos. Which doesn't make sense to people unless they know her. Hero lives to fix things. Nothing stresses her out more than someone in pain that she can't help, so it makes perfect sense that she wants to dedicate her life to fixing people's permanent mistakes.

Once I got drunk with this girl I was hooking up with and let her do a stick-and-poke tattoo on my boob. Hero was furious that I didn't ask her to do it, and she had a point—it was supposed to be a sword, but looked more like a dick in sober daylight. But Hero fixed it into a badass resistance fist. She's been drawing tattoos of my nightmares for years because when she's licensed, she's going to tattoo them on my body with a big sword splintering them into pieces. Thinking about it is part of what makes the nightmares bearable.

Hero should be at Pratt or something; I honestly don't know why she spent four years at Harvard.

Well, I do. I just feel guilty about it.

"What do you want to do today?" Hero asks when I'm dressed.

"I don't know. What *is* there to do?"

"We could go to the beach. Although it's a little chilly. I could ask Meg. Maybe we could do a girls' day or something."

I smile. Hero is so shy that the idea of a girls' day is her worst nightmare. But she knows that people distract me. And that distraction is just what I need.

"Sure."

"I'll text Claudio and see where everyone is."

"How's that going, by the way?" I say as we leave my room. "You guys have been together, what, three months?"

"Six," Hero says, heart eyes lighting up her face. "But we've been close for so long, it feels like longer. I mean, you know that."

I do. For years both of them have been known around campus as HeroandClaudio. They studied together, went to movies together, they were effectively dating for *years* before Claudio made it official. Which is what makes me so wary of him. He leaned on Hero for the emotional support you'd expect from a partner without the respect of committing to her.

Hero insisted the whole time that they were "just friends" but I'm not an idiot. Claudio was into her and didn't do anything about it until our last year of college. And I have no idea why.

"I've never been able to just talk to someone like this," Hero says. "Like, I'm not worried about the fact that we graduate in two months and he lives on a different continent, because I just feel like we can get through anything. I've never felt this close to anybody ever."

It stings to hear Hero say that the closest she's ever felt to another person isn't with me. And to be reminded that college is over in nine weeks, and that I've been too shell-shocked from Trump's win and the rise in hate crimes to apply for a job.

"Cool," I say. "So—where are they?"

Hero checks her phone and smiles. Which makes me feel worse. "They're actually at the beach. It is, like, the nicest day we've had all spring." Hero turns to me. "Wanna head out?"

"Let me just get some books."

I throw my huge-ass philosophy textbook into my backpack before meeting Hero in the foyer. The driveway is huge and covered, not in gravel or tarmac, but broken white seashells. That must have been a great cause to throw money at. It's not like the Southern Poverty Law Center or BLM could have used that money or anything.

Ben's family probably voted for Trump, though. And they totally have guns.

Hero and I are only walking for, like, ten minutes before I start to hear the ocean roaring. The sea smells sweetly salty, which is not a turn of phrase I'd ever think could be accurate.

We walk down a pair of rickety steps, flanked on either

side by wispy beds of seagrass, until we reach a nearly deserted beach.

Claudio jumps up and starts waving enthusiastically when he sees us. Hero smiles and waves her hand twice before letting it fall back to her side.

"Sup," I say when we reach a huge, maritime-blue umbrella that Ben, Meg and Claudio are lounging beneath. Meg's on her side, her head resting on her hands and dark sunglasses covering most of her face. She's dressed in the most un-beach-like attire I've ever seen—black combat boots, gray skinny jeans, a black turtleneck sweater, and a skull and crossbones scarf.

Damn. Respect.

Ben, by contrast, looks frozen. He's sitting next to Meg and actually looks dressed for the beach, wearing no shirt and salmon pink swim shorts dotted with the Lacoste logo. And while it's warm enough to be pleasant, it's nowhere near shirtless levels. Ben's torso is covered in goose bumps, and he's as hunched over as possible without obviously being cold. An uncapped highlighter is clamped in his teeth and he's frowning down at—I do a double take—*Mansfield Park*.

"Do your gym buddies know you've got a boner for protofeminist lit?" I ask as Claudio kisses Hero on the cheek and she sits beside him.

Ben drops the book and glowers at me. "I'm in Jane Austen and Rebellion. I have to read this."

"Why the hell are you in that class?"

"I need a humanities credit."

"So out of all the humanities courses, you went with Jane Aus—"

"It's an easy A, alright?" Ben says, grabbing his book and shifting his eyes away from me. "I'm reading the predecessors of cliché rom-coms, not *Ulysses*."

"Oh, right, I forgot the work of sexist male pigs is automatically worth more brain space than that of feminist icons."

Although honestly, *Ulysses* is kind of my jam. James Joyce was a prick, but that book is wack in a way that makes it totally dope. But this dipshit doesn't have to know that.

Ben ignores me and highlights a passage. I'm surprised. I've never seen him so into something that he lets me win an argument.

I realize that John's not here, which is a relief. Neither is Peter.

"Where's your brother?" I ask Meg. She looks up and moves over so there's room for me to sit between her and Ben. I see Ben shoot her an evil look, but she smiles like they've got some sort of secret. My stomach tweaks.

"Peter stayed home today," Meg says as I sit down.

"And John?" I hold my breath as I imagine possible answers.

"He flew to Jamaica for the weekend," says Ben, taking the highlighter out of his mouth and running it over a passage.

Wow.

"I can feel judgment wafting off you," Ben says without looking up.

"I mean, what other kind of response do you expect from 'he flew to Jamaica for the weekend'?"

"It's not *that* weird," says Ben, still engrossed in the book. It's kind of hot—even as a comp lit major, it's hard to find guys who read Jane Austen that closely. "Like, I know it's not normal, but out of everything that's different about my family, I wouldn't have guessed—"

"No, it's weird, bro," says Meg, lifting her shades to peer at Ben, who finally looks up from his book. The fact that he looks up when Meg talks to him but not me makes a toxic feeling I'm not familiar with crawl through my stomach. Ben's body naturally straightens as he faces her, and he immediately hunches back down, trying to suppress a shiver.

"Dude, just put your shirt back on," I say, although he's so fucking ripped that I'm going to miss not being greeted by his abs whenever I look at him. "You're clearly cold."

"No, I'm not."

"You look like sandpaper." I reach behind Ben and toss him a T-shirt I assume is his. "No one's gonna care. Just be comfortable."

Ben looks down at the shirt in his hands, running it through his fingers. Then he looks around before quickly pulling it over his head.

"Better?" I ask quietly after Meg rolls over, her back facing us.

"I guess."

Then he does something I don't expect. He knocks his foot against mine and shoots me a smile.

A shock runs through me when his toe brushes mine. And the degree to which I want him to touch me again makes me want to run into the ocean and swim as far away from my feelings as possible.

5

BEN

I look down at *Mansfield Park*, trying to make my mind focus on the words and not on how close Beatriz is sitting. She's not any closer to me than she was at the hospital, but it's different without armrests between us. And without the hostility that's been raging for years.

I wouldn't go so far as to say that I enjoy Beatriz's company. But I don't *not* like being around her either.

She unzips her backpack and takes out a thick textbook.

"Wait, are you both studying?" Claudio asks, leaning around Hero to stare. "Guys! We're on holiday!"

Claudio is always complaining about how fast-paced life is in America. Once a professor marked his grade down because he was consistently five minutes late to class, and Claudio said, "But I was having my coffee," like this was a perfectly reasonable explanation.

"Some of us have papers due the literal day we get back," I say, highlighting my favorite passage of *Mansfield Park* (I may have read it before…twice) and trying not to think about the only grad school program I've ever googled—a program in Jane Austen studies I only pull up when I'm drunk.

"I mean, there are worse places to do schoolwork than the beach," Beatriz says, taking out three pens and a highlighter.

"Fair enough." Claudio lies down next to Hero, kissing her hand.

"I don't understand them," I say, mostly to myself but sort of to Beatriz too. Instead of answering, she reaches into her backpack for her phone and starts writing a text. My phone goes off.

Beatriz: just text me they might hear us. r u saying u DONT find nauseatingly adorable pda enticing? im shocked

Ben: It's more I don't get why it took them two fucking years to get together, and now that they are together, they're acting like teenagers on a first date instead of people in their early twenties. I have no interest in relationships, and even I think that's weird.

Beatriz: honestly, thats kind of why I came. Claudio taking so long to ask her out, I mean

I shoot her a confused look.

Ben: You came to chaperone them? Seriously?

Beatriz: no dumbass, im not out to protect her maidenhood. im worried Claudio took so long to ask her out so he could fuck other people. and Hero deserves someone who respects her

Oh. I mean, Claudio definitely slept with people in the time between meeting Hero and asking her out. A lot, actually. But I feel it would break our bro code telling Beatriz that.

Ben: He was probably just nervous. He's the softest dude I've ever met. And anyway Hero seemed okay waiting?

Beatriz: i guess. her romantic affinities ARE closer to those in the book in ur lap than a normal person, maybe she liked the pining

Ben: Ha ha, that doesn't surprise me.

Beatriz: so ur capable of writing 'ha ha' and not just saying it.

I roll my eyes and drop my phone next to me before looking back at *Mansfield Park*. I glance at the book in Beatriz's lap and do a double take.

"Holy fucking shit."

I thought I was a copious notetaker—because I actually take notes—but the margins of Beatriz's textbook are covered in color-coded annotations. They alternate between blue and purple ink and are all connected to lines Beatriz underlined. I look at the second page to see that she's highlighted the subheading of the chapter. Does she do that with *every* chapter?

"What?" Beatriz asks, looking from her book to me and back again.

"That's—insane." I bend over to get a better look at her notes. "What's your technique?" I'm closer now and I've never noticed that Beatriz has the vaguest of freckles peppered across her face. Or maybe it's acne scarring. Is that the only place she has freckles? How did she get them? Does she like sweet potatoes?

I move away from her.

"W-what do you mean, 'what's my technique?'" Beatriz asks.

"You clearly have a system." I point to her textbook, glad to have a subject to latch on to because I don't know where the eruption in my head just came from. "The color coding, where you highlight as opposed to where you underline, etcetera. I'm just curious—I thought I was a serious notetaker, but that's nuts."

But to my surprise, Beatriz looks embarrassed. I've never paid her a compliment before, but this isn't the reaction I expected. Or wanted.

She curls her toes into the sand, not looking at me. "I dunno."

"Really?" I'm trying to keep my tone light. Beatriz has, on multiple occasions, made it clear that I'm an asshole, but it wasn't really until last night that I started to see where she's coming from. I don't totally get what she means, but I don't want to make her feel *bad*.

Which is another feeling I didn't expect.

Beatriz looks at me. "You won't take it seriously."

My heart lurches. She's looking directly into my eyes in a way that makes it clear that's not an option. She chews the inside of her cheek and I remember with a jolt the last time I saw her do that. Her nails were digging into my back, her body gently opening as I pushed myself—

"Look, I'm really into school, okay?" I say, more loudly than I mean to. "I think I could learn something from you, that's all. But if you're gonna be weird about it, fine." I pick up *Mansfield Park* and shove it open.

Beatriz: i have a learning disability ok? color coding and writing everything out is the only way i can retain information and the only way i was able to get my gpa high enough to get into harvard

Well, I'm a dick.

Ben: Oh. Well, that's actually pretty admirable, why wouldn't you have said that out loud?

Beatriz: bc i didnt know if you'd believe me

Ben: What? Why wouldn't I?

Beatriz: bc every prep school prick ive met thinks its bullshit. i heard someone say once that i probably only got in because of affirmative action

Ben: I'm sorry.

Beatriz: thanks

Ben: No, I mean it. That's shitty.

Beatriz doesn't respond but nods, half to herself and half to me.

"So are you gonna explain your technique to me or not?" I ask quietly, knocking my highlighter against the edge of her book.

She sizes me up. "You won't be a fuckface?"

"You've already seen my fuckface." It comes out before I can stop it, a hiss that only Beatriz can hear but that I can't believe I've said aloud.

She inhales sharply. I brace myself for her to slap me—which honestly, would be fair—or scream at me, but she doesn't. She stares at me, her mouth partially open.

And for a crazy second, I think she wants to kiss me.

Something gets tight in my pelvis. When I look down, I'm horrified to see that my body is responding.

"Actually, I'm hot," I mumble, getting up before Beatriz can look down too.

"Wha—"

But I run into the ocean before she can finish her sentence.

BEATRIZ

We stay at the beach until sunset. After I'm done studying, I spend a few hours scrolling through social media on my phone. Wondering if Ben will text me again. Not liking how much I want him to. And really not liking how hungry I felt watching him flirt with me, get hard, pretend he wasn't hard and submerge himself in seawater until his clothes were clinging to him in a way that highlighted every muscle in his body.

The sky is pink as we head back to the house, shaking sand out of our shoes before entering the foyer.

"Anyone getting hungry?" Ben asks, setting the beach umbrella in front of a stained glass window by the door.

Meg looks at her phone. "It's only, like, 5:30."

"I know, but I was thinking of cooking tonight, if—if people would be into that," Ben says, kicking off his shoes before walking into the kitchen.

"You cook?" Hero asks.

"Oh, he's brilliant," says Claudio. "My first night here, he made a ton of bread and pasta to help me feel more at home, all homemade. It didn't taste as good as my mum's, but still."

Ben shoves Claudio and he laughs.

"I'd be down with that," Meg says, opening the fridge and taking out a bottle of wine.

I watch her, chewing on the inside of my lip. I catch Ben's eye and see the look on my face reflected on his. I try to give him a consoling expression, but honestly, the last time I consoled someone I was, like, three, so I have no idea if I'm pulling it off. Ben shrugs in a *What can you do* sort of way.

"I'll help you, bro," Claudio says, patting Ben on the back and pulling out a few cookbooks.

"What can I do?" asks Hero, ever the helper.

"You guys should go hang out," Claudio says to Hero before smiling at me. "I've totally monopolized Hero since we've been here. You should have some family time."

I'm grateful to Claudio for understanding the importance of girl bonding, but I don't like the way he's looking at me— like he *knows* he's being considerate and is waiting for me to praise him for it.

Meg uncorks the bottle and pours wine into her glass, almost to the brim. I glance at Ben to see him watching Meg nervously.

"Why don't you come too?" I ask Meg. Someone should probably keep an eye on her.

"Okay!" Meg takes a huge swig of wine as she leads the way toward the stairs.

"Um, what's in that room?" Hero asks, pointing around the staircase to a room I didn't notice when we first arrived.

"Oh, that's just a room."

Hero and I stare at Meg.

"Guys, this is an eight-bedroom house," Meg says, hopping off the stairs. "Therefore, you have too many spaces for just a living room and a den and stuff. So you just have lots of rooms with no purpose."

"Yeah, that checks out," I say. Man, every girl in every final club would drop their panties for Ben if they saw he lived in a house like this. Then the thought of hundreds of socialites trying to fuck him makes my stomach churn.

"I guess you could call this a second living room?" Meg says, leading us through the door frame. There's a brick fireplace against one wall, shiny hardwood floors and furniture so color-coordinated it looks like a spread from *Architectural Digest* (which Uncle Leo reads cover to cover). A grand piano sits by the window seat with sheet music piled on each side of the stand.

"God, I haven't played a real piano in forever." Meg sets her wine down on a bookcase and pulls out some music.

"You play?" Hero asks.

"Yeah, I'm such a fucking stereotype." There's a hardness to Meg's voice that makes the way she chugs her wine even more worrisome.

"Doesn't matter, if you enjoy it," says Hero. Meg just has another sip.

"Which Montgomery plays?" I ask, trying to distract her.

"None of them." Meg doesn't look up as she flips through the music.

I snort. "Why would you own a grand piano if no one plays?"

Meg shrugs. "I don't know. It's just a rich people thing." She sets the music on the piano stand, smoothing it flat. "You guys don't mind if I wreak havoc on your ears, do you?"

Hero shakes her head, and I say, "You do you."

Meg squints at the music then starts to play. It is *far* from havoc. It's not perfect—Meg clunks through wrong notes here and there, and often starts a section over, but I feel more listening to Meg play than I have hearing classical music anywhere else. It's like Meg's hands give life to something sterile. Shapes on a page become a story I can't let go of until the last note.

"Holy shit," I say when Meg's done.

"You're *so good*," Hero says, giving Meg a shy hug. "I feel lucky that I got to hear you play."

"Thanks." Meg starts a different piece and plays for what might be hours while Hero sketches and I walk around the room inspecting the books. There are floor-to-ceiling bookcases on most of the walls, and given the way the spines crack when I open the books, they've clearly never been read.

"Well, I need a refresher," Meg says after a while, draining her wineglass as I look up from a first edition of *Dubliners*. "You guys need anything?"

"I'm good," I say. Hero sketches quietly until Meg reappears, swaying as she carries a tray holding another overfilled glass of wine and a steaming mug.

"So, how's it going in the kitchen?" Hero asks as Meg sets the tray down on the coffee table.

"A-ma-zing." Meg enunciates every syllable as she picks up the mug and hands it to Hero. "Claudio made this for you," she says, and I recognize the smell—it's this loose-leaf tea Hero's obsessed with that you can only get online because it's made in England. "He said you seemed tired at the beach, so he made a whole pot if you want more."

Hero smiles and closes her eyes, sipping the tea.

"But—how does he have that?" I ask, nodding at the tea. "It's not easy to get."

"He got some for me as a Christmas present when he went home," Hero says, warming her hands around the mug. "It's cheaper there." She turns to Meg. "Coffee gives me a stomachache, so this is really my only caffeine fix. And I usually have some around this time at school. It's sweet that he remembers."

I didn't know that.

"Aww. You guys are, like, married already."

Hero blushes, smiling like she knows something she's not telling me. My gut twists.

An incredible smell wafts in through the kitchen. My stomach growls as Meg inhales.

"Oh my god, I'm so glad John peaced. Ben's been dying to cook since he came home, and no one cooks like him." Meg flops onto the couch, her wine spilling a little. She doesn't notice.

I remember how willing Ben was to make me mac and cheese last night. My stomach growls again, but not because I'm hungry.

"I'm glad no one suggested takeout." Hero sits next to Meg and sips her tea.

"Oh, Ben totally set this up. He only cooks when John's not here. I could practically hear the culinary wheels turning in his head when John said he'd be gone for the weekend."

Hero frowns. "Why does he only cook when John's gone?"

"Because it's John, and 'men don't cook.'" Meg raises her eyebrows. "Are you really surprised?"

"I guess not."

"How come he's such an asshole?" I ask, even though I know the answer.

Meg pauses. "He's not always an asshole," she says quietly, zoning out as she stares into the fireplace. "Ben just...gets him going."

"What does he do?"

Meg's eyes sharpen, and she shrugs. "Exists."

Claudio's voice announces that dinner is ready and Meg leaps off the couch, bounding out of the room.

"Wow," Hero says as we follow her. "I feel bad for Ben. Sucks if that's really all he has to do for his brother to be so shitty to him."

I feel hollow as we walk into the kitchen. I don't realize why until I see Ben crouched over a stove in an apron he wouldn't be caught dead in if John was home.

I feel bad for Ben too.

6

BEN

I turn off the stove as everyone piles in, pulling the way-too-pink apron over my head. Tonight, Claudio and I made soft-shell tacos where everything from the tortillas to the fillings is homemade. We've perfected it by now—we make it at least once every time Claudio stays with me, which at this point has been upward of ten times. Although, my parents think Claudio makes it and I just helped instead of the other way around.

"Whoa." Hero leans over the stove, wafting up the smell. She smiles right at me for the first time ever, I think. "Dude, this is *unbelievable*."

"Thanks, uh—you," I say stupidly. She's never called me "dude" before, and weirdly, she sounds just like Beatriz when she does.

I look behind Hero at Beatriz. And my stomach drops.

She looks—angry. And a little upset?

Why?

She looked absolutely fine a second ago when she and Hero came in. But now her eyes are narrowed, she's breathing heavily, and it's clearly because of me.

But I didn't do anything. And I'm one hundred percent sober, so she can't be mad about something I don't remember. Again.

I go over and over everything that could possibly have happened in the ten seconds between Beatriz entering the room and the look she's giving me now, and the more I mull it over, the more my stomach ties itself in knots. I don't know what I did. I don't know why I care.

"Um, actually, I think you underdid it, Benny," Meg says, dipping a finger into the salsa and pretending to wrinkle her nose.

"Ha ha." I look at Beatriz, wondering if she'll laugh. She doesn't.

She doesn't even look at me when I hand her a plate, and she's silent for all of dinner. Claudio and Hero are busy babbling to each other in Italian, and I'm too focused on watering down Meg's drinks without her noticing to talk to Beatriz.

So Beatriz just stares at her phone. Not scrolling and not talking to anyone.

After dessert, Hero and Claudio wash the dishes while I play Scrabble on my phone with Meg. Beatriz leaves, and the alcohol I've consumed makes my thoughts even harder to disentangle than usual.

I want to follow her.

But do I want to follow her to find out why she's mad at me, or to tell her she has no reason to be mad at me?

Or do I want to go after her because I need to know how it makes her feel to be reminded she's seen me come? I need to ask her if she still wants me, to tell her if I don't touch her before we graduate, I'm going to lose my—

Once the dishes are done, Hero wanders off to find Beatriz, Meg tagging along. Claudio sits beside me as they disappear upstairs, pouring the last of the mojito pitcher into my glass.

He looks at me once they're gone, all excited like a goddamn puppy. "Magic?"

Magic: The Gathering is this card game that Claudio taught me the first time he stayed with us, summer before freshman year. It's something the nerds I made fun of in high school played, so I never considered it a worthwhile pastime.

But I've been hooked for almost four years. Maybe it's because Claudio taught me as a distraction when we were hanging out upstairs, and were forced to listen to my dad scream at my mom until she was crying. And ever since then, Claudio keeps decks he's built for me in his suitcase to distract me whenever it happens again.

Claudio's the only one who knows MTG is my jam. If John ever found out I spend my trust allowance on a card game where you pretend to be a wizard casting spells and summoning creatures, he'd find a way to make it sound like this game is interfering with how seriously I take the family assets, so that Dad would either lessen my allowance or throw out all my cards.

John's good at making my hobbies sound like the end of the Montgomery name. Even though a dorky card game is definitely better than what he spends his allowance on.

"Sure."

Claudio and I go to our rooms to get some decks. As I pass the den, I see Meg, Beatriz and Hero all watching that British baking show Meg is obsessed with. Meg's black-and-pink hair is now in two short French braids, and Beatriz is braiding Hero's hair in a circle around the top of her head.

Beatriz can French braid?

Claudio's shuffling his deck in the downstairs living room when I come back clutching a four-pack of beer. He pulls up the score-keeping app on his phone and we start to play. Three games in, I'm just drunk enough to not feel like a pussy by asking, "Things good with Hero?"

Claudio grins. "They literally couldn't be better."

I nod and finish my turn.

"So, like...why her?" I say as Claudio plays a Land.

"What do you mean?" Claudio attacks me and I block him.

"You just...seem to be all about her, and she's alright, I guess, but I don't see why you're so whipped."

Claudio thinks for a second. "We just...get each other. We're aligned, you know? Like, we have the exact same deal breakers."

"Such as?" I draw a card and weigh my options before playing a creature.

"We both want to get married before we're thirty. We want to have a house and kids and pets. Oh, and cheating is the big one."

"What do you mean?"

"You know, we agree that people who cheat are bad people."

I pause. Claudio's dancing around something we've never talked about. An event that shattered his family that I only know about because I was in the room when it imploded.

"That's kind of black-and-white, don't you think?" I say, trying to gauge his reaction. There isn't one. "Like, I agree that cheating's bad, but...sometimes good people make dumb decisions," I say, thinking about Meg. "That's just...a pretty bold statement."

"Doesn't mean it's not true." Claudio finishes his turn.

"Bro," I say softly. "I—do you really think your mom's a bad per—"

"Your turn," Claudio says, his eyes flashing darkly in a way I've never seen before.

I swallow and draw a card. "Well, luckily, it seems like Hero is literally incapable of cheating, so I think you're good," I say, hoping I sound cheerful.

"Yeah." Claudio smiles like he didn't just look as if he wanted me dead. "She's perfect." But he bites his lip.

"You okay?"

Claudio nods. Then he puts his cards down and looks at me. "I'm probably only telling you this because I'm wasted," he says, fidgeting his knee. "But...I'm gonna propose to her at graduation."

"WHAT?"

I yell so loud that Meg screams from upstairs, "SODOM-IZE IN SILENCE," and Claudio makes shushing motions.

"You—what—*propose?*" I barely manage to keep my voice down.

Claudio shrugs. "I only have a year on my visa after we graduate. I was planning to just go home after uni, but...I want to be with Hero. It just makes the most sense. But I also know how much she loves romance and this would definitely count as a big romantic gesture. I'm going to talk to her about it to make sure we're on the same page, but...yeah. If all goes well, we'll be married by this time next year."

I gape at Claudio. All that comes out of my mouth is, "Are you insane?"

"I mean, I'm in love, so depends on who you ask."

"In *love?*" This is too fucking much.

Marriage isn't about love. It's about convenience. I don't remember the last time my parents voluntarily spent time together. They're only ever in the same room if John or I are there too. Right now, they're "in Europe," but everyone knows that means my mom is visiting friends in France, while my dad's in business meetings all day before spending nights with…well, not Mom. When I was in high school, and actually experimented with monogamous relationships, my dad told me I should see other girls and tell my girlfriend about them to make her "work harder."

It's not that my parents hate each other. They just always made me think of marriage as a business arrangement and children as assets. Love's not part of the equation; it's easier that way. Fewer feelings means fewer opportunities for everything to get fucked and the family money to fall apart. I literally don't think my parents have ever gone on a date. They wouldn't be able to make conversation for the length of dinner.

Claudio rubs his eyes and says, "I think I'm too pissed to keep playing."

"Me too," I say. It's not true, but I feel unsettled and want to be alone.

"I'm gonna see what everyone else is up to." Claudio gets up and stretches. "Wanna come with?"

"I'm good." I check my phone as Claudio leaves. One in the morning. Better start sobering up in case I need to take Meg to the ER.

I head into the kitchen and am about to drain my second glass of water when I hear stumbling footsteps.

Shit. Probably a drunk Meg to whom I'll have to deny alcohol.

I'm surprised when I hear not-Meg's-voice say, "Oh."

I turn around, and Beatriz is standing in the entryway.

"I, uh, thought you and Claudio turned in," she says.

I shake my head, holding up my glass of water. "In case Meg…you know."

She nods. "Yeah, I definitely can't drive tonight. Meg made

screwdrivers." Beatriz walks over to the farmhouse sink and turns on the faucet. I'm about to offer her a glass when she bends over and sucks directly from the gushing stream.

"What the hell are you doing?" My mouth is open as I stare at her.

Beatriz wipes her mouth. "Um, drinking water?"

"I would have gotten you a glass. How…that's such a barbaric way to consume water."

Beatriz glares at me. "Honestly, do you hear yourself? You say the most snobby and pretentious shit, then get all holier-than-thou when someone *dares* to call you out on it."

Something feels different about the way she's yelling at me.

"What's up with you tonight?" I say, putting my glass down and turning to face her.

"What do you mean?"

I take a few steps toward her. "What do you mean, 'what do I mean?' You sound really fucking mad."

"That shouldn't be surprising." Beatriz holds her ground as I get closer. "I'm mad at you 99 percent of the time."

"Not like this." I'm standing in front of her now, her eyes stormy as she looks up at me. "Not that I care, but—"

"That sentence is only ever uttered by people who do care."

"I don't like when people are mad at me!" I shuffle toward her again and she doesn't step back. "And I didn't even do anything, I don't understand why you just decided to be—"

"Ben, drop it."

I freeze, not just because Beatriz sounds like she wants to kill me, but because she's never said my name like that before. She always calls me "dude" or "asshole," but hearing her say my *actual* name makes it undeniable that things are different now. Different in a way I've tried to fight—but I'm not sure how much longer I can.

I stare down at her as she glares at me. "Fine," I finally say before walking over to the fridge and refilling my glass. When I turn around, Beatriz is gone.

I scroll through my phone at the island, finishing my water. It's edging closer to 2 a.m. now. I should probably go check on Meg.

I wander into the den, scanning the couches for Meg's frail body. She pretty much has her own room here, but for some reason, she prefers sleeping on a couch in the den. I glance around but don't see her.

Weird. Then I notice a light slipping out from under the door of the theater. She's probably watching *Taskmaster* or something.

But when I open the door, it's Beatriz sitting there on the love seat, hugging her knees to her chest, her face buried.

I lean against the door frame. "Uh, hey."

Beatriz jumps. "God, what?"

"Dude, chill. I thought you were Meg."

"Meg went to bed a while ago. I checked before going downstairs."

A soft feeling spreads through my body. No one's ever helped with Meg before. No one else has ever known.

I sit on the love seat beside her. Beatriz looks up, her face making it clear she wants me gone. I open my mouth to say something, anything, but my mind goes blank. So I say the first thing that pops into my head.

"I'm surprised you know how to French braid."

She leans away. "Were you stalking me?"

"No! I was getting something from my room and saw you guys."

Beatriz eyes me wearily. "Okay…why are you surprised?"

"Well, for starters, you—" Is what I'm about to say offensive? "Don't have hair?"

"Yeah."

"I mean, I wasn't born bald."

I raise an eyebrow at her, and she sighs. "Well, I guess I was, but you know what I mean. I haven't *always* been bald. I shave my head because my hair is so aggressively thick and curly that it's just easier not to have any at all."

"Okay…" I still don't know what this has to do with French braiding.

"So I came to that decision after years of trying countless ways of styling my hair so that I wouldn't be hot as hell all the time, but could also be confident that I didn't look gross," Beatriz says impatiently. "I learned how to French braid when I was like eight. It was the only way I could keep from fainting in the summer."

She opens her phone, but her face looks strained.

"Everything okay?" I ask.

"Yeah, why?"

"You just…seemed a little upset when I came in."

"We're not friends, man," Beatriz says without looking at me. "You don't have to check in with me."

My mind is racing, yet my sluggish brain's not alert enough to separate what I'm thinking from what I should say. "Maybe I want to."

Beatriz stares at me, her face struggling to stay impassive. "Why?"

I feel my heartbeat in my throat. Beatriz keeps looking at me, not letting me get away with saying nothing. I open my mouth, but nothing comes out because her eyes are boring into mine, and they're so dark and passionate, and—

"Beatriz," I say, my voice shaking.

She bites her lip. I lean toward her.

That's when she sighs and says, "Fine."

And I still. I don't want "fine." Not when she says it like that, like she's doing me a favor. The night we first met, I didn't care how she felt because I was a teenage asshole but now…she's a person and not just a body. And I'm not comfortable being with her if part of her doesn't want to be with me.

So my lips stop inches from hers. I whisper, "Why are you mad at me?"

Beatriz lets her head fall back. "Ben…"

"I know you're upset about something I did." I move as close as possible without intruding on her part of the couch.

"I'm not," Beatriz says softly, looking away from me.

"Yes, you are. I know you. I *know* you, Beatriz, and you know me. We don't have to like each other to get each other."

"The fuck you know me." There's fire in her eyes but I can't tell if it's the kind that destroys or the kind that—

"What did I *do*?" I know I'm begging, but I'm too drunk and too desperate to care. "Please, tell me. I don't know why you're mad at me."

"*Exactly.*" Beatriz's eyes flash. It's a fire that's going to destroy me, alright. "You. Don't. *Remember.*"

"I want to. Look, I know it was forever ago but—I don't want you to be mad at me."

"Then maybe you shouldn't have—" Beatriz stops talking, breathing fast.

"What?" I whisper. "I shouldn't have what?"

"It's nothing."

"Then why did you—"

"Shut *up*," Beatriz yells, gesticulating angrily as she leaps up. "Shut up, shut up, SHUT UP."

"I will when you tell me!" I yell back, following her.

I expect her to scream at me again, but she doesn't. She turns toward me and stares, her eyes tracing my face, and—

"What?" My voice cracks.

Beatriz looks at me again. "I hate you so fucking much."

Then she slams me against the door and kisses me.

Fuck.

Thoughts try to come together, but everything short-circuits as Beatriz bites down on my lip and all I can think about is kissing her back. I feel so on fire that it takes everything in me *not* to rip her clothes off, pull her into me and, and—

I want her. No, I *need* her. And I didn't realize it until this very moment, as she's pressed against me—one hand in my hair, the other under my shirt. I hold her face, and Beatriz makes a noise that sends my hands under her crop top, fumbling with the clasps of her bra.

"Fuck, I'm too drunk for this shit." I break away and look down her back.

"Just let me do it." Beatriz pulls the straps through the armholes of her shirt, dropping it before she kisses me again.

"Hey," I say, gently pulling away and wondering if I've gone insane.

"What?"

I run my hands along her sides before spreading them across her hips, holding her here so she has to look at me. "Are you—are you sure?"

Beatriz nods.

"I'm just really drunk, and you're probably drunk, and if you think this might be a mistake, we don't have to—"

"It is almost definitely a mistake." Beatriz hooks a finger around the waistband of my chinos. "But I really fucking want it."

And her shirt's off.

She pulls me toward the sofa, which is good because the

sight of her has blown a fuse in my brain and I don't remember what walking is.

Beatriz straddles me on the couch. She bends down to kiss me and waiting for her lips to find mine is the longest two seconds of my life.

There are no words to describe how much I want this girl. She doesn't carry herself the way anyone else I've hooked up with does. She's here to fuck, and she doesn't fuck around as she spreads her legs even further. My hips involuntarily push up.

"God," she hisses into my mouth. I spread my arms across her back and pull her close, feeling the sharp points of her shoulder blades as I touch as much of her as I can.

Beatriz pulls away, her eyes boring into mine, making me wait. I inhale sharply. I don't think I really *looked* at Beatriz the last time I saw her topless. Rookie mistake.

She slowly lowers her face back to mine, lightly brushing her lips against my mouth before moving them across my cheek and jaw, kissing her way across my stubble.

"Do you want to go to my—" I start to say, but then Beatriz sucks on my neck and words have no meaning.

"No, I need you now." She tightens her knees around me to make it clear she's not kidding. I close my eyes as her hands slide down my chest, tugging at my shirt, all while her mouth is still on me. I can't get my shirt off fast enough.

"Jesus Christ," Beatriz says, leaning back as it hits the ground. "I seriously hate how hot you are."

"Oh yeah?" I smirk. "You seem perfectly satisfied to me."

"Fuck you." Beatriz rolls her eyes, but I'm done waiting. I pull her face down with one hand, the other closing around her breast. Beatriz moans, her hands diving into my hair as we fall backward.

My hands slide under her jeans, and when I feel something lacy beneath my fingers, I know for sure that when the world ends, this is how I want to die.

"Take your clothes off *now*." I fumble with the snap of her pants.

"No, you." Beatriz slaps my hand away and tries to undo mine.

"No, YOU," I say more loudly, reaching for her again, but she pushes my hands away screaming back.

"NO, YOU!"

It never occurred to me that our spats were the way our repressed minds found an outlet for the sexual tension mounting between us for too long. And there's no other explanation for what's happening now, as I get more and more turned on watching her yell at me to take my clothes off.

"You're fucking annoying," I breathe, pulling her back to me so I can feel her skin against mine.

"If I'm annoying, you're a goddamn nightmare." Beatriz's words are lost in my mouth as she kisses me like she's out of time—sucking on my lip, her chest on mine. Her hands feel me hard beneath her, and Beatriz groans. "You better let me take your clothes off now—or else."

I've never been so willing to concede.

Beatriz pulls my chinos and boxers down to my ankles, and I kick them onto the floor before reaching up and yanking down the zipper of her jeans. Beatriz's underwear are bright red, and I have no time to appreciate how sexy they look because all I can think about is getting them off.

And then we're naked.

Beatriz plants her hands on my hips, moving them up as her body moves down. She comes back to me gradually, and I'd forgotten how much I like holding an ass that actually fills my palm. Her fingers tangle into my hair, and I need this to happen soon.

I want three more pairs of eyes so I can look at every part of her body and still watch her eyes bore into mine. I catch sight of my own skin as I watch Beatriz get lower, and almost burst out laughing.

"What?" Beatriz asks, a slight quake in her voice.

"I'm so fucking pale." I cover my face with my hand, laughing into my palm. When I peek through my fingers, I see Beatriz smiling too.

"Yeah, that's accurate." She lays her arm across my chest so the stark difference in our skin tones is even more obvious. "This is fucking nuts," she says softly. I wonder what she's thinking.

This shouldn't work.

This shouldn't feel as good as it does—I shouldn't want someone so different from me, someone who's everything I've been raised to avoid.

But I do. I want Beatriz with such alarming clarity that right now, I don't care what anyone else thinks.

We're still for a second—then I lunge toward Beatriz just as she throws herself at me. We meet in the middle, everything frantic and dirty and perfect, because it's her.

My heart is beating so fast it feels like a drum thundering through my chest, and I feel Beatriz's thumping at the exact same rhythm. She presses her hips against mine, whispering something that sounds like "fucking shoulders" and I'm pulsing all over.

We look at each other again—one last chance to cop out before it's impossible to go back.

"Hey." Her voice is quavering, a sliver of the vulnerability I saw last night peering through.

"Y-yeah?" I say, afraid she's going to back out as she looks into my eyes and remembers who I am. Ben Montgomery—the capitalist womanizer who stands for everything she hates.

But Beatriz lowers her head into the crook of my neck. Her breathing is jagged, her voice delicate and maybe a little scared as she mumbles, "I want you, Ben."

My breath hitches. Her pelvis moves slightly, and I *feel* her.

It happens slowly. I wrap my arms around her waist and push deeper and deeper, until we're completely connected.

"Fuck," I say as she starts rolling her hips. It's different from last time. We'd been even drunker, both on beer and the high of being in college. I'd been so consumed by the idea of fucking whenever I wanted that I didn't care who I actually fucked.

And it's been so long since someone has fucked *me*. I forgot how much I like it, how much I like watching a girl I'm insane for take control of everything and want me along for the ride. Beatriz pulls me close as our bodies keep meeting. I let her and it's everything.

When I finish—more quickly than I would've hoped—Beatriz keeps her body flush with mine.

"Shit, we don't have paper towels or anything."

"Use my shirt." I carefully reach down and toss it to her.

When she's sufficiently clean, Beatriz starts to get dressed.

"Wait." I put my hand on her arm. She looks confused. "Did you come?" I didn't think she did, but I've been with girls who said they had when I didn't feel anything change.

"No." Beatriz shakes my hand off and pulls on her underwear. "That's why I'm leaving."

"You're…going to get yourself off?"

"Yeah, I know how this works." Beatriz pulls on her jeans.

I frown. "What do you mean?"

"You got what *you* came for, so we're done." Her shirt's on, her bra swung over one shoulder. "Straight guys never want to help girls after."

"I do," I say quietly, swinging my legs off the couch and reaching for my boxers as I get up.

Beatriz frowns at me. "You didn't last time."

Jesus Christ, Montgomery. I'm ashamed I can't remember. "Seriously?"

"Um, yeah."

"Fuck. I'm sorry. Can I make it up to you now?"

She looks at me skeptically. "For real?"

I don't say anything, but cross the space between us. I put my hands under her shirt and let my mouth roam along her skin until her breathing's uneven and she whispers, "Can we go to your room? More comfortable...and private."

"Yeah, of course."

I wad up my shirt and follow her out the door. Before we leave, I make sure no one can tell anyone's done anything in here besides watch a movie.

Then we're in my room. I lock the door and grab Beatriz's wrist as she starts toward the bed.

"What?"

I kiss her lightly because *finally* I'm allowed to. It's soft. And sweet. And so different from the epic mistake we just made in the theater. But Beatriz pulls herself close, and I bend to pick her up.

"I'm heavy," she says quickly, like she's afraid.

I lift her up and she smiles. We kiss our way to my bed.

I set her on the bed's edge, holding her face with both my hands, inhaling everything about her and kissing her until my lips are numb. These past few days have been fucking torture—seeing Beatriz in my house and being close enough to touch her without pressing my lips to hers, and letting her do horrible, incredible things to me.

"Ben," she moans, and something deep inside me roars. I slide her shirt off, nudging her onto her back so I can make quick work of her pants.

"Is there anything specific you want me to do?" I ask, removing her underwear.

"Um." She looks down at me, biting her lip nervously.

"What?"

"It's embarrassing," Beatriz mumbles, breaking eye contact. I put a thumb under her chin and gently make her look at me.

"I don't care. I want you to feel good."

Beatriz's eyes grow wide and she nods. "Can you—can you just kiss me all over, and—and tell me things you like about me?"

"Sure."

"But like...won't that be hard for you?" Beatriz asks, still looking apprehensive. "I mean...you don't like me that much."

I stare at her for a long time before saying, "I don't hate you as much as I pretend to."

My lips ghost over hers before finally making contact, and I hope to god that both of us forget what I said in the morning.

Beatriz reaches down and starts touching herself. I trail my mouth across her face, letting my lip catch on her chin and kissing my way to her ear. I suck on her earlobe before whispering, "I like how smart you are."

Beatriz's head arches back on the pillow, encouraging me to keep going.

"I like how many books you've read."

Beatriz laughs a little. "Nerd."

I smile too, glad her eyes are closed and she can't see.

Listing things I like about Beatriz isn't as hard as I thought it'd be.

In fact…it's maybe a little too easy.

As Beatriz gets close, I feel like I might come again just from watching her say my name. I kiss her, and kiss her, and kiss her, my mouth absorbing the sound of her finishing.

We break apart, and I watch her sit up, wrapping herself in the comforter from the foot of my bed. I strip down to my boxers and shut off the light, wondering if Beatriz should go back to her room so we don't attract attention in the morning.

But I don't want her to.

BEATRIZ

I wake up with my head throbbing. My eyelids are heavy as I lift them and look out on—a room that's not mine. I don't get a chance to register much besides its unfamiliarity because that's when I realize I'm not alone.

"Oh shit."

Ben is asleep beside me, blond hair swooping across his face in zigzags, and his mouth slightly open.

I slept with Ben last night.

Shit, shit, shit, SHIT.

It's coming back now—the visions are hazy, but the memory of how good it felt is burned into my mind, like my body memorized every stroke of his hand and touch of his lips.

Then something slides sharply into focus: we didn't use protection.

I was so drunk, both on alcohol and the dude I'd been low-key fantasizing about, that it didn't occur to me to use a condom. I have an IUD, but still. Ben is the biggest womanizer at Harvard. What if he has something?

God, I'm such a pendeja. I *know* how to have sex safely; I've been doing it since I was fifteen. But apparently, I don't know how to have sex with Ben safely. Maybe in more ways than one.

I poke Ben until he groggily mumbles, "What?" His eyes open, and I watch the hungover wheels slowly turn in his head. His eyes go wide.

"Ohhhh no," he says, running a hand slowly down his face.

"I know."

"We didn't—"

"Oh, we did."

"Fuck, fuck, fuck." Ben sits up and pushes his hands through his hair while he leans against the headboard. It looks too hot to be allowed.

My treacherous eyes scale his torso as he sits up, the sight of his taut stomach and smooth chest deepening something inside me that's clearly not finished.

"It was a mistake, right?" Ben says, looking down at me. I sit up and the comforter falls off, exposing my bare chest. Ben looks down, and for the second time in under a minute, I watch his thoughts align with mine.

"Almost assuredly," I say, my voice shaking.

Ben watches me, his face showing all the hunger for me that I feel for him.

"Fuck it."

Ben's hands close around my cheeks and he's kissing me. It's hot and raw, and it doesn't taste great, but morning breath is the least of my concerns.

I try to ignore the pulse in my head as I feel my way down and under the elastic of his boxers. Ben's teeth clamp down on my lip when he realizes what I'm about to do. His mouth breaks from the kiss as his forehead falls against mine, his eyes squeezed shut.

I just watch him. His features are blurred because of how close we are, but I can't help marveling at how different Ben is when he's like this. During the day, he exudes this air of stony snobbery and stolid masculinity—he's everything wrong with privileged white men and is a walking manifestation of all the things I want to bring crumbling down.

But when Ben is so close that I can feel the sweat in his hair, and his features are blissed out as he moans my name, I can't shake the feeling that I'm lucky to see him like this.

Which is dumb. Ben fucks more people in a month than I've fucked in my whole life.

But still. It feels different, and I don't know why.

When he's done, Ben kisses me deeply before working his mouth down my body to repay the favor. He stays between my thighs until I'm biting my lip to keep from crying out, and my body arches closer and closer to his mouth. Oh my god—I don't ever want him to stop, I—

I come back to earth slowly. The cresting intensity left in Ben's wake catapults me so fucking high that it's several seconds before feeling returns to my limbs and reality sets back in.

And I remember why I woke Ben in the first place.

"Dude, we didn't use a condom," I say as Ben slouches off the bed and pulls a shirt out of the dresser beside it.

He freezes.

"Oh *fuck*." He looks like I just told him I'm pregnant. "You—are you on—"

"I have an IUD."

Ben looks relieved.

"But we should both get tested to make sure neither of us has any infections. And you should get tested again in a month 'cause that's how long it would take for new ones to show up."

He pauses halfway between pulling his shirt on. "Why are you being so thorough?" he asks, his head emerging. "Do you *have* something?"

"I'm being thorough because we just had raw sex." Saying it out loud makes me feel queasy. "And for all I know, *you* have something."

"Please, you have way more sex than I do." The look on Ben's face makes it clear he wouldn't have said that if he wasn't hungover.

I narrow my eyes. "Wow, it's real classy to slut-shame someone *right* after they've fucked you."

"I'm just stating a fact." Ben tugs his shirt down so aggressively he stretches the fabric. "I'm not calling you a slut. I fuck a lot too, that would be grossly hypocritical."

"Doesn't stop most guys."

Ben's eyes bore into mine. "Would you be here if I was like most guys?"

Cocky motherfucker. But...he's also not wrong. Instead of answering, I say, "How would you even know how much sex I have?"

"Because Hero stays in our room every time you're hooking up with someone," Ben says. "Which...is a lot."

"How do you know she's not there just to snuggle with Claudio?"

"Because she sleeps on the couch." Ben unplugs his phone from the wall and shoves it into his pocket like it's done him a personal wrong.

"God, what's wrong with you?"

"If it would make you feel better, we can get tested," he says coldly, completely ignoring me. "I can drive us to a clinic."

I start pulling my clothes on, the reality of what I did becoming way too real. "What are we gonna tell people if we just go off together?"

"I don't know, *you* think of something." Ben's eyes are ice as he types on his phone and starts scrolling. Before I can say anything, he adds, "You should go back to your room. It's still early, but people might start waking up soon."

I pause buttoning my jeans. Ben's brashness is…hurting my feelings.

I shouldn't feel this way; when was the last time Ben Montgomery did something that elicited an emotion besides fury or, as of last night, ecstasy?

"Fine." I yank on the rest of my clothes and leave his room before he can say anything else.

My mind spins as I lock the door to my room and collapse on the bed.

I'm so fucked. Of all the people I could have slept with, *why* Ben? I'm on hook-up apps. If I wanted to get some, I should have fucked somebody who's *not* the person I hate more than anyone else.

I groan into my pillow. I only slept with him because he's hot. That's it. And we have freakishly insane chemistry that scientifically cannot be restrained. Our bodies probably recognize each other as a diverse addition to our respective gene pools.

Ben's ancestors are probably all inbred, so that makes sense.

My phone buzzes.

Ben: There's a clinic nearby. If we go now, we could be back before people wake up.

Beatriz: what if we're not

Ben: I don't know. Tell people you went for a walk or something, and I was out getting coffee when I bumped into you and drove you back.

BEN AND BEATRIZ

Beatriz: ...u kinda had that locked and loaded

Ben: It's not THAT detailed; YOU could have thought of it in less than thirty seconds.

Oh my god. Does Ben seriously use *semicolons* when he texts?

Ben: Are you coming, or not?

I think about last night—how intense it was, how *good* it felt—and try to reconcile the guy who made me feel those things with the guy I'm talking to now. It's such a stark turnaround with absolutely no warning.

It's reminding me why I don't hook up with rich white guys. And why Ben is the reason I made that rule in the first place.

Beatriz: no ill get hero to take me

Ben doesn't respond immediately. He's probably pissed that I'm not praising him for actually taking responsibility for fucking me without a condom, and I could not care less.

Ten minutes later, my phone goes off again.

Ben: Did I piss you off?

Oh. My. God.

Beatriz: ur doing that thing again where u so obviously acted like an asshole and then r surprised when someone blows u off

Ben: What did I do?

I can't with him right now. I put my phone on silent before heading into the bathroom and taking a shower, pretending the water is washing away everything about last night. It can't happen again. And if this is how Ben acts after we hook up, then I don't want it to.

I finish my shower and pick up my phone to check the time before I get dressed. Jesus—there are three more texts from Ben.

Ben: Can you please tell me what I did?

Beatriz?

Fine, don't

Whoa. Of all the words I've used to describe Ben Montgomery, *needy* has never been one of them. I still don't want to talk to him, but it's nice to see he's human.

Instead, I text Hero. u up yet?

Hero: Yeah, what's going on

Beatriz: plz dont ask any questions, but i need u to drive me somewhere

Hero: Where? Are you okay?

Beatriz: yeah yeah. i just need to go to a sexual health clinic

Hero: Meet me downstairs in five

Hero's the fucking best. I remember all the times I called her drunk at a party at 4 a.m., and she had to sneak the car out without Uncle Leo waking up, and she never lectured me about it. She just showed up, brought me home and slept in my room in case I started barfing in my sleep.

I grab a sweatshirt and leave my room. I half expect Ben to appear in the hallway when my door clicks shut but he doesn't.

Hero's waiting in the foyer when I come down.

"How'd you get here so fast?"

Hero blushes. "What do you mean?"

Alright, now I'm suspicious. "I mean, you texted me—" I check my phone "—literally less than a minute ago to meet you in five, and you're already here."

"I just walk fa—"

But Hero is interrupted by Claudio coming out of a room just off the foyer, saying, "Darling, you left your phone in—" He stops when he sees me. "Oh hey," he says sheepishly, holding the phone out to Hero, who takes it quickly.

"Oh my GOD," I whisper when Claudio disappears. "Did you—did you guys finally—"

"No!" Hero says, too quickly for it not to seem defensive. I frown.

"¿Qué pasó?"

"Nothing."

"Did he pressure you?"

"No! He'd never do that!"

I give her a look.

"I'm serious, Trizita," she says. "I'm just…still not ready."

"He better be chill with that. Or I will take a carrot peeler to his face."

Hero snorts. "He is. We were just snuggling."

"Ew."

Hero laughs and pulls a set of car keys out of her purse.

"So where am I taking you exactly?" she asks, opening the door to the garage.

"Oh. Whose car are we taking?" I didn't think about this part.

"Ben's parents give Claudio a car to use when he's here." Hero walks down the garage's many bays before unlocking the doors to a BMW.

"This…is their spare car? Also, who just *gives* someone else a car to use whenever they're here?"

"I mean, it's pretty generous." Hero turns the key in the ignition as I shut my door. "Maybe it's the car designated for guest use, not just Claudio." She puts the car in gear and backs out.

"Whatever."

"Oh yeah, where am I going?" Hero asks, hitting the brakes.

"I actually have no idea." I take out my phone and google it. I almost tell Hero that Ben said there was a clinic nearby, but that would lead to questions about why Ben, of all people, knows I'm looking to get tested.

"There's one like ten minutes away." I start a navigation and put my phone in the holster attached to the windshield.

"Righto."

"So…are you not gonna ask me why I texted you before 10 a.m. asking to be driven to a sex clinic?" I say a little later, as the GPS informs us that our destination is on the right.

Hero shuts the car off. "I mean, you said you didn't want to talk about it."

"That doesn't always stop you from asking."

Hero shrugs. "I figured you drunkenly got with someone from Tinder after we all went to bed, and woke up to realize you hadn't used protection or something."

Well, 75 percent of that is true.

★ ★ ★

"So what freaks you out about sex?" I ask Hero as we drive home from my appointment. "Like, it's totally fine if you're just not ready, but…is it something you even want?"

Hero thinks it over. "I don't think I'm asexual, if that's what you're asking. I definitely…like stuff."

She blushes and I have to keep from snorting. "Then what is it?"

"It's just…really fucking scary." Hero's face wrinkles with emotion.

"Hey." I reach over and gently put my hand on Hero's shoulder. She takes a deep breath, but her expression doesn't change.

"Pull over here."

Hero pulls into a parking lot on our left, shutting off the car once we're in a spot.

"What's going on?" I ask. "Does Claudio make you feel scared?"

Hero shakes her head. "No, the opposite. Like he's up-front that he wants to whenever I'm ready, but said he wants me to be in control when it happens. So, like, when we're making out and stuff, he never puts his hand under my shirt or anything unless I place it there."

Wow. Maybe he's a better dude than I gave him credit for.

"But when he touches me I just…*feel* too much." Hero pulls her hair into a ponytail. By the time we're done talking, I bet it'll have gone through at least four different hairstyles.

"Okay?"

Hero pulls the ponytail out before she's finished tying it and starts a braid. "No one's touched me before, Trizita," she says like this explains everything.

"Okay?"

"I've never gotten goose bumps from not being cold!" Hero bursts out, dropping her hands so her half-braided hair falls limp. "I didn't know sounds could come out of my mouth without my permission! I didn't know you could want someone to bite you. I feel like I'm not me anymore." Hero's voice breaks and I see tears in her eyes.

"Hero," I say gently, unbuckling my seat belt and pulling her into my arms. "That's all normal."

"It doesn't feel normal," Hero sniffs. "It feels—it feels—" She doesn't finish.

"Feels what?"

"Too good," she mumbles. "I—it's just not something I was prepared for."

I'm quiet. I want to help Hero but I can't relate to what she's talking about at all. The first time I kissed someone, I wanted more. The rush that comes with physical intimacy was never something I feared, it was something I chased. I know Hero's different, but I can't wrap my head around being afraid to feel good.

"I just feel like I don't know myself anymore," Hero says softly. "It's like—we're about to be real adults and I thought I had everything figured out. I've got my apprenticeship, I'm looking for apartments, I'm as prepared for the next chapter as I can possibly be."

Like I need any more reminders about how fucked *I* am come May.

"And then the most basic thing I feel in control of— my body—becomes foreign. And it's just…shit timing. I'm twenty-two and can't even lose my virginity to the guy I'm in love with."

I squeeze her tighter. "Life doesn't always go to plan, I

guess," I say, knowing I'm being cliché as fuck but I don't know what else to say.

Hero snuggles into me. "Has your life turned out differently than you thought it would?"

My heart lurches as I think about the night Hillary lost. The job applications I'd been researching for a year staring blankly at me from my laptop. The due date passing because I was too exhausted from doom scrolling to entertain adult life with a fascist running the world.

Then images of Ben flash through my mind. Something else I didn't expect and don't know what to do about. I start to remember what he said to me last night, and how I asked him to do something I've always wanted but have never had the guts to ask for.

"I mean, not any more than it did when I was nine," I say, pushing Ben out of my mind. Or trying to.

"Right, sorry." The desperation melts from Hero's face and she takes my hand. "I didn't mean to...of course your life hasn't turned out like you thought it would."

"It's okay," I say, finishing her braid. "Moving in with you and Uncle Leo has made my life a lot better than it would be if I hadn't."

I still remember the day Leo and I got the last of my stuff from my mom's house. She wasn't supposed to be home, but of course she was—hiding behind a trash can in the backyard, only emerging when I went out alone to get my soccer ball.

"Mami—" She was thinner than the last time I'd seen her, her ribs showing through her filmy tank top. Her skin paler than I'd ever seen it, dark circles under her eyes.

"How could you do this to me?" she choked. "Do you not love me?"

"I—"

But then Leo started calling my name.

"If you tell him I'm here, you're dead to me," my mom said. "Do you understand?"

I nodded, trying not to cry, not understanding how I could feel so numb when my mom was saying things that should have hurt me. She sank back behind the trash can, I picked up my soccer ball, and Leo took me home.

Now, looking at Hero, I'm reminded both of how much I lost and how much I gained. I just wish this trade-off didn't come with nightmares that never cease, and depression that I sometimes worry will pull me under.

Hero holds out the hair tie and I finish her braid.

"Thanks for being my therapist," she says quietly. "I think I really needed to vent."

I smile. "Anytime. Playing therapist is the only thing I'm actually good at."

7

BEN

I hear Beatriz's door slam and her footsteps stalk down the hall only thirty minutes after she was in my bed. I stare down at my phone, but she hasn't responded to my texts. I read and reread the unanswered messages and feel more and more humiliated every time.

What the fuck is her problem? She makes such a huge deal out of what an oblivious asshole I am, but then when I try to get her side of the story she shuts down? This is why we're always at each other's throats—if I'm not aware enough, or woke enough, to do exactly what she thinks is right, I'm not worth talking to. Even if all I'm trying to do is understand what she means.

I clench and unclench my fists before grabbing *The Last Olympian* and heading downstairs to eat.

"Morning, mate." Claudio walks in as the coffee machine beeps.

"Hey." I take out two mugs and fill them with coffee, leaving room for Claudio to add milk. Which he only does if no one else is around. Everyone in his family drinks it black and he didn't even realize you could add milk until he stayed with me.

"Cheers." Claudio takes the mug and smiles. I must look extra grumpy today because Claudio glances down at the book under my arm and says, "Uh-oh. What's wrong?"

"Nothing." I throw the book down on the island and pull out a stool.

"You only read Percy Jackson when shit's really bad."

"No, I don't." I didn't realize Claudio knew I still read it at all.

Claudio just looks at me. "Dude, when John sent you that 'care package,' you had the entire series stashed under your bed for months."

My stomach twists as I remember the package of literal worms John sent me once, with the attached note of, "They missed their daddy."

"I don't—just—fuck off."

"Okay." Claudio squeezes my shoulder before getting cereal and two bowls.

As he fills our bowls with milk and cereal, I stare at the same page in my book for five minutes. Part of me wants to tell Claudio everything—to ask him about the weird, corrosive feeling that took root in my stomach when I remembered the times Hero showed up at our door because Beatriz was fucking someone who wasn't me. It felt awful and so unfamiliar that it made me drive Beatriz away just minutes after I made her come.

But the other part of me doesn't want Claudio to know—

not just that I hooked up with Beatriz, but that I care when she hooks up with other people.

So I go for a combo. "I slept with someone last night."

Claudio looks up from his phone, raising his eyebrows in surprise. "Who?"

"Just someone around here." That's believable enough; Claudio knows that there are a couple local girls I hook up with whenever I'm home.

"Okay…" Claudio waves his hand in a *go on* motion.

"And… I don't know, it was great, and then this morning she got all bitchy."

Claudio just looks at me.

"Dude, what?"

"I doubt that's what happened," Claudio says, not unkindly. "Look, you're my best mate, but you do tend to—"

"What?" I'm getting pissed now. I shouldn't have said anything.

"You're just…kind of sensitive," he says. "Not in a bad way," he adds quickly, when he sees how clenched my jaw is. "I mean, it makes sense. I've been here like twelve times, and there's never been a time John hasn't—"

"What are you getting at?" I want this conversation to be over. But Claudio looks at me like he wants to help—not like he pities me, or like he thinks I'm an asshole. He just sees me. So I don't shut him down.

"You just react to everyone like they're your brother, even when it's someone like me, who's never intentionally—what's the word?—dissed you." Claudio sips his coffee and grimaces. He's always complaining about how appalling American coffee is. "And that makes sense because John *does* shit on you in really subtle ways so he can easily deny them. It just…shouldn't be surprising if you lash out at someone and they don't want to be around you."

Jesus Christ. Claudio observes so much more than other people. Like when he made Hero that pot of tea yesterday. She didn't ask him for it—she probably hasn't even told Claudio that she has a pot of tea at six o'clock every day. But Claudio noticed.

And sometimes the fruit of these observations is a psychology paper on why I'm an asshole.

"I guess that makes sense," I say.

Claudio pats me on the back as he puts his empty bowl in the dishwasher. "Should we finish up that Magic game?"

I shake my head. "No, I—I have to do something."

"Alright." Claudio takes a last sip of coffee and squeezes my arm. "You're a good bloke, Ben. You just…try really hard to be your dad."

I shrug. Not wanting to admit that Claudio might be right.

I get up, grabbing my keys from the counter. I don't even know what I'm going to do, but I know I want to see Beatriz and maybe she and Hero haven't left yet.

I walk into the garage just as the car Claudio always uses pulls in. My heart sinks when I see Beatriz in the passenger seat, talking animatedly to Hero.

"Hey, Ben," Hero says to me when she opens the car door.

"Hey." I shift my gaze to Beatriz. Her face is hard to read—it's not angry, but it's not happy either.

"Where are you off to?" Hero asks as they pass me.

"Uh—"

"Getting coffee?" Beatriz's voice is slightly hard.

I feel myself flush. "Yeah. You guys need anything?"

"I'm good," says Hero, looking down. Beatriz doesn't even respond.

When they've disappeared into the house, I start my car, heading out of the driveway to the nearest sex clinic.

I get home half an hour later, and see Hero and Beatriz lying on a couch in the piano room, their legs piled on top of each other. Hero's reading this book called *The Hate U Give* that I've seen all over the internet. Beatriz is reading—*Dubliners*? I must be seeing things.

I look again and see that I'm not. But at the beach she called James Joyce a sexist male pig.

I kind of want to talk to them but can't make myself do it. Instead, I climb the stairs to my bedroom. Maybe I can finish *Mansfield Park* and start my essay before hitting up the gym.

But I stop cold when I pass the den.

John's back.

Looking significantly tanner and just as douche-y.

I walk over to where John's sitting with Peter. "I thought you were going for a couple days."

"Had business to attend to." John gives me a look and I know exactly what he means.

"Come on, man," I say, looking down and seeing what's spread on the coffee table between him and Peter.

Meg pops her head up from under the coffee table. "Benny!"

"What the hell are you doing under there?" I start pulling her to her feet. She's gone all limp; it's like holding a rag doll. I put her arms around my shoulders as I hoist her up and see something that makes my heart stop.

Track marks.

"Why do you have those?" I ask, almost shaking Meg. She slouches as I try to make her stand, and we both topple onto the couch.

"Shhhhhhh." Meg brings a finger to her lips. "It's a secret."

"What the actual FUCK, John!" I yell at my brother, wanting to hit him so bad that it's good there's nothing nearby I could throw at him.

"Meg's a big girl now, she can do what she wants," John says, like my rage is an inconvenience. "Don't blame me if she's finally ready to have fun."

"John said I'm fun," Meg whispers, giggling into me.

"It's not even ten in the morning!" I turn to my best friend, holding her up so I can have a better look at her—at this person I've been trying to protect since we were thirteen and I found her drunk in a closet. Who I'm letting slip through the cracks.

How long has Meg been doing heroin with them? John and Peter have been shooting up forever, but Meg has an addictive personality—her aggressive indulgence of alcohol makes *that* clear. John knows that, and frankly, I'm surprised Peter is idly watching his baby sister do smack.

But come to think of it, Peter never says no to John. None of us do.

I want to rip John limb from limb and melt the pieces, *Breaking Bad* style. My chest starts heaving as my hands shake.

John's face darkens as he looks at me.

"Don't cross me, kid genius," John says, his voice serious for once. "Just because you're Dad's favorite doesn't mean you're anything to me."

My chest goes cold. John's right—it's just the first time either of us have admitted it.

The last time John was happy, *he* was the one being groomed for the six-figure job right out of college. It was his name falling from the lips of every hot socialite trying to get a piece of the Montgomery name. I could walk around the house reading fantasy books without Dad saying, "I already have one failure of a son. I don't need another."

John's hated me since I was nine and skipped fourth grade—

when he started flunking out of school because he couldn't read things properly. But Dad had too much pride to get him help, Mom was too scared to stick up for him, and John had too much pride to admit he needed her too.

He started stealing Mom's oxy when I was top of my class every year, then he picked up heroin when Dad started introducing us as, "This is Ben. And that's my other son," all the while developing a hatred for me I didn't realize went this deep. Because the way John's looking at me now is scary.

He won't think twice before seriously fucking up my life.

"Meg, come on." I loop her arm around my shoulders and start to pull her up.

"You can take her away, man," John calls as I drag Meg out of the den. "Doesn't mean she won't come back."

Something heavy crushes my chest, and I know that the second I've got Meg settled in her room, I'm going to freak out. I tuck her into bed as quickly as possible, put a glass of water on the bedside table, lock myself in my room, and sink to the ground.

I'm breathing so heavily that my body rocks with every inhale and exhale. My head feels foggy. My vision blacks out. I curl my arms around my knees, hiding my face because I know what comes next. Tears flood down my cheeks as I breathe like I'm drowning, tears that have no feeling because I'm completely numb as I rock back and forth. I only know I'm crying because the tears are hot when the rest of my body feels cold.

I freak out for, like, half an hour before I start to get a headache from all this dumb crying. I wipe my face, blow my nose and put on gym clothes.

I pass the den on my way to the basement and see that John and Peter are gone. But all their drug paraphernalia is still splayed across the table.

Anger rakes through my body and I'm picking up everything from the needles to the drugs themselves before running back to my room. I stash them behind my Norton Critical Jane Austens. It's the last place John would ever look.

John can break me as much as he wants. But I will not let him break Meg.

I go down to the gym and work out until I'm so sweaty, my hands leave imprints on the floor. I go back to my room, shower and read *Mansfield Park* until my eyes hurt.

It's dark out when I leave to check on Meg. She hasn't moved from the bed I put her in hours ago. I check her pulse and tuck the covers around her once I feel a steady beat.

Back in my room, I open my laptop to start an outline for my essay when there's a knock at my door. I frown. Meg always barges in without knocking, and Claudio texts me if he wants to hang out.

I open the door and Beatriz is in front of me.

"Hi," I say, something fluttering through me as I see her standing there. She's wearing a black hoodie that says Freedom with the BLM logo on the arm, and red pajama pants with Ruth Bader Ginsburg's face all over them.

Gee, can you tell she's horny for social justice?

"I thought you never wanted to talk to me again," I say, noticing that she takes out some of her many ear piercings when getting ready for bed.

"Not that I care," she says icily, "but—"

"That sentence is only ever uttered by people who do care."

Her eyes narrow. "You need to not right now."

"You're the one knocking on my door."

"Well, Hero and I heard yelling earlier, and then you just disappeared. Don't want people to think I murdered you for your problematic adoration of Kerouac."

I don't say anything. Which Beatriz takes as a cue to walk toward me, so I have no choice but to step aside.

"Yes, by all means, come into my room." I shake my head as I close the door.

I turn around to see Beatriz staring openmouthed at my bookcases.

"What?" I say, realizing too late that I've never let anyone besides Meg in here. I don't want people to see that, in addition to Dickens, George Eliot, Austen and Joyce, I've also got Philip Pullman, Harry Potter, multiple Rick Riordan series and Kate DiCamillo scattered all over my room.

Beatriz walks over to my Jane Austen bookcase. "Dude… you're a nerd."

"I'm not—"

"How did I not know you *do* have a boner for proto-feminist lit?"

I try not to laugh, so I shrug. "It's not something I advertise."

"But why?"

I shrug again, not wanting to tell Beatriz that I tried reading Jane Austen in the living room when I was twelve and John gave me so much shit for it that I couldn't read any books for a week without crying.

"Why are you just noticing this now?" I ask, walking over to stand beside her. "You were here last night."

"Yeah, but…I was distracted." She looks at the ground, the color in her face deepening. For the first time all day, things don't totally suck. "Now I see why you like how many books I've read."

Her tone is light, but when I meet her eyes, they're nervous.

"I do," I say softly, turning around to sit back down at my desk. I really hope she doesn't remember what I said only moments before that.

"So why do you have an entire library of Jane Austen?"

Beatriz sits in the armchair in front of the bookcase. I purse my lips but don't say anything. "What?"

"You can't tell anyone," I say, not really knowing why I'm gearing up to tell her this anyway. Maybe it's because Beatriz remembers what I say to her when things are too intense for words, or because—for once—someone came to make sure *I* was okay instead of the other way around. "I've read the complete works of Jane Austen."

"No. Way." Beatriz sits up in her chair, glee taking over her entire face. "On *purpose*? I did not see that coming. So, why are you taking Austen and Rebellion if you've already read all her books? I know you need the credit, but it just seems like that would bore you."

I hesitate again.

"Dude, I won't tell anyone." Beatriz holds up two fingers in a Scout's honor. "This is way too juicy for me to risk not hearing more."

"See, I felt okay until you said that."

Beatriz laughs. "For real, I won't let it slip to anyone if you don't want me to, not even Hero."

"Really?"

Beatriz nods.

"Well… Jane Austen is actually my favorite author," I say, stacking some pencils scattered across my desk neatly behind my laptop. "Her character work is unparalleled. And I just wanted more insight into her work. You can consult Wikipedia all you want, but it's no substitute for learning from a professional."

"Have you read the annotated ones?"

Wait, she knows about those? "The huge ones that are, like, coffee-table-book-sized?"

Beatriz shakes her head. "I'll show you." She leaves, giving me a few moments to try and get my body to calm the fuck down because if Beatriz knows as much about Jane Austen as I do, I'm going to jump her bones right now.

"I mean these ones," Beatriz says, closing my door when she comes back and holding out a thick paperback copy of *Pride and Prejudice*. The spine is creased in so many places I'm worried the book will split in half if I open it.

"Wait, there are annotations for the *cover*?" I say when I see the first page. I look at her, knowing there's a smile breaking across my face because my cheeks hurt, and Beatriz is looking back at me with the exact same level of enthusiasm.

"Right?" she says, coming closer. She smells like pinewood soap and a scent that is so distinctly Beatriz it's hard for me not to kiss her. "These editions are *amazing*. The dude who annotates them is so thorough, it feels like you're reading a contemporary novel. He explains all the tiny things you don't even realize you don't know."

"Oh my god, I need all of these." My voice is hushed as I sit in my desk chair, carefully thumbing through the book in hungry awe.

Beatriz sits back down in the armchair. "You can borrow that if you want."

"Really?" I'm shocked. Letting someone borrow a book this worn is like letting them borrow your soul.

"Sure," says Beatriz. "I mean, I'll be here for a while, right?"

I nod. I assume she means staying here for the rest of spring break, but part of me hopes she could mean something else too. "Thanks," I say, because there are no words to describe how holding this book makes me feel. It's like before Beatriz came into my room I was freezing, but now I'm wrapped in a fleece blanket and feel just a little more at peace.

"No problem." Beatriz stares at me.

"What?" I say holding her gaze. My heart is beating too fast for me to even think about breaking it.

"So you *do* like Jane Austen," she says, her voice as soft as her eyes.

"And you like James Joyce," I say just as quietly, knowing she's remembering our exchange on the beach. "I saw you and Hero earlier."

"Maybe you're not as much of a fucker as I thought."

I laugh. "Don't get your hopes up."

"I w—" But Beatriz stops talking.

I look at her, my heart beating even faster at the thought of what she was about to say. Part of me hopes it was, "I want to."

But Beatriz doesn't say anything. Instead, she pulls a book from my bookcase and starts reading as I begin my outline. Well, as I try to—the truth is, Beatriz sitting in my room reading my books is such a fucking turn-on that I can't look at anything besides her body curled into that armchair for more than five seconds.

"Well…it's late," she says after a while.

My head jerks up. I can't tell if she's just commenting on the hour, or if she's implying we should—

"Maybe I should go to bed."

Damn it. "Okay."

Our eyes meet as she gets up, hers asking the question that's burning in both our minds.

Her sweatshirt rides up as she walks away, and I see the flash of a belly-button ring she wasn't wearing last night.

Oh my god. What the fuck am I doing?

This girl is not just out of my league, we don't even play the same sport; we're not *supposed* to play the same sport. We belong in lanes that are never supposed to overlap.

But I want her so bad.

"No," I say quickly, standing up. Beatriz's hand drops from the doorknob and she looks at me, her face open. "You can stay if you want." I try so hard to sound like I don't care.

Beatriz's face slips a little. "Do you want me to?"

Yes, yes, yes, YES.

But also no.

If I sleep with Beatriz again, something will be different. Two drunken hookups are very different from sober sex.

I glance down at the book in her hand—*Jane Austen and Philosophy*. It's a book I got from a graduate school syllabus one of the times I drunkenly researched advanced literary degrees. And suddenly the idea of smart, nerdy Beatriz, the girl who knows maybe more about Jane Austen than I do, leaving my bedroom without tangling her body with mine is too unbearable to consider.

"Yes." I push my chair aside, making quick strides to close the space between us. "I really fucking do."

"Are you s—" But Beatriz doesn't have time to finish her sentence because my mouth is sliding into hers.

She tastes like pizza and ginger ale, and I probably taste like microwave burritos, but I don't care. I'm too caught up in the noise Beatriz makes when I push her against the wall, and the unbearable way her skin feels under the soft cotton of her sweatshirt.

I brace my hand on the door as Beatriz heaves into me, her thigh rising to hook around my hip. This is the first time we're hooking up sober, and I'm almost enraged by how much better it feels.

Before, when Beatriz slid her tongue over mine, everything felt like fire, but this—the white-hot sensation burning through me—is pyromania.

"Wait, fuck," Beatriz says, tearing herself away as I groan. "I just remembered—"

"What could you possibly remember that's worth talking about right now?" My eyes are closed as I trace my lips across her throat, pulling at the hood of her sweatshirt as I try to kiss her shoulders.

"I got tested today and haven't gotten the results back."

"Oh." I stop. "Shit, right." I won't be getting my results back until tomorrow at the earliest.

We look at each other. Beatriz bites her lip as she stares at me, and I want to touch it so badly.

"What do we do, then?" I say, taking her hand. For a second, I'm embarrassed, but then Beatriz's fingers close tightly around mine and I don't feel embarrassed at all.

Then, a look crosses her face that makes my heart fumble. She pushes me off her and walks toward me so I have to back up. She backs me against the edge of the bed until I have nowhere to go but down.

I expect Beatriz to shove me like she did last night, but instead she sits down beside me and scoots back, pulling the collar of my shirt until I'm crawling along above her. She slowly pulls off her clothes, pushing my hands away when I try to help, and I'm already hard.

When Beatriz is naked, her fingers travel south on her own body, and I bend down to slide my tongue across her neck, down past her shoulders, and onto her chest.

"No," Beatriz says, pushing me off. "Watch me."

Holy. Fucking. *Shit.*

I can't *not* watch her. This is sexier than any of the porn I've ever watched.

When it sounds like she's close, Beatriz pulls at my shirt and says, "Please do it too."

My clothes hit the ground and I'm naked beside her. We finish together and I look down to see her holding my other hand.

Just as I feel something buoyant rising through my body, Beatriz gets up much too quickly. My hand falls limply on the bed.

"What—what are you doing?" I ask because she's throwing her clothes back on like we're fucking on a couch and her parents just got home.

"It's late," she says, disappearing under her sweatshirt.

"Oh. Do you usually go to bed early?"

"No." Beatriz pulls on her RBG pants. "I just… Hero might have a nightmare or something, and I need to be in my room if she comes looking for me because she can't find me in here, and I just think it'd be better if I—"

I have never seen Beatriz Herrera babble. It's so out of character that I look for reasons she might have to be freaking out.

Then I realize—the reason is me.

Or at least, the me she got this morning after we hooked up. The me who was so jealous that I pushed her away. And if I don't say anything now, I'll push her away again.

"Beatriz." I reach out, closing my hand around hers like I did by the door.

"Yeah?" Her eyes are so vulnerable it makes me ache.

"I want you to stay."

Beatriz looks confused.

"I was shitty this morning," I mumble. Beatriz's eyes widen. "Um…yeah. So if you want…please stay."

She turns off the light and crawls in beside me. She doesn't let go of my hand as we fall asleep.

Beatriz is asleep the next morning as I pull on workout clothes. I wonder if I should leave her a note telling her where I'm going, then I realize that this is (a) embarrassingly 90s, and (b) way too personal for someone I've only slept with three times (four if you count freshman year).

She's gone when I return. I close my bedroom door after changing, wondering if I should text her, when someone calls my name.

"Benny!" I turn around to see Meg skipping down the hall.

"Hey," I say, my eyes darting to her pupils. They seem normal. "How'd you sleep?"

"Oh fine," she says, not meeting my eye. Odd. I open my mouth to ask her to elaborate, but she bursts out, "You know what we should do?"

"Uh, what?" I ask.

"Go on a whale watch!"

Oh god. I hate whale watches. As a concept, they're fine, but *every* time my parents host friends from Europe, it's the first thing they want to do. I have been on more whale watches than the number of years I've been alive.

"But—why?" I ask.

"Beatriz and Hero have never been!"

I perk up. "Did they say they wanted to go on one?" I ask as we walk downstairs.

"Dunno!" Meg jumps the last few steps and runs into the kitchen. Beatriz is sitting there, scrolling through her phone, but she looks up when we come in. Her eyes dart between Meg and me before quickly looking away.

"Good morning!" Meg hops over to Beatriz and gives her a hug.

Beatriz looks startled. "Are you always this happy in the morning?"

"Depends on the morning." Meg gives Beatriz an exaggerated wink and Beatriz's lips tighten. "Anyway, we should all go on a whale watch later," she says. "It's a Cape Cod requirement."

"Do you just…watch whales?" Beatriz asks, looking like this is the worst possible way to spend time.

"Yeah, but you get to be on the ocean and it's majestic and shit," Meg says, scrolling through her phone. "There's one in like an hour." Beatriz is still wary. Meg rolls her eyes. "John is away for the day if that affects your decision."

Beatriz snorts. "It does, actually. I guess I'll go if Hero goes," she says, sliding off her barstool. "I'll see if she's up yet."

But just as Beatriz has disappeared upstairs, Hero and Claudio emerge from Claudio's bedroom.

"Morning!" Claudio says, starting to make coffee.

"Sup." I nod at Claudio. "So Meg is making us go on a whale watch."

"Ooh." Hero's face brightens. "That sounds fun."

"Yo, Beatriz!" Meg calls up the stairs. "Hero's in!"

"Ugh, fine," Beatriz calls down. She comes into view looking as excited about this as I am.

"Anchors aweigh, mateys!" Meg says, racing toward the garage door and starting down the stairs.

So I guess we're going on a whale watch.

"This. Is. *Freezing*." Beatriz's arms are wrapped around herself as she shivers. We've just left the dock, Beatriz and Hero sitting on a bench while Meg stands at the railing with Claudio and me. Meg leans on me as she looks down at the ocean and I scroll through Twitter. Claudio's posting everything to his Instagram story, like he hasn't been dragged on almost as many whale watches as I have during his tenure as a Montgomery houseguest.

The boat is surprisingly busy for a Cape whale watch in March. It's mostly cetacean nerds who are hoping to spot a specific breed of whale that's most common in the spring. The driver is doing his usual announcer thing when a lone flipper emerges from the water. "And that's a humpback whale," a voice booms over the intercom. "That flipper has as many bones as you have in your arm and hand."

Sea spray whips me in the face, and sitting seems like it's

the better option. I approach the bench where Beatriz and Hero are perched.

"Why the fuck didn't you tell us it would be so cold?" Beatriz says the second I sit down.

I blink. "Because I figured sailing through the ocean while there's still snow on the ground would have made it obvious," I say, trying to sound scornful. I don't exactly know what's going on with us—if we're going to hook up again, or if she even wants to—but I feel like I should act like nothing's changed in front of everyone.

"You suck," Beatriz says, and I think I've made the right call. Hero rubs her hands up and down Beatriz's arms to try and warm her up.

Meg slumps down on my other side and I look up to see Claudio slide in next to Hero. They smile at each other in a way that conveys more than I've ever said in a five-thousand word essay.

"God, I think the last time I was on a whale watch I was still with Harper," Meg says, crossing her legs under her.

"Shit, really?" I say. Harper was Meg's only serious relationship, back when we were in high school. "That was forever ago."

Meg nods. "She's at Brown now."

"An ex?" Beatriz asks, taking a break in her shivering to talk to Meg.

Meg nods. "I liked her a lot, but she ended things once she found out I was bi." She shrugs like this isn't a big deal, but I remember how cut up she was when it happened. There was an unexpected ER trip that night.

"God, that sucks," Beatriz says, turning to face Meg. "I'm sorry."

"Thanks." Meg smiles weakly.

"Wait, why would she do that?" Claudio says, leaning

around Hero to see Meg. I wish he was sitting next to me so I could elbow his side.

"Um…" Meg looks uncomfortable. "Because biphobia's a big thing in the queer community?"

"What's that?"

"Wow, really?" Beatriz looks at Claudio like he's dirt.

Claudio shrugs. "No one talks about stuff like this back home," he says. "I like to learn!" Claudio smiles and Hero rests her head on his shoulder.

"Biphobia is exactly what it sounds like," Beatriz says snappishly. "People being phobic of, or erasing the identities of, bisexual people."

"Oh, huh," he says. "So why would your ex break up with you just because you're bi?"

"Um, she had some bad experiences with girls saying they were bi just to hook up with her," Meg mumbles. "Because they wanted a story, or whatever. So she didn't really trust anyone who was bi not to cheat on her."

"Yeah, it's fucking bullshit," says Beatriz, angrily. I wonder if she has a lot of queer friends.

"Well, hold on," says Claudio. "Just to play devil's advocate—" Beatriz tenses beside me "—wouldn't sleeping with a guy make you less queer? I mean, if the 'queerness' of bisexuality comes from liking the same gender, you would *technically* be less queer than someone who is fully homosexual. Like, you'd be 50 percent queer whereas a lesbian is 100 percent queer."

"That's not how sexuality works, asshole," Beatriz snaps.

Claudio holds up his hands in surrender. "I was just being hypothetical."

"Well, don't." Beatriz gets up and walks over to the side of the boat, looking out over the water. She wraps her arms around herself and I see her visibly shivering.

I walk over to her. "Here," I say, slipping out of my jacket and handing it to her.

She raises her eyebrows at me. "No way. It smells like a country club."

"You are clearly cold," I say. "No one's gonna care. Just be comfortable."

A smile tugs at Beatriz's mouth because I'm repeating verbatim what she said at the beach the day before yesterday.

"Fine."

BEATRIZ

The first thing I do when I get the email saying I have no STIs is fuck Ben in a bathroom. We're all out to dinner after the whale watch—Ben, Hero, Claudio, Meg and even Peter, which honestly surprises me since he doesn't usually hang out with us.

Although I did see him slip Meg's ID off the table and into his pocket while she was studying the menu. So maybe Ben's not as alone in taking care of her as he thinks he is.

I see the email pop up on my phone and glance at Hero, making sure she's not watching. I look across the table at Ben when I open it. He's watching me quizzically. I take a screenshot and text it to him, knowing it doesn't matter if Hero sees. Ben and I gave each other fake names in our phones.

A smile that absolutely destroys me spreads across Ben's face as he types. A screenshot pops up on my phone—Ben's negative test result. My heart skips as he keeps typing. Who knew responsibility could be this sexy?

The words that pop onto my screen are so salacious that all I can manage through the pound of my heartbeat is, bathroom five minutes.

The second the door's locked, Ben presses his lips to my neck with an almost angry urgency, guiding me forward until my crotch meets the edge of the sink. I can feel how ready he is as he crowds up behind me, and I fumble in my pocket for the condom I put there this morning. His hands slide under my shirt and across my stomach, and I feel a brief stab of fear because he's feeling how not-skinny I am. But Ben pulls at my skin in a way that makes it clear he wants me, and as he toys with the button of my jeans everything inside me melts.

How is he so good at this? And why is it making me so weak?

"I wanted you so bad earlier," he says, teeth grazing my neck.

He slips the condom on, pulling my underwear aside, and then he's inside me. He moans and I can't believe we spent the majority of our day not having sex. Halfway through, Ben stops and turns me around so I'm facing him.

"I know bathrooms are gross but I need you naked." Ben's voice is deep and desperate but his eyes are like they were back at the train station—asking my permission and being okay with hearing no.

I rip my shirt over my head as he lifts me onto the sink.

"You too."

Ben pulls his shirt off as my legs close around his back, pulling his hips to mine. "Fuck—you—" Ben mumbles when he feels how wet I am.

"That's kind of the point." I arch toward him and he slides back into me. Ben's forehead smudges the mirror as he fucks me deeply.

"You're gonna make me come," Ben moans when it feels so good I can't breathe. I gasp, "Yes," and Ben's mouth is hot against my neck as we get there together.

I open my eyes to see him smiling at me. It's hard not to smile back.

"Satisfactory?" His eyes are glinting as I pull my clothes back on.

"I didn't think you'd need verbal confirm—"

Ben kisses me before I can finish, and I feel his grin widen.

But then I remember the nude he got mere days ago on the T. And how he told me to "get in line" on the drive here. The line of blonde, skinny white girls I've watched him make out with all across campus.

Ben's only sleeping with me because that line is miles away.

I pull away from him and button my jeans. "So, we're not telling anyone, right?"

"Oh. Right, yeah."

"Cool."

He picks his shirt off the floor and I watch his skin disappear under a long-sleeve Lacoste. It's easier this way. The sex will be better too.

But I also know that Ben would want this to be a secret even if we didn't have history. Because Ben Montgomery III would sooner lose his trust fund than admit he's attracted to someone like me. Which is honestly fine. It's better, actually, because it means that sleeping with Ben poses no threat to my equilibrium. He's a dirty capitalist who's only at Harvard because of Daddy's money. I'm a first-generation immigrant attending Harvard on scholarships. There's no way feelings could fuck it up.

After Ben leaves, I wait five minutes before following.

"But I don't see why you'd want to do sit-ups in a restaurant bathroom," Claudio's saying as I take my seat next to Hero. I look up to see that Ben is *flushed*, like he's just taken a long walk on the beach without sunscreen.

"I needed to earn the pasta I ordered," Ben says, playing with his napkin.

"I thought you got a lobster roll."

"So, Meg, where do you go to school?" I say, because Hero's looking at me like she's putting the pieces together.

Meg looks embarrassed. "I, uh—don't go to school. I tried, but…" She doesn't elaborate.

"Oh, that's cool," I say, suddenly remembering that Meg *told* me she'd barely finished high school when she brought me the snickerdoodles. Oops.

"Honestly, you're lucky," Ben says quickly, looking at Meg in a way that makes my jaw tighten. "When it's January, and I'm crossing Quincy Street on the way to Lamont from Mem Hall, I would much rather be at home in front of a fire than going to the library."

Meg smiles appreciatively, and my stomach clenches.

"That is *not* the fastest way to Lamont from Mem Hall."

Ben looks surprised for a second, but matches my tone when he responds. "It's definitely faster, I've clocked it."

"Why would you clock a six-minute walk? That's so du—"

"Because when it's five degrees and gloves make my hands look weird, one minute makes a big fucking diff—"

"Are you seriously vain enough to not wear gloves when it's *five degrees*?"

"You don't wear a hat when it's five degrees, and you don't even have hair!"

The food arrives before I can respond. Claudio nudges Hero and they both start laughing.

Ben asks what's so funny, but I barely register Claudio's "Sorry, inside joke" because I can't take my eyes off Ben's mouth.

I want him. I didn't know I liked it when he yells at me, and now there's nothing stopping me from taking out my phone and texting, when ur wrong, ur mouth does this thing that makes me wish we hadn't left the bathroom.

Ben: There's a lot more my mouth can do to you in a much more comfortable setting.

Beatriz: like what

Ben: Come to my room tonight and you'll see.

Beatriz: and if i dont?

Ben: You'll spend all night wondering how many times I could get you there.

At midnight, I'm in Ben's room, his clothes on the floor and mine coming off. He's on me, then under me, then we're side by side and my hand's getting him close. Then his mouth is between my legs and I'm screaming into a pillow, and when we finally collapse into each other, Ben turns off the light and I whisper, "Hey."

"What?" Ben sounds exhausted.

"Nine."

He opens his eyes. "Huh?"

"The number of times was nine."

Ben grins more widely than I've ever seen. I turn around as my head hits the pillow, so he can't see that I'm itching to smile back.

It's like once Ben and I hooked up on purpose, we couldn't stop.

At first it was enough to see him naked every night. Then it was doable to intermittently sext him during a movie and go down on him in a closet. But after two days, that's not enough, and we're straight up fucking in an empty bedroom while everyone watches a movie.

"Hey," I say between kisses.

Ben stills.

"Is there anything you want to do differently?" I ask, pulling his shirt over his head. His chest is covered in hickeys since secrecy forbids tattooing them on his neck.

Ben just stares at me. "Am I doing something wrong?" he asks, sounding flustered.

"No, not at all," I say, brushing his hair out of his face. He pretends not to melt into it and I pretend not to notice. "I just…sex is better if you actually talk instead of just guessing, you know?"

"This feels like a trap."

I roll my eyes. "Forget it."

We keep kissing and I'm about to put the condom on him when Ben takes my wrist. "Can I—um…? Can I fuck you… here?" He gently cups my tits.

Oh my god.

I've never needed a dick between my breasts before but all of a sudden I *really* do.

"God, yes."

Ben holds them together and slides between them, saying, "Oh, *fuck*," and moaning over a part of me I've never wanted.

A few minutes later, it's not enough. My hips are bucking and Ben smiles because he knows how much I need him. He pulls away, trailing his mouth down my sternum. He sucks on my rib cage as he finally puts the condom on, slipping inside me like he's savoring every second. I cry out, and Ben curls his arms under my back, clutching me to him and saying my name. We forget about volume so completely that it's good everyone's watching a movie with lots of explosions.

There's something sweet and gentle about the way he comes this time. And it makes me ache.

Ben holds me after, staying inside a little longer than he has to. Then we separate and pretend nothing's changed.

When everything has.

Because he's the first cishet white guy I've actually *wanted* to sleep with. I've always passed when they offered because it was clear they only wanted me to add "dark skinned mama" to their list of sexual conquests. And they always asked for a threesome the second they heard I was into girls.

And when I met Ben, I treated him like I treat every pretentious white asshole who talks down to me. And instead of pissing him off, it made him want more.

Every time I match him, he wants more.

I waste away the day with Hero and Meg, checking my phone because I want Ben to text me. He doesn't. But every time Meg mentions something about Ben that I don't know, I get pissed.

The weather is shit the next day. Rain pours down the windows so we decide it's a movie marathon kind of afternoon. Meg insists on watching "the Oscar noms" so we traipse through *Moonlight* (dope, but sad), *La La Land* (fucking stupid, but Hero loved it) and *Manchester by the Sea* (fuck Casey Affleck) until Ben declares he needs a break.

"My eyes are gonna fall out," he says, stretching as he gets up. Ben leaves and my phone goes off.

Ben: Our closet. Now.

"I have to pee," I say quickly and head down to the ground floor. I see Ben approaching the coat closet that's spacious enough to hook up in when the doorbell rings. Ben pauses, looking at the door confused.

"You expecting someone?" I ask, walking over to him.

He shakes his head. "And who would go out in this?" He gestures just as thunder booms overhead.

I stand in the foyer as Ben opens the door to three blonde girls dressed like they're about to go clubbing.

"Uh—hi," Ben falters, glancing at me and looking terrified.

"Montgomery!" one of them squeals, throwing herself at Ben so that her cleavage, so ample it looks painful, rubs against his chest.

I hate her.

"Thanks for inviting us!" another one says, pushing past Ben and setting a brown bag I'm sure is filled with alcohol on the island. None of them have even looked at me.

"I—uh—didn't?" Ben says, closing the door and looking confused. But the door barely clicks shut when someone pushes it open from the other side. More girls file in, all looking like clones of Gigi Hadid and Cara Delevingne.

"Oh my god!" one of them says, grabbing my arm like we're best friends. "You're so tan!" She rubs her finger along my arm, like she's checking if my skin color will rub off. "That's some quality shit. You'll have to tell me what brand you use." She gives me an air kiss and walks away without asking my name.

"I brought hard seltzers, bitches!" says a girl in a backless lace number. She opens the refrigerator and studies it. "Hey." It's a second before I register she's talking to me.

"Uh, yeah?"

"Can you help me?" she says, nodding at the fridge. "My hands are full."

My eyes narrow. "Why me?"

"You're not carrying anything." The girl readjusts her grip on the bag that, in all honesty, does not look that heavy.

I'm about to point out that no one else is carrying anything either when Ben appears behind me. "I'll take it," he says, walking over and rearranging stuff in the fridge. "Is that enough room?" he asks, looking at the girl. I see his eyes quickly dart down her lace neckline and my blood starts to boil.

"Yeah! Thanks for being so *helpful*," she says. That's when I choose to leave.

I'm on my way upstairs when I run into Meg. She looks guilty for a brief second. I look down to see her cocktail glass is empty.

"Uh, I heard voices?" she says, leaning on the banister.

"Yeah, a fuck-ton of blonde Amazons just descended upon the house," I say, nodding back down the stairs.

Meg frowns. "What? How many?"

"At least ten."

Meg raises her eyebrows. She pushes past me and, against my better judgment, I follow her back down.

Meg takes in the scene in the kitchen—all the girls sidled around Ben as he looks supremely uncomfortable. "What the f—"

"Enjoying my surprise?"

I turn around to see John leaning against the wall, looking so smug I want to smack him.

"What are you talking about?" Meg asks. Ben disentangles himself from the gaggle in the kitchen and walks over.

"The fuck did you do?" he snarls at John.

"Just thought it was getting a little boring around here," John says. "I don't see what the problem is here, Benny. I mean, they've all been here before." He looks significantly at Ben, who turns pink.

"Well, if you're going to invite a bunch of people over at least be a good host," Meg says, pushing John toward the kitchen. "Take their coats or something."

I turn to Ben once they've disappeared. "What did John mean?" I ask.

Ben says, "Huh?" but in a tone that makes it clear he knows what I mean but doesn't want to answer.

"When he said they've been here before," I say. "The fuck did that mean?"

"Oh," Ben says, looking like he's just eaten a lemon. "They, uh—I mean, they're—I've sort of—"

Ben babbles for at least thirty seconds before it hits me. I turn around and look at all the girls dressed like it's hunting season and they're determined to snare someone. I watch the way they all keep glancing at Ben. The way their eyes narrow when they see him talking to me.

Good god. I'm standing in a room full of people Ben has fucked.

I consider just hiding in my room until all the Barbies leave. Then I realize that if I do, I'll hear Ben bring someone into *his* room since our rooms are next to each other. And the idea of that makes me want to punch someone.

Because he's got to, right? The only reason Ben was fucking me is because he had no other choice. Now a Cape version of the line waiting back for him at school has descended en masse. I don't care who Ben fucks, but that doesn't mean I want to listen to it.

So instead, I stick to Hero like glue—which means I spend most of the night listening to girls ask Claudio countless questions about living in Italy. And watching Claudio bask in it a little too much.

My pocket buzzes.

Ben: Kill me.

I fight a smile.

Beatriz: i wouldve thought this is Montgomery heaven

Ben: There's a reason none of them have ever been back.

Beatriz: u poor soul

The girl across from us on the couch starts telling Hero about the wonders her plastic surgeon could do for her nose.

"Fuck off," I tell her, standing up. "Come on, let's get a drink or something," I say to Hero.

She nods, but then Claudio says, "But we're having such a great discussion." He pouts at Hero. If by "discussion" he means girls treating him like he's a sex god because he's from Italy, then yeah, it's *riveting*.

Hero hesitates. "I'll, uh, catch up with you later," she says to me, sitting back down next to Claudio.

"But—"

Hero turns back to the girl who basically told her she needs a nose job. I head to the kitchen because if I'm going to get through this night, I'll need a drink.

I take a bottle of wine out of the wine rack on the kitchen counter. Ben is trapped in the breakfast nook with three girls. He's in the middle so there's no way for him to casually leave. I meet his eye and he subtly holds up his phone. I pull mine out of my pocket.

Ben: I've never smelled so many cotton candy scented people in my entire life.

I snort.

Beatriz: and u know its all called 'unicorn fanfare' or some shit

Ben: Why do people even wear scents? It's weird to go up to a person who smells like a tree instead of a human.

Beatriz: ur asking the wrong person

"Oh my god, 'horny cis asshole' is totally what I'm gonna call my ex next time he drunk texts."

A girl appears next to me, looking down at my phone. I place it facedown on the island.

This girl's the only one actually dressed like it's raining out—cozy cable-knit sweater, yoga pants and fuzzy socks on her feet.

"Yeah, it describes most of them," I say, feeling my phone buzz.

Ben: I like that about you.

"I'll drink to that." The girl raises her glass of wine in my direction. For a second, I think she means Ben admitting he likes something about me, but then I realize she must have meant what I said before.

"I'm Carly," she says, extending her hand.

"Beatriz," I say. "Thanks for actually introducing yourself to me."

"No prob." Carly sips her rosé. "So, how do you know the Montgomerys?"

"I go to school with Ben." I look for the surprise in Carly's eyes that all white people have when I tell them I go to Harvard. I expect her to say something like, "Harvard, like in Cambridge?" or "Which Harvard?" as if there's a different one that dark-skinned people attend.

But she doesn't. She just nods and says, "Cool."

I respond to Ben while she sips her wine.

Beatriz: i got 99 problems but liking u aint one of them

Ben: ☹

"What about you?" I ask, looking at Carly. "What's your in?"

"I used to date Ben."

"Is there anyone here who hasn't?" I say, hoping it comes off as a joke.

Carly laughs and sips her drink. "It's a small town," she says, wiping wine off her lip before putting her glass on the island. "Trying to fuck a Montgomery is one of the only worthwhile pastimes."

My stomach churns. I drain my wine bottle and head back to the rack for another.

"So, Harvard," Carly says, following me and picking out her own bottle of wine. I hand her the corkscrew once mine is opened. "It must be nice to know you're basically guaranteed a job when you graduate."

I choke on my wine. "What makes you say that?"

"I mean, you must have your pick of the litter," Carly says, tilting her head to one side.

"Not really," I say, trying to squash the anxiety in my stomach. "It's uh—been a rough year."

"God, tell me about it," she says, taking a long sip from her bottle. "My parents voted for Trump."

"Shit, really?" I say, even though it shouldn't be a surprise.

Carly nods. "I didn't because *I* actually care about human rights." She says this a little too pointedly and I want to roll my eyes so hard. "We're basically fighting all the time," she continues. "It sucks."

Yeah, fighting with your parents is definitely the worst outcome of Trump becoming president.

I glance at Ben again and he holds up his phone.

Ben: Is it creepy to say that you look sexy drinking wine from the bottle?

"Ben, don't your parents have, like, three yachts?" someone loudly asks him.

"Jesus Christ," I mutter, turning around so I don't have to watch.

Beatriz: yes

Ben: Sorry.

Beatriz: i didnt say i minded

"Right?" says Carly. "Honestly, everyone here is trying to get back in Ben's pants. I carpooled with some of them, and they would not shut up about how a Montgomery vacation would help their brand. Yachts, and scenic Insta backdrops, blah blah blah."

"Wow," I say, not looking up from my phone.

Beatriz: apparently on the way over here everyone was talking about how ur vacations could make them influencers

Ben: I just love being wanted for my money.

I know Ben's kidding, but something pinches in my stomach.

"So who is 'horny cis asshole'?" Carly asks, nodding at my phone and making me jump. "Your ex?"

"What, no," I say, quickly. "Just, uh—someone I'm seeing." My phone buzzes again. Carly glances over my shoulder at Ben.

"Ohhhh," she says. "Got it."

Ben: It's nice that you don't.

"Well, I've gotta run," Carly says, setting her bottle of wine down.

"Do you, though?" I ask, because that was rather abrupt.

"I mean, even if I didn't," Carly says, smirking at me. "Your mind is clearly elsewhere." She winks before taking her leave. I feel hollow.

I go to Ben's room the second everyone's gone. He pulls me in, and we're kissing, and before long I'm on my knees, and he's groaning, then our bodies are flush and I am riding so fucking high.

"This is all I thought about," he says, slowly running his hand over my curves before cupping my ass. "All fucking night."

He sounds like he means it.

I look away from Ben when we're done and see the half-drunk bottle of wine I brought up smashed all over the floor.

"Oh, shit," I say, nodding at it. Ben tears his eyes from mine and looks at the floor. He starts laughing.

"How did that even happen?" I ask, disentangling myself from him and reaching for some tissues.

"I mean, we were going kind of hard," Ben says, smiling softly as he starts picking up the pieces of glass. He puts a hand on the bedpost and starts shaking the bed, the table where the wine was perched wobbling as he does.

"Ah."

I reach for my phone when we're done, checking Instagram as Ben tosses the glass before climbing back in bed and doing the same. A text pops onto my screen.

i am now regretting my decision to read finnegans wake

I laugh.

"What?" Ben looks down at me.

"My ex wants to shred *Finnegans Wake*," I say as I type back, literally unreadable.

"Why's he texting you?" Ben says, his voice tight.

"*She's* texting me because we're still friends."

"Jesus Christ, is *everyone* bi?" Ben shoves the covers aside and gets up. "First Meg and now you."

"What's your problem?" I ask as Ben stalks into the bathroom and brushes his teeth. I don't know why he's so shocked; I figured he would have picked up on the fact I'm queer from the whale watch.

Ben pretends not to hear me over the faucet. "For the record, I'm not bi," I say when he turns out the bathroom light.

"So you don't hook up with girls?"

"I do, but I'm pan. I hook up with people, not genders."

Ben leans against the door frame, arms crossed. "So are you making plans to get back with her the second school starts?"

I sit up in bed, the sheets falling away. Ben doesn't look at me. Interesting. "What if I am?"

Ben doesn't answer, but throws pajamas on before sitting across the room from me. I raise my eyebrows.

"Why are you all the way over there when there's a naked girl in your bed?"

Ben doesn't respond but goes pink. Something clicks into place. A smile spreads across my face.

"Holy shit. You're jealous."

Ben jumps to his feet. "No, I'm not."

I start laughing.

"Shut up," Ben says, crossing his arms. "Stop laughing!"

"Make me."

Ben takes that as a challenge and pulls me out of bed, taking my hands and placing one on his crotch, and the other under his shirt. I yank it off, eyes closed, running my hands along his shoulders, and I feel something I didn't notice before. I open my eyes and see that his shoulders are covered in stretch marks.

"Oh hey, you too," I say, breaking away and running my hands over them. Ben's face hardens and he quickly moves my hands off.

"What?" I ask, pointing at my belly. "Dude, I have them too."

He looks down at the stretch marks that wave across my hips, a battle scar from puberty. "Wait, really?"

"Yeah. Dude, they're normal."

"Oh." Ben's eyes are unfocused.

"How do you get them there, anyway?" I ask, slowly touching his shoulders again. Ben doesn't push me away.

"Working out," he mumbles, not looking at me.

"Oh. What sport do you play?"

"I don't."

"Then why do you work out so much?"

Ben's eyes are focused on a dirty sock under his bed. "Exercise is healthy."

"Dude, we more than fill our exercise quota by walking, like, three miles around campus every day."

"Maybe that's not enough for me."

"What do you mean?"

Ben sighs, his nostrils flaring. "Why are we talking about this?"

I raise my eyebrows. "Why are you avoiding it?"

"I'm not."

"That is the textbook way to avoid a conversation."

"Well, you're being annoying."

"Ben!"

"What?"

"Why do you—"

"No one will want me if I don't look like this, okay?" Ben

moves away so quickly I practically fall over. "You didn't know me before I started going to the gym. I was scrawny and nerdy and girls never noticed me. *No one* would want me if I wasn't this ripped."

"That's bullshit."

Ben snorts. "It's impressive how delusional you are."

"What the fuck is that supposed to—"

"You *hate* me, Beatriz!" I've never seen Ben's face so screwed up. "The fact that I look like this is the only reason you're sleeping with me. And that will clearly be over soon if you're talking to your ex seconds after we've—"

"What's wrong with talking to my ex?"

Ben just stares at me. "It's your *ex*," he says like it explains everything.

"So?"

"Why would you want to talk to someone you've already been through?"

I sigh. "For the record, I don't hate you, but Christ, you make it hard sometimes."

I expect Ben to snark back but he doesn't. Instead, his voice gets small and he says, "You don't?"

I inhale sharply. I didn't expect my heart to skip at Ben sounding vulnerable. "No," I say softly. "I mean, I don't like that you had a job handed to you, or that you're rich enough to have your pick of all the final clubs. But—you're wrong that—" Ben's eyes widen, and it makes it hard to talk. "I like people, not genders, remember?" I say again, attempting to lighten the mood. "I wouldn't be here if I really hated you."

"Really?"

"Yeah, dumbass. Who else is going to quote Jane Austen to me while I'm riding them?"

Ben laughs, and I kiss him hard, so hard that his body jerks in surprise before his hands close around my ass and we fall into bed. It's not long before we're twisted up together, having sex again.

Ben's going really deep and it starts to hurt. It's something I don't usually comment on because it usually happens when a guy is close, but for some reason I say, "Hey, Ben?"

He stops and looks at me. "Yeah?"

"Can we—like, would you be upset if we stopped?"

"Nope," he says. "Like for a second, or are you done?"

"Um…done?"

"Okay." Ben rolls over so he's next to me, slipping the condom off and tossing it in the trash. "What?" he asks when he catches me staring at him in disbelief.

"I'm just waiting for you to stop pretending you're not mad."

Ben looks confused. "But—I'm not."

"Really?"

"Why would I be?"

"Because we've been fucking like animals and I asked you to stop when you were literally about to blow."

Ben wrinkles his eyebrows. "Dude, I don't want to have sex with you if it makes you uncomfortable. That's, like, rape-y."

I'm still suspicious. "Really."

Ben nods.

A knot I didn't know was there loosens in my chest, and I want Ben again. I kiss him and he responds like we were never interrupted, which immediately makes me stop.

I push myself away from him. "This is one of your strategies, isn't it?"

"Huh?" Ben looks dazed.

"Telling me it's okay to stop so that I feel safe and want you again."

"Is that something guys do?" Ben sounds so disgusted that

I'm thrown. "Oh my god. That's *sick*. That's even more rape-y than the other thing."

"So…you were really okay with stopping?"

"Yeah." Ben sits up and takes my hand. His knuckles are knobby and I want to kiss them. "I mean, I like what we're doing, but if you want to stop, we'll stop. If you want to not spend the night after, you don't have to. If you want to stop having sex altogether and form a proto-feminist-lit fight club, I'm down."

I laugh so loud that Ben's hand covers my mouth. I lick his palm, and he smiles. His eyes are shockingly blue, and the arrogance that has always repelled me isn't there.

He means this. The ropes that formed the knot in my chest disintegrate and morph into a feeling I've never had when hooking up with someone.

"What do you want to do, then?" he asks.

"It's embarrassing."

I feel Ben kiss my ear. "I like how cute you are when you're embarrassed."

"No, but really."

"Can I guess?"

I give Ben a look that makes him laugh.

"You want to find all Trump voters and castrate them."

I smile. "Yes, but no."

"You want to scour the internet for RBG's home address."

I shove him. "You read too much into my pajamas."

Ben grabs my hand and sucks on a finger. "You want to go back in time and assure yourself that I am indeed more than just a nice bod."

"Fuck you."

He laughs. It's not until he's been on his phone for twenty minutes that I work up the courage to finally say, "Can we snuggle?"

Instead of responding, Ben tackles me, planting kisses all over my forehead until I'm laughing and pulling him close. We hold each other until we're both asleep.

Sometime in the middle of the night, I jerk awake. It's a few seconds before I realize my mom's not actually chasing me through our old house. I glance at Ben, but he's still out.

I get a drink of water from the bathroom. I'm just passing the Jane Austen bookcase when the flashlight on my phone catches something weird. A black case with a zipper poking up behind the Norton Critical edition of *Northanger Abbey*.

I unzip it. My heart stops.

"Ben," I say loudly. He doesn't move. "BEN."

He jolts up. "Wha you doing?" he mumbles sleepily, turning on the light. "Why are you—" Then he sees what I'm holding. "Oh shit."

"You do smack?" I wish my voice would stop quavering.

"No, I swear to god I don't," Ben says, coming toward me and trying to take my hand, but I throw the case on the ground between us, the needles and drugs falling out.

Ben steps back. "Dude, what the fuck!"

"How could you do this?" I shout, forgetting that it's three in the morning.

"Oh my god, chill out!" Ben whispers as ferociously as he can. "I already told you it's not mine. Why don't you believe me? Why are you so bent out—"

"The fuck it's not yours." My voice cracks. God fucking dammit, I am *not* going to cry. "Why else would you be hiding it?"

"Oh yeah, I'm just going to display illegal opioids on my bookcase, what a fitting ornament for the works of Charles Dickens."

Ben looks at me, and there's humor behind the frustration in his eyes. I look daggers at him.

"Dude, are you seriously not going to comment on how fitting it would be to display opioids next to Charles Dickens?"

"Stop trying to make me laugh!" I step toward him and a sharp pain stabs through my foot. "Ow!"

I look down and see why. Blood is slowly, and quickly, pooling out from under my foot. I lift my foot and see a piece of glass poking out of it.

Fuck. The bottle of wine that shattered. Apparently we missed a piece.

How fitting.

"Oh shit." Ben books it to the bathroom and comes back with a first aid kit.

"How?" I say as Ben kneels and uses a Kleenex to mop up the blood.

"Glass is a motherfucker." Ben looks at me, and I know what he's asking. I glare at him but sit down, letting him gently take my foot. He uses tweezers to get the tiny piece of glass out and applies pressure until the blood has subsided. Then he disinfects the wound before handing me a Band-Aid.

But I don't take it. Because for a second, I'm not in Ben's room anymore. I'm in the living room of my mom's house, *her* needles scattered on the floor. Blood pouring down her arm from where I pulled one out, heroin still left inside.

"Beatriz?" Ben is kneeling next to me, his hand on my arm. I blink and realize the Band-Aid is now on my foot.

"When did you do that?"

"Just now?"

"But—"

"Are you okay? You looked kind of weird."

"I'm fine."

Ben tries to hug me, but I push him away. "What?" he sounds exasperated. "I'm trying to help!"

"I don't want you to." My voice cracks, and I *am* crying because this isn't the first time I've heard those words when a needle is lying discarded on the floor. Except last time, they were coming from my mouth. "I can't do this, you can't be—"

"Beatriz, it's John's," he says quietly. "I'd never—I haven't even done shrooms. Wait, you're leaving?"

I walk toward the door. "I can't do this with someone who shoots up." I turn the handle.

"But *I don't*." Ben is beside me. I expect him to close the door, or put his hand over mine, but he doesn't. "Look, go if you want but… I just don't get why you won't believe me. I thought we were—"

"What?"

Ben shakes his head, like he's got water in his ear. "Nothing. Go if you want to."

Back in my room, I feel like shit. I can't believe this is happening again. I can't believe I was *stupid* enough to let it happen again. And I *really* can't believe that Ben would—

Ben: I know you may not believe me but—I had that stuff because Meg has just started using. John's been doing it forever, but he recently got her into it too. I just kind of lost it when I found out and I took their shit so Meg would be safe.

I feel worse. okay.

Ben: Okay as in…

Beatriz: as in okay?

Ben: Do you believe me?

Beatriz: does it matter?

Ben: To me.

Beatriz: why?

Ben doesn't respond. I put my phone down and try to sleep. But hours later, I reach for it again.

Beatriz: i do believe you

Given that it's 5 a.m., I don't expect Ben to respond. But he does.

Ben: I'm glad. Do you want to come back?

Beatriz: im kinda too tired to fuck

Ben: We don't have to. I just sleep better when you're here.

I don't respond, but I go next door. Ben looks exhausted as he smiles weakly at me. He spoons me when we reach his bed, and I didn't realize that I sleep better when he's here too.

8

BEN

Every morning, I leave Beatriz asleep in what I'm starting to think of as our bed and go work out. I've always worked out in the morning, but recently it's because the way I feel when I see her sleeping is really overwhelming and confusing, and I just need to bench-press about it.

Meg always pops by when she and Peter get here, usually to fuck with my music and make fun of the grunts I make when lifting. Although, since I found her using five days ago, she's been coming around less. Which is something else I need to bench-press out.

"Sooooo, how's it going with Beatriz?" she asks this morning, her hair tied back with a bandana. Like everything is normal and she hasn't been avoiding me.

I sigh. "The same. She's still a socialist nightmare."

"Are you sure?" Meg asks. "You seem different."

"Unlikely." I don't like the way she's looking at me.

"You do, Benny. Your face is less frowny in the mornings now."

I don't say anything, just finish my rep.

"Alright, fine," Meg says, before changing the Pandora station to old-school Taylor Swift. "I'll just say that I know you, dude. And whatever is going on, or not going on, with you and Beatriz is a good look for you."

Meg leaves, and I'm glad because there's no way I can't smile.

Claudio and I play Magic all morning, and I lose every game because I'm thinking about Beatriz. About how she melts when I kiss the bridge of her nose. About how she insists that Emma and Harriet are in love, and that's why *Emma* is a romantic tragedy. About how I feel like everything is easier when she's around.

She walks by with Hero, who's dragging Meg as she mumbles about saltwater taffy. Beatriz looks at me and my stomach lurches so intensely that my hands shake as I reach for my phone.

I tell her everything I want to do with her, but she doesn't respond.

"You alright, mate?" Claudio asks when I've lost my third game in a row.

"Yeah…"

"You sound funny."

"Um… I'm not feeling well," I say, getting up because I need to be alone. Meg's words swirl through my head, and I remember how much I loved curling Beatriz into my body as we fell asleep last night. How fighting with her felt worse than taking Meg to the ER, and pulling her into me when it was over felt—

My heart is going to jump out of my chest, and I need my books.

"I'll see you later."

I walk back into my room, pull random books off the shelf and try to read. Try to lose myself in words but it's not working so I pull out my laptop. I start writing. Pouring out everything I feel because if I don't, I'm worried I'll freak out worse than I did after I found Meg high.

I write until it's dark out and Beatriz knocks on my door. I jump because I know what I have to say to her. And it's not something I want. But it's something I have to do.

I open the door, my heart beating through my mouth as I'm about to tell her how I feel. Then she says, "I don't think I can do this anymore."

My heart stops beating. "Oh."

Beatriz nods.

"That's, uh—okay—honestly, that's kind of a relief because I was just trying to figure out how, um—to tell you the same."

Beatriz looks like I just punched her. I hate it. But her voice is steady as she says, "Cool, good we're on the same page."

"Yeah, totally." I run a hand through my hair as I look around the room. "You have, uh—all your clothes and shit?"

"I think so." Beatriz walks around my room. "So this is it, then."

I turn around. She's standing in front of me, a few earrings in her hand. I swallow as I remember tracing them with my tongue. "I guess so."

I feel like I should say something else but…I don't know what. What do you say to someone you can't stop thinking about, but who will never fit into your life?

We look at each other. My eyes close. Hers do too.

"This is the last time," she whispers when our lips are inches apart.

"I know."

I push my mouth against hers and she inhales sharply. It's desperate. And slow. Usually when Beatriz and I come together, everything is fast and frantic, but this time—I need to remember every second. Every moment of Beatriz's eyes rolling back into her head, of her lips opening mine, because when we're together, no part of our bodies is ever closed. Of her telling me how and where she wants me, and me telling her not to stop, ever.

It's the best fucking orgasm I've ever had.

And then it's over.

I turn around while she gets dressed, because I'm scared that if I watch her put her clothes on, I might start crying. I wait for the sound of the door closing, but it doesn't come. I turn around.

Beatriz is standing with her hand on the doorknob, frowning.

"Um…aren't you leaving?"

Beatriz looks at me. "My mom is a drug addict."

That is the last thing I expected her to say. "Oh."

"Since this is over, there's no point keeping it from you. And…since you weren't always shitty to me, I figure you deserve to know why I freaked out last night."

"O-okay."

Beatriz nods and turns the handle.

"So—is that the real reason you came here with Hero?" I ask. "You didn't want to go home?"

Beatriz's face darkens. "I haven't seen my mom in thirteen years. I've lived with Hero and her dad since I was nine."

Oh my god. So much about Beatriz makes sense now—why she's so guarded, why she couldn't believe me when I said I wasn't using, why—

I'm falling for her.

I always liked that Beatriz was tough, and smart, and doesn't take shit from anyone. But I didn't know that she walks through life having been dealt the shittiest hand I can imagine, and instead of pissing and moaning, Beatriz fights her ass off to make the world better. And knowing that makes her the most attractive person I think I've ever seen.

I've spent days, maybe years, falling for her brain and her body. But it's not until now that I'm falling for her heart.

Which is why I need to let her leave. Because I'm a Montgomery before I'm Ben.

"So yeah, that's why I freaked last night."

I nod. "Okay."

She turns the handle and leaves.

After Beatriz is gone, I'm walking past the den on the way to the gym when I glance in and see something horrific.

Meg and John sitting on a couch.

Making out.

"Hi," I say so loudly that both of them jump. Black lipstick is smeared over both their faces, teeth marks on Meg's neck. They look at me like I'm the fucking Grinch.

"What do you want, loser?" John asks, absentmindedly playing with Meg's hair.

"Um, what the fuck?" I say, gesturing at them. I stare at Meg, wanting to ask her a million questions, and she stares back like she doesn't have any answers.

"I mean, we were going to get up to something more fun," says John, moving his arm down Meg's shoulder and tapping her arm. "But all my supplies seem to be missing."

I clench my teeth but say nothing. Hoping my face stays impassive.

"So this is the next best thing." John pulls Meg into him so territorially, that the words *NOT MY SISTER* burn through my head. It says a lot that when looking at Meg and John, the person I feel brotherly protection for is not my brother. I just stare at Meg.

"What?" she finally says, her voice lower than usual, like she has a cold.

She doesn't look good. And not just because she's doing drugs. She looks…bummed. Completely different than she did when she fucked with my music this morning. And I really don't like the fact that Meg's feeling depressed while John's tongue is in her mouth.

"Fuck off," John says before kissing Meg again and I have no choice but to leave before I start vomiting all over them.

I'm passing through the kitchen on the way to the gym when I hear voices from Claudio's room.

"That's insane," Hero says.

"Hear me out!" I can tell just from Claudio's voice that he's smiling. "I actually think that Ben and Beatriz would be good together."

I stop cold.

"If you think about it, they're *so* similar. Just in really different ways."

"That doesn't make sense," Hero says, laughing a little.

"They're both supersmart, they're both stubborn as fuck, and they're both really passionate."

"Yeah, but I don't know if that means they'd be a good couple. Although…"

"What?"

"I think Bea might like him," Hero says quietly. My stomach drops.

"Wait, seriously?" I hear the sheets of Claudio's bed rustle as he moves around with excitement. "Maybe this could really happen, then!"

"I mean, I don't know for sure. And you definitely can't tell anyone," she says, her voice dropping an octave.

"Hey, I know," says Claudio, and I hear him kiss her.

"She just…looks at him differently now. And whenever he's not around, she's always checking her phone. And whenever we pass you guys, she stares, like *stares,* at him."

"I really hope that's true," says Claudio.

"I mean, it's only good if he feels the same way."

Claudio's quiet. "I think he would if he chilled the fuck out for two seconds."

"But is that likely?"

Claudio laughs. "Probably not."

Hero yawns. I hear Claudio say, "You wanna go to bed, mi amore?" Hero must have nodded, because I hear Claudio get up and I duck behind the island. But all he does is turn out the light and close his door.

Oh. My. God.

The truth is, I'm used to hearing that girls have feelings for me—either from texts, or angry DMs from their friends, or on the dry-erase board outside our room. But that's nothing compared to how it feels hearing that *Beatriz* might.

I know it's just speculation, but it's Hero's speculation. And she knows Beatriz better than anyone. If she thinks Beatriz likes me—it means she probably does.

I don't understand. Not only am I wrong for Beatriz in every way imaginable, but if you feel that way about someone, why would you push them away? Why would you barge into their room, tell them it's over, fuck them, then let them go?

Wait.

That's exactly what *I* did.

Holy shit.

BEN AND BEATRIZ

I was wrong. I'm not falling for Beatriz.

I'm already there.

Maybe I've been slowly falling in love with her from afar and the past week just kicked it into high gear. It would explain why I haven't been able to stop thinking about her since we met. And why she popped into my head every time I was with someone else for three fucking years.

Great. That's just great.

I figure out how I really feel about the person I've had under me for almost a week who gets me better than anyone, and who told me she never wanted to see me again. Great timing, Montgomery. *Brilliant.*

I'm considering whether or not I should slap myself when my phone buzzes.

It's Beatriz.

BEATRIZ

The morning after I find the drugs and Ben snuggles me to sleep, I wake up to find him gone. He's always gone whenever I wake up, and I have no idea where he goes. Hero and Claudio usually hang with me until Meg and Peter get here, so I have absolutely no idea who Ben could be hanging around with.

Sometimes I worry he fucks other girls the morning after being with me so he can stop feeling ashamed about it. I know he had that option when John invited his past hookups over, and I know he didn't take it.

But that's not enough to shake the feeling I get whenever I see his pale stomach pressed against mine. Like this is wrong. Like sleeping with Ben is just a reminder that everyone in his life thinks I'm less than. And I can't stop wondering just how ingrained that might be in the person whose body I share.

I wander down the hall into Hero's room and am surprised to see her sketching on the bed, her headphones on. She's usually still with Claudio this early.

"Hey."

Hero looks up and takes off her headphones. I hear a long, sustained note and instantly recognize it as *Les Mis*. Hero loves long, boring musicals.

I lie next to her on the bed. "I thought you snuggled up with Claudio every morning."

Hero rolls her eyes. "I *do*, but he's FaceTiming with his family right now."

"Cool."

"So, what did you get up to last night?"

"What? Nothing." I sit up so fast my head hurts.

Hero looks at me, her eyebrows practically disappearing into her hair. "Um…you okay?"

"Yep, fine, why wouldn't I be?" I don't think she knows. If she did, she'd look smug.

"Because I asked you how you spent your evening and you reacted like I told you someone leaked your nudes."

"I keep my nudes very well hidden."

Hero doesn't say anything. But when I look up, she's smirking.

"Hey." Meg saunters into the room looking so chill, I'm worried she'll fall over.

"Hi, Meg!" Hero smiles, scooting closer to me so there's room for Meg on the bed. Instead, Meg falls into the nonexistent space between Hero and me, knocking Hero's sketchbook to the floor.

Weird.

Oh shit. Maybe she's high.

I strain my ears and hear John's voice coming from the den.

"Hey, let's go somewhere," I say. Hero gives me a confused look, but I ignore her. I stand, pulling Meg to her feet.

"Too much effort," Meg mumbles.

"Hey, Hero," I say, looking desperately at my cousin. And even though she doesn't know why, Hero gets up.

"Yeah?"

"Haven't you always wanted to get saltwater taffy on the Cape?"

"Oh, for sure!" Hero says, taking Meg's other arm. "Let's go to that place you told me about yesterday."

Meg wrinkles her nose. But when Hero takes her hand and pulls her out of the room, she doesn't protest.

Claudio comes out of the living room as we pass by. "Hey," he says, smiling at all of us before looking at Hero like she's the center of his universe. "I'm going to hang out with Ben for a bit," he says softly, like he and Hero have a special tone of voice they only use for each other.

"Have fun." Hero smiles and Claudio kisses her hand before he walks back to the living room, taking a deck of cards out of his pocket.

I glance inside and see Ben's blue eyes staring at me. His hair is wet. A post-sex shower? I quickly look away.

Hero shuts the front door behind us, and I wonder if Ben will text me. Sometimes when we run into each other during the day, he looks at me in a way that makes my stomach cave and texts me dirty things his eyes have failed to communicate. I never respond because he can't know how much I like it.

Ben: Sometimes when you're gone all I think about is that sound you make when I come inside you, and it's all I can do to not burst into whatever room you're in, carry you out, and kiss you until your body melts into me.

I swallow and don't respond.

"Who's been texting you nonstop for the past few days?" Meg calls from behind Hero. "Ben?"

I almost stop walking. Did he...did he *tell* her?

"Why would Final Club Twat text me? He doesn't even have my number." I shove my shaking hand into my pocket.

"Dunno. He's been in such a good mood every morning, I thought maybe you guys aren't at each other's throats anymore."

Oh my god. Is *Meg* where Ben goes every morning? Does he go to her house, fuck her, then drive her and Peter over?

"That's a pretty big conclusion to jump to," I say, kicking a pebble on the sidewalk.

"I know Ben," Meg says, and I want to kill her. She looks right at me. "Trust me."

I feel sick. I knew it was possible that Ben fucked the memory of me away with white girls he's "supposed" to be with, but for some reason it hurts more that he's washing me off with another person of color—like it's not my lack of whiteness that disgusts him, but how dark I am exactly.

My phone goes off again.

Ben: I would be lying if I said that I wasn't counting down the hours until I can feel you beside me again.

I hate him. I hate him so much.

But for some reason, the hate for Ben Montgomery that's coursing through my body makes me want to cry, when before it made me want to scream.

I wander blindly around the candy shop Meg and Ben have

been going to since they were kids. I try to block out everything around me, try to focus on the color of the candy barrels, or the sweet smell of the store. Lorna calls these grounding exercises, and she wants me to do them whenever I feel like my life is slipping out of control.

And never in a million years did I think Ben Montgomery would be the cause.

I don't see Ben for the rest of the day, and after Hero's gone to bed, I tell him it's over. He responds by telling me he was planning to dump me anyway.

Class. Act.

Since we head back to school tomorrow, I start packing everything up. I'm about to zip up my suitcase when there's a knock at the door.

I open it but no one's there. Just a note on the floor.

Just in case I wasn't clear before, Ben REALLY likes you. But he's too dumb to do anything about it. You're cool, I'm glad I got to meet you. Have a good rest of school—Meg

Um. WHAT.

I look up and down the hall but no one's there. Did Meg seriously just abandon this bomb so she wouldn't have to watch it detonate? And what if it's not even *from* Meg? What if it's Ben's weird way of telling me he might—

I try to feel how soft the rug under my feet is, and notice how bright the moonlight is—and how beautiful Ben looks when he's half-asleep, and how the first thing he does whenever we snuggle is sigh like I'm the only thing that matters, and how when I talk about Jane Austen he looks at me like he's hanging on every word, and—oh shit.

Do *I* like Ben Montgomery?

Yeah. I do. A lot.

Well, hold on, maybe I don't. He did just dump me. For no reason. Maybe I only feel this way because I can't have him anymore. That's the kind of fucked up shit my brain would pull. Like, if Meg told me yesterday that Ben was into me, would I have said "AWESOME," or "FUCK"?

I have no idea. And can only think of one way to find out.

Beatriz: i know we already had our last time

How should I put this? My thumb starts to delete and accidentally hits Send. Shit. I write, but, then hit Send so he knows I'm not just telling him a fact. But I'm at a loss of what to say next.

Ben responds before I can say anything.

Ben: I need you.

9

BEN

The second I'm back in my room, there's a knock on my door.

Beatriz.

"Hi," I choke when I see her.

"Hey," she says.

We don't say anything. I need to say something because I can't let her leave. I *need* to tell her how I feel because even though it's embarrassing, I have this feeling that if I don't, I might regret it.

"Beatriz, I—"

She kisses me before I can get it out. I hear the door close and feel her arms pulling me in, and it's fucking ecstasy.

Now I get why breakup sex is a thing—because feeling Beatriz's hands in my hair wakens an intensity I know is there because I thought I'd lost her, but for some reason she chose to come back.

She pushes me toward the bed, her hands removing my clothes so swiftly that I hardly realize she's done it until I'm sprawled out beneath her, feeling the bedding brush against my bare skin.

Her lips kiss me gently as I pull off her shirt, her pants, her everything. Then the condom is on and she's about to take me inside her when I say, "Wait."

She stops. Her thighs are hooked around my hips. My heart is beating in my throat, like it's trying to fight its way out of my body and into the hands of the person it belongs to.

"Beatriz—I want you."

"Yeah, that's why we're doing this."

"No, I mean…" I try to say it. I really fucking do. But it's like my mouth doesn't know how to form the word. "I care about you. *A lot*," I manage.

"You like me?" she says, her voice quiet.

No. "Yes."

Her eyes are so foreboding that for a horrible second I'm scared she doesn't believe me—scared that she thinks I'm saying that just to get her into bed. When I've never been more serious about anything in my whole fucking life. When I would go back in time and erase Jane Austen's works from history if it meant that Beatriz Herrera would say she felt the same way.

Beatriz must see something in my face, because her eyes soften. "You—you do? Are you sure?"

I burst out laughing. I can't help it. "I'm more sure than Emma figuring out she wants to bone Knightley."

Beatriz rolls her eyes. "Emma is in love with Harriet. I've *told* you this."

I laugh. Beatriz smiles, then her face changes. "I like you too."

"Really?" My voice cracks. It's so embarrassing and I could not care less.

Beatriz nods. "I think I might have for a while."

"Me too," I say, my chest heaving. "Kiss me. Please." She does, and every second Beatriz makes love to me is a second I realize that I have probably just made the worst decision of my life.

So I don't understand why it also feels like the best.

BEATRIZ

I'm on my phone after Ben and I have sex four times in a row when I get a text from Hero.

Hero: your prima is the happiest girl in the whole fucking world

Beatriz: ???

Hero: I'll tell you tomorrow, it's too exciting to say over text

Beatriz: okay?

Hero: I'm so so so so happy. Claudio's the one, bea

Whoa.

Beatriz: how do u know?

Hero: I just feel it. He's it for me. I've never been this happy

My stomach hurts. But I manage to text back, i'm glad ♥
I look over at the guy passed out beside me. Wishing my

feelings were that clear-cut. I like him. So fucking much. Which is weird because—even though I'm almost done with college—I've never *liked* someone before. At least not like this. I've been attracted to people's personalities, but never enough to assign a word to it. I've only hooked up with people who wanted something casual because relationships always seemed like a waste of energy. Which was why I let this thing with Ben happen.

But I *really* like him. I suddenly like that he's a little arrogant, because it means he feels passionate enough about his opinions to be a dick about it. I like that he wakes me up in the middle of the night by kissing my head in his sleep. And I like that when I told him about my mom, he looked not like he felt sorry for me, but like he was seeing me for the first time.

And I like that by some bizarre twist of fate, Ben likes me back.

And the fact that I'm feeling all this for the most cishet white guy I've ever met is freaking me the fuck out. What does that say about me? *Does* it make me less queer? Am I a traitor to everything I stand for? Will people take my opinions less seriously if they learn that I have passionate sex with the enemy on the regular?

And *is* Ben the enemy? Before any of this started, I was so sure he was. He looked and played the part; he was Ben Montgomery III—heir apparent to one of Boston's biggest bank firms—but now… I don't know what to do now that he's just Ben.

"Baby," I whisper because Ben's asleep and can't hear me. But he smiles without waking, sighing so contentedly I almost drop my phone. I didn't know I could make another person that happy. That's how Ben feels without any filters or barriers. He wasn't fucking with me.

"Baby," I say again, and Ben opens his eyes sleepily.

"That's me." He holds out his arms and I bury myself in them. I don't care what anyone else says. I want this person.

I sleep with no nightmares for the first time all break.

My bags are packed and I'm waiting in the foyer. Hero's next to me, her hand intertwined with Claudio's, and I'm trying not to watch Ben talking to Meg in the kitchen. It doesn't look good.

They were sitting at the island when I came down with my bag, and Meg stopped talking the second she saw me. She looked awful. Dark circles under her eyes, and her face—which usually sports an obscene amount of black makeup—was clear of any makeup at all. Her hair looked dank, like she hasn't washed it for days.

She looked so much like my mom.

I glanced at Ben. The way he looked at me made it clear his feelings since last night haven't changed, but he quickly looked away and waited until I was gone before saying to Meg, "I don't like that you're hanging out with John so much."

"What, are you jealous?" I hear Meg ask scathingly.

I hold my breath.

"No!" Ben says, and I let it out. "I'm worried about you."

"Well, don't," says Meg. "I'm fine."

"Meg—"

"Hey, did I do anything weird last night?"

I freeze. Weird like leave a hit-and-run matchmaking note?

"Weird like how?" Ben asks.

"I don't know… I just remember that I did something I may not have done if I hadn't been…" She doesn't finish the sentence. She doesn't need to. "I'm just worried I did something that might come back to bite me in the ass."

Does she regret telling me Ben likes me?

"I mean, you were making out with John," Ben says and

my mouth falls open. "If that's not a big fucking mistake, I don't know what is."

There's a pause. "He's not that bad, you know," Meg says quietly. "Like…I know he's not great, but…he's not the worst."

"Meg, what the *fuck* is up?" asks Ben, articulating my thoughts exactly. "I know you're…going through something right now, but like—"

"What's *that* supposed to mean?"

"You're just…toeing the line more than normal. Like, drinking is one thing but heroin—"

"You don't get it, Ben." Meg's voice rises enough that Hero and Claudio look up. "You don't get to come home and judge me just because you had this perfect, Ivy League life handed to you. Not everyone's gifted a six-figure salary before they even graduate. Some of us don't even *get* to graduate." Meg exhales in frustration. Ben tries to cut in, but she doesn't let him. "I'm employee of the month at fucking McDonald's, Benny. John is the only person around who gets me and can make things bearable. So don't fucking judge me when *you're* the one who's left me behind."

"*What* is going on?" Ben sounds so desperate I want to hold him. "That's—*none* of that is in response to what I'm saying, I'm just worried about y—"

"Well, stop worrying," Meg snaps. "And I would watch your back, Ben. John's…" But she doesn't finish her sentence. Instead she says, "I'll see you next time you're home," and disappears.

John saunters in an hour later, saying, "Alright, kiddos, let's get you back to school."

I follow Ben down the stairs, but when we reach the Tesla, Ben steps aside to let me put my bag in first, while he glares at

John. Once John realizes he can't shut the trunk on me again, he shrugs and gets in the driver's seat.

I nod at Ben and say, "Thanks." He looks around to make sure no one's watching, but everyone's piled inside the car. Then he squeezes my butt and kisses my head before getting in. I stand there for a second so I have enough time to hide my smile.

Hero sits between Ben and me on the ride back to the train station, which is probably good because I don't think I could stand my leg touching his for over an hour without also taking his clothes off.

When Hero unlocks the door to our room, the sight of my desk reminds me how much I slacked off over break. I'd been planning to do all my work for this week when instead all I did was...well, Ben. I sit down and start working immediately.

"Aww, shit," I hear Hero say behind me.

"What?" I ask without looking up.

"I left my favorite dress at Ben's."

"That sucks." I write a note in the margins of my textbook.

"Should I ask John to send it to me?"

I put my pen down and turn around. Hero's leaning against the dresser, frowning.

"Maybe ask Claudio to get it?" I ask. "Do you really want John having your number?"

"Claudio's really busy with...stuff." Hero smiles and blushes in a way that makes me think she doesn't mean schoolwork. "I don't want to add one more thing to his plate."

"What kind of stuff? Does it have anything to do with what was too important to tell me over text?"

Hero shrugs and blushes deeper. I hear the noise of a text being sent. "I asked Claudio for John's number so I can ask him myself. And forget I said that, it's not that important."

"What's going—"

But Hero gives me a look that shuts me the hell up. I go back to my philosophy homework. After a few hours, Hero asks if I want to grab dinner. I'm not even a quarter of the way through the homework due over the next few days.

"Naw, I'll eat later."

"Okay. Claudio and I are going out after, so I'll be back around like ten."

"Don't get pregnant."

Hero shoves me on her way out the door.

"Love you!" I call. I work until it's 9:45 and my brain feels like mush. My stomach growls. I wish I could say it's from hunger, but it's a different kind of ache. An ache that's still new but that makes me reach for my phone.

Beatriz: i never thought i would miss ur ridiculously huge house

Ben: Oh, yeah? What do you miss about it?

Beatriz: the multitude of rooms we could sneak off to at all hours of the day

Ben: What could you ever miss about those?

Beatriz: im not sure, i may need help remembering

Ben: I miss shoving you into that closet on the first floor

Oh god.

Beatriz: i miss feeling u take my clothes off in the dark because people would be able to see the light under the door

BEN AND BEATRIZ

Ben: I miss the surprise of your lips on my chest because I go temporarily blind whenever you look at me like you want me

Beatriz: i want you all the time

Ben: Me too

Beatriz: Ben i want you now

Ben: Me too

Beatriz: if u dont find a way to get ur body next to me in the next hour im going to

There's a knock at the door. I sigh and open it. Ben is in front of me.

"What are you—" But Ben kisses me before I can finish, slamming and locking the door as my stomachache shifts lower and my pelvis is throbbing.

"I missed you," Ben hisses, pulling my shirt over my head as I fumble with his pants' button.

"Hero gets back in ten," I murmur as Ben pushes me against the ladder to my lofted bed, nudging my head aside with his nose so he can suck on my neck.

"Then let me fuck you."

I push Ben to the floor; there's no time to climb to my bed. I'm on top and Ben's mumbling about how sexy I look when I'm riding him.

But just before he's about to come, Ben opens his eyes. He looks straight at me and says, "I like you so fucking much."

And I come so intensely that I hope Hero's not down the hall because I'm sure that's how far people can hear me.

Ben throws his clothes back on, kisses me and flies out the door. Less than three minutes after Ben leaves, Hero opens it.

"What happened to you?" she asks. I look in the mirror and realize that I'm flushed. Two orgasms in eight minutes will do that to you.

"I went running."

"You hate running."

"Thought I'd give it another chance."

I sit down at my desk and glance out the window. My heart jumps. Ben's walking down the sidewalk outside my room when a skinny blonde girl stops him.

Jealousy twists my stomach. When the girl playfully touches his arm, I turn away and feel slightly sick.

When I turn around, they're both gone. Did they go off together?

A chill runs down my body when I realize that I can't fault him if they did. And that if Ben sleeps with her…I'd be devastated.

"I'm going to Claudio's tonight," Hero says. I was so busy freaking out that I didn't realize she'd packed a bag.

"What about Ben?" I say.

Hero shrugs. "He'll find another bed to sleep in."

I'm worried he already has.

Hero leaves and I stare at the same page of my textbook for ten minutes.

I want to text Ben. But it suddenly hits me that we're at school again. The line of girls is back. And what if feelings aren't enough for Ben Montgomery to let me skip the crowd?

My phone goes off.

Ben: I know I just saw you, but Claudio's going to invite Hero over if you want me to, uh, come back.

190

BEN AND BEATRIZ

My jealousy subsides but doesn't disappear. Just because he wants to spend the night with me doesn't mean he's not lining up other people.

And I don't want Ben Montgomery in anyone's bed but mine.

Beatriz: get the fuck back here

10

BEN

I'm in love with this girl. And it's scarier than kayaking in the middle of a thunderstorm.

I've never wanted to kiss someone this much. My favorite thing to do is trail a path of kisses across Beatriz's forehead, down her cheek and around her entire face because she sighs so happily when I do, and hearing her feel that good makes me want to do it until my lips fall off.

I was on my way to my dorm when her first text came through, going the unnecessarily long way just in case I ran into her when I went by her building. And thank god I did because she wanted me with only ten minutes to spare.

But when I go back to her room later, she seems a little off. Sort of standoffish and not totally present. I'm trying not to freak out about it.

"Are you okay?" I ask when I plant a kiss on the bridge of her nose and she doesn't react.

"Yeah," she says too quickly. "Why?"

"You just…seem upset, maybe?"

Beatriz doesn't respond.

"I just—want to ask you something but…but don't know if I want to know the answer."

That doesn't sound good. "Okay?"

She scrunches her face up, thinking. "Actually, if I don't ask, it'll drive me crazy."

"Okay…"

"When we were at your house—" She stops, biting her lip.

"Yeah?"

"Where—where would you go every morning? You were always gone when I woke up."

Is that it? "To the gym."

Beatriz looks at me, her eyes tense. "…Really?"

"Yes? Why?"

She doesn't answer. "Did you—I mean, not that it matters now, but—did you tell Meg about…us?"

"What? No! Didn't we agree not to?"

"I just thought—you guys are close so…"

"I mean, did you tell Hero?"

"What? No."

"There you go, then," I say. "You didn't tell your best friend, I didn't tell mine."

Beatriz bites her cheek again. "I thought Claudio was your best friend."

I move my leg so it's touching her thigh. "He probably is, in like, the actual definition kind of way—Claudio's for sure the best friend that I have. But Meg's…like my sister. The only words I can think of to define her relationship to me is calling her my best friend."

"So you guys have never…" Beatriz trails off and I don't understand what she's asking until she makes a lewd gesture.

"Oh my god." The thought of having sex with Meg makes me feel sick. "No. Jesus Christ, *no*. Meg has told me to my face that seeing me shirtless makes her want to barf."

Beatriz perks up. "Really?"

I nod.

"Okay." She puts her hand on my cheek and I close my eyes because her fingers lightly stroking my face is better than being valedictorian. Her lips find mine and I drink her in. Then something occurs to me.

"Hey, wait." I pull away and it takes Beatriz a second to open her eyes.

"Yeah?"

"Were you jealous because you thought I ditched you in the morning to go fuck Meg?"

"What, no." Beatriz is pulling at her fingers and I know she's lying. I just didn't know it would make me feel like there's a fucking parade dancing through my stomach.

"You totally were," I say, pulling her closer. Beatriz doesn't look at me but she doesn't object when I slide my hand onto her back and trace her spine.

"I was not," she says breathily.

"You're territorial."

"I'm not," Beatriz says so quietly that my hand stills. She doesn't look at me.

"Are you?" I say softly, this time completely serious.

"Am I what?"

"Territorial."

"Like in general?"

"Yeah, and…about this?" My voice is quiet too because feelings are hard to talk about.

Beatriz looks at me. And for the first time ever, she looks breakable.

"I—maybe—did you hook up with that girl who talked to you outside my room?" she bursts.

It takes me a second to remember what she's talking about. Someone I'd hooked up with a couple times stopped me as I was leaving Beatriz's room earlier and made it clear she'd be down for it to continue. But—

"No," I say softly. Because the idea of sleeping with someone else and not telling Beatriz made me feel dirty, and not in a good way.

"Really?" Beatriz looks relieved.

I shake my head. "I—just—want *you*," I say, practically coughing the words out. "And—"

Beatriz kisses me. Her bare chest against mine as we slide deeper into her bed. I try to say something, but she bites my lip and I just kiss her harder. Eventually, we break apart, both breathing heavily, a hickey starting to form on her neck.

"I just—" Beatriz looks breakable again. "I want you to be mine," she whispers.

And I'm shocked at how easily I say, "I want that too."

"You do?" Her voice cracks.

I nod, taking her face in my hands and closing my eyes as my forehead rests against hers. "It's all I want."

"Ben." She hugs me tightly.

Darcy and Elizabeth ain't got nothing on us.

"Anything else you wanna ask me?" I say, figuring that if she's going to learn something about me that will make her leave, I'd rather know now than in a few weeks.

Beatriz stills in my arms. "Yes…but I don't know if I want to know the answer."

I shrug. "It's up to you."

Beatriz pauses, then shakily asks, "Did your parents vote for Trump?"

Well. I feel like I just ate poison. "Yes."

Beatriz nods but doesn't look okay.

"You alright?"

She shrugs. "I mean, I suspected, but it just sucks that the parents of the dude who spends every night inside me literally don't care about my rights." She looks at me, fear in her eyes. "You—*you* didn't—"

"Oh my god, *no*." I move close to her. "*No fucking way.* Dude's a lunatic."

"Your parents still voted for him, though."

Her tone pisses me off. "I mean, they didn't *actually* think he'd win," I say. "They just wanted to stick it to Hillary."

"So they preferred treating the election system like a joke to voting for a qualified woman."

I scoff. "The election system *is* a joke."

"Are you fucking serious right now?" Beatriz sits up, her eyes blazing.

I sit up too. "Do you seriously think our political system is functional?"

"No, but it's not dysfunctional enough that your vote has no power."

"Chill out, Massachusetts went blue."

"That's not the point, Ben!" Beatriz pulls her shirt back on and climbs down the ladder. When she looks up at me, I'm shocked to see that her eyes are wet. "I'm so fucking sick of this," she says quietly. "I just…can't get away from it."

The sight of her crying melts my compulsion to win an argument. "From what?" I say, climbing down the ladder and reaching my hand out. She doesn't take it.

Her eyes are fixed on the ground and when she finally looks up at me, she looks—*so* sad. A specific kind of depression that I don't understand. But the fact that it's on Beatriz's face means that I want to.

"Hey." I slowly take her hand, and this time she lets me.

"What?"

"I want to understand."

Beatriz narrows her eyes at me. "You can't."

Anger flares. "I know, I ca—" I stop and take a deep breath. "I want to understand as much as I can. If you want," I add quickly because Beatriz looks exhausted. "Like, you so don't have to, I know it's not your job, I just—"

"I mean—" Beatriz sizes me up. "There's not like one definitive answer. How would you propose I go about dismantling generations of internalized racism?"

I shrug. "Maybe…is there like…I don't know, a specific event that you've experienced you'd want to tell me about?"

Beatriz's eyes become sharp. "Oh."

"You don't have to," I say again. "I just—"

"I want to," she says, looking right at me. "I do."

"Okay." We climb back into bed, and I hold her so she's leaning against my chest, my arms wrapped around her while my head rests on hers.

"Well, on my first day of classes I was speaking Spanish with one of the cleaning staff and a professor told me to stop chatting and clean the bathroom. Even though I literally had a backpack on."

"—What?"

Beatriz nods. "And when I told her I was a student, she said I shouldn't talk to them if I wanted people to take me seriously. And she acted like she was doing me a favor, like I was uneducated and it was a teaching moment."

Wait. That's exactly what I assumed about Beatriz with the whole mise en place thing at my house. Holy fuck.

Am *I* racist?

"It happens all the goddamn time," Beatriz continues. "White people acting like they know more about me than I do, and getting pissed when I don't thank them for it."

"I mean, do you know for sure they mean it that way?"

She stiffens again. "I won't tell you if you're gonna be like that," she says, starting to pull away.

"Like what!" I say, getting frustrated. She doesn't answer. "God, why are you being so sensitive?"

"Because my *life* is being 'so sensitive'!" she almost yells, moving away from me. "You *don't* get this, you *don't* understand how something as small as a glance or a tone change from a white person to someone like me can make it clear that I'm inferior. You will *never* understand how it feels to know that 46 percent of the country voted for a man who thinks people like me belong in cages. I'm *scared*, Ben—" Her voice cracks.

I feel horrible.

"I'm sorry," I say, reaching for her but she doesn't come back.

"I'm such an idiot," she mutters to herself as she climbs back down. "I should have known better. This is why I don't hook up with white guys, this is why I couldn't get a fucking job, *this* is why I've always been scared of—"

She just looks at me. And something inside me roars.

I can't fix this. And I've never encountered something in my life that I can't fix. Meg gets alcohol poisoning? I'll be around to take her to the ER. I have an accident in the Porsche? Dad'll pay to fix it. But I can't change Beatriz standing in front of me, looking like she's afraid to move.

I've never felt helpless before.

And then I realize. Helpless is how Beatriz feels all the time. Helpless is how those DACA kids must feel when they're being kicked out of the country. Except I have the choice to ignore it. And they don't. I look at Beatriz and a hole opens up inside me as I wonder if *she* could be kicked out of the country.

Holy shit.

I start to understand how it feels to have problems money can't fix. The reality of Trump's presidency—a presidency that my parents support, that puts the person I care about in danger—hits me in a way it hasn't before. And I know what I want.

"Beatriz," I say, my voice deep as I climb down after her. "Beatriz—" God, I'm shaking. "I want to be with you."

She stares blankly. "You are with me," she says, looking around at the tiny room we're in.

"No, I mean more than just sleeping together exclusively. You know," I say quietly. "I want to be your boyfriend."

Now she stares at me like I've gone insane. "*You* want a relationship?"

I grin. "I know, right?"

"With me."

"Only with you," I say quietly, my gut writhing.

"We graduate in eight weeks," she mumbles.

"I don't care," I say. "We could graduate tomorrow, and I'd still want to be with you."

Beatriz's mouth falls open and her eyes blaze, and for a second I'm worried that I've scared her.

But then she says, "That might...be okay."

Oh my god. "Really?"

She nods. "I've never really liked anyone before," she says softly, looking as embarrassed as I feel, which makes this a little easier. "But I really, *really* like you."

"Enough to go out with me?"

Beatriz nods. "At least...I want to try."

I smile and pull her close. I kiss her, and if I'd known this was how it would feel to have a girlfriend, I would have asked Beatriz out the second she was first in my arms.

Beatriz is too exhausted to keep the previous conversation going, but she lets me hold her as we fall asleep. She lets me touch her and kiss her and do everything I can to tell her I love her without words.

But something jolts me awake as we're falling asleep that night. "Beatriz?"

"Mmm?"

"So—now that we're a thing—like, what does that mean for you being—not straight?"

She's quiet. "Honestly...I don't know," she says, turning around to face me. "I'm still figuring that part out."

"Should I be worried?" I try to sound lighthearted.

Beatriz frowns. "Why would you be?"

"Like..." I remember what Claudio said on the whale watch. How "hypothetically," being in a hetero relationship when you're queer could lessen it. "Will being with someone like me make you feel...not like you?"

"No," Beatriz says, and she looks surprised by how authoritative she sounds. "I feel the most like me when I'm with you," she says. "Other people may not see it that way but that's their problem." She speaks slowly, like she's only believing the words as she's saying them.

I snuggle closer to her. "Okay."

She smiles but it's tight. "I just...never thought I'd be here, you know?" she says. "So... I'm still trying to wrap my head around it."

I lift my head up to see her better. "What do you mean?"

"You're like the *most* cishet white guy I've ever met," she says, smiling affectionately. "And those are all things that, before you, I consciously avoided. It's like I spent my whole life never seeing the color red and now I'm bleeding for the first time. I never knew something like that was inside me. That's kind of a weird metaphor," she says, scrunching her eyebrows together. "But you get what I mean?"

"I think so?"

"Basically, it's a me problem," she says reassuringly. "This is something I'll have to process with my therapist, but it has no effect on how I feel about you. We can talk about it more if you want, but…I'm all in," she says, looking sheepish. "I want this."

Relief floods through me as she closes her eyes. And it's like I can feel myself loving her just a bit more.

BEATRIZ

Ben leaves in the morning. But this time, I know he's not going to see anyone who's not me. And it makes me so happy that when Hero gets back, she takes one look at my face and asks me why I'm in such a good mood. I don't tell her Ben is my boyfriend, though. I don't know why, but I just don't want to.

A few days later, I'm coming out of a lecture when Ben texts me.

Ben: Want to do something tonight?

Beatriz: is the answer ever no?

Ben: ☺ I meant more like go somewhere

Beatriz: like a date?

Ben: Maybe ☺

What the fuck am I going to wear? I may hook up a lot, but I don't usually go on dates.

After dinner with Hero, I meet Ben at the Memorial Church in Harvard Yard. I didn't really dress up, and I'm relieved to see that Ben didn't either. Maybe there is a good reason we're together.

"Hi." He smiles at me.

"Hey."

He leans down to kiss me, and for a second, I'm surprised he's doing it in public. I know we're a couple or whatever now, but there's still a part of me that's scared Ben wants to keep me a secret.

He takes my hand and holds it the entire time we walk through Harvard Yard and into Harvard Square.

"I didn't put any thought into this, by the way," I say, while we wait to cross the street.

"I mean, neither did I," he says. "I figured we'd just hang."

"I knew there was a reason I liked you."

Ben grins. "Wanna go there?" he asks, nodding at the Harvard Book Store as we cross the street.

Which was not the campus bookstore—which I learned when I tried to order textbooks online freshman year and didn't understand why I couldn't find half of them—but an independent bookstore that's been in Harvard Square since 1932, according to the sign swaying in the wind.

"Sure."

It's one of the most inviting-looking bookstores I've ever seen. The storefront isn't a wall, but six huge windows repping things like "New in Paperback" and "Used Books." Once Ben and I get inside, I see nothing but walls and tables lined with books. I can see why he'd want to go here on a date.

We wander around, holding hands, Ben making a beeline for the Lit Crit and Biography section. As I watch him hungrily pull books off the shelves with titles like *Hamlet in Purgatory* and *The Cambridge Companion to Jane Austen*, I realize that given his *Star Trek*-level nerdiness for all things literary, I'd been assuming Ben is an English major. But now that I think about it, I'm pretty sure if he was his parents would disown him.

"What are you going to do when school's out?" I ask, noticing that right behind this section is Women's, Queer and Gender Studies. I already know the answer from Meg but I'm curious to hear how Ben would put it.

Ben looks sheepish.

"What?"

"You're gonna judge me," he mumbles.

I put my hand on his lower back and kiss his shoulder. "But I'll still like you."

Ben smiles and rests his head on mine. "I'm starting at my dad's firm in the financial district the day after graduation."

"Jesus, that's fast." I look at him. Ben's eyes are soft in a way I now realize is just for me.

"It's been in the works for a while," Ben says, sliding out a blue tome called *The Literature Book* and scanning the table of contents. "He wants me to get to work as soon as possible."

"But you'll have just finished *college*. You should have a break."

Ben shrugs. "That's not really his biggest concern."

I frown. As much as I like Ben, I don't like this part of his life. And I don't know how to reconcile the hot nerd I'm falling for with the elitist WASP he's expected to be.

"What's *your* biggest concern?" I ask, eyeing a book in Joyce studies.

Ben furrows his eyebrows. "What do you mean?"

"Do you think you should have a break between finishing a degree at an Ivy League and starting a demanding job?"

"Gee, how do *you* feel about it?" Ben asks, smiling. Then his face falls a little. "It doesn't matter what I want. My dad needs me to take over the family assets someday, and we have to start that process as soon as possible."

"Ben—"

"So who's your favorite feminist scholar?" he says, taking my hand and pulling me toward the Women's, Queer and Gender Studies section. He raises an eyebrow when he sees the look on my face and says, "Don't think I didn't see you making googly eyes at this section."

After a few hours, Ben and I wander around Harvard Square before eventually finding our way back to his room, where we get naked on the couch.

When he kisses my name into my ear, I lean back slightly. I need to see his face.

I take in his hair, which my hands have pushed in all directions, his brow furrowed. His lips curl into a smile when he sees me watching, and something unwanted and unburdened bursts through my chest.

I gasp.

Ben kisses me, his lips lingering on my cheek. "I've always wanted you," he says softly, tracing my body like it's something holy. "Since before we even met."

I murmur his name, and his face is undone. Ben comes inside me, and that's when I know.

11

BEN

Two weeks later, I'm fucking around on my phone while Beatriz works in the library. She's going to come by my room when she's done. I scroll through some old social media posts and come across one of Meg and me at the beach last summer. My stomach twinges and I realize that I haven't talked to her since getting back to school. Every time I think about her—and what she was about to say about John when I left—I get so anxious that it's just easier to focus on how obsessed I am with my girlfriend.

But I should really call Meg. Make sure things are okay.

"It's Meeeeeeeeeeeeeeeg," her voice mail says. "Okay, bye."

I hang up and text her.

Ben: Hey. I haven't heard from you in a while. Wanted to make sure you're okay.

I feel nauseous but manage to breathe through it. An hour later, she texts me back.

Meg: wow you even text girls like a pussy

Holy fuck. That's not Meg.
It's John.
Something heavy weighs on my chest as I type back, Where the fuck is Meg.

Meg / John: in my bed

No. *No.* The weight on my chest starts sinking, and the heavy breathing starts. I have no other way of contacting Meg. She's closed to DMs on Twitter and Instagram, always saying, "I'll text the people I wanna talk to." And I never thought *I* would be someone she wanted to avoid.

My phone buzzes again.

Meg / John: so hows hero

My body starts to tremble. I put my phone down and try to keep from choking up with rage. Another text comes through.

Meg / John: u can ignore me all u want doesn't mean ill stop

Ben: Why the fuck are you texting me from Meg's phone, SHE WILL BE ABLE TO SEE THIS.

Meg / John: aww meggie doesn't care we're tight now

Ben: Then why the fuck are you asking me about Hero.

Meg / John: in case i need fresh meat

I almost throw my phone across the room. I try deep breathing in the way that's supposed to calm you down, but it just makes me feel light-headed.

Meg / John: what she's not still with claudio is she

Ben: Of course she is, why the fuck would she leave a relationship with a good guy who's actually in college and isn't a freeloading junkie who couldn't even get his shit together to graduate high school.

Meg / John: you better fucking apologize asshole

I can feel my heartbeat in my ears.

Ben: Make me.

John doesn't respond.

My brain is foggy. My stomach is suddenly unsettled, and there's not enough of my brain left to talk me out of calling Beatriz.

"What's wrong?" she says when she answers and hears me wheezing.

"I'm—it's nothing—"

"Are you in your room?"

"Yeah, but—"

"Stay there." She hangs up. Ten minutes later, she knocks on my door. I'm sitting on the floor, shaking, but somehow I get the door open. Beatriz looks at me and I brace myself to see shame in her eyes—that her boyfriend is a weak-ass pussy who melts down and is pathetic enough to ask his girlfriend for help.

But she doesn't.

"Hi," she says quietly, sitting down beside me and putting her hand on my shoulder.

"H—hi—I'm sorry—"

"Shhhh." She reaches into her backpack and pulls out a Kleenex packet and a water bottle. I don't realize I'm crying until she puts the tissue on my face, and it comes back wet.

"I'm a m-mess," I manage.

"Nope, you're just having a hard time," she says, kissing my cheek. She puts her hand on my lower back. "Breathe here."

I do. Her palm moves up and down as my lungs expand, and it makes me feel a little calmer. I keep breathing into her hand until the rocking stops and my head is aching. I notice that Beatriz put a bottle of water next to me. I drink some.

"Sorry," I say, trying to lower my voice. "I…I just freak out sometimes."

Beatriz nods. "How long have you been having panic attacks?"

I stare at her. "I don't."

Beatriz looks like I just told her my eyes aren't blue. "Okay, I know you have this bullshit macho meter, but you literally just showed, like, all the symptoms. I would know, I've had tons."

"I just lost my shit a little. I'm fine."

Beatriz looks like she wants to say more but doesn't. She just sighs and takes my hand. "Do you feel like telling me why you lost your shit a little?"

My stomach seizes, and I start to wheeze.

"You don't have to," Beatriz says quickly, putting her hand on my back again.

She's so…kind. No one's ever been kind to me before. People have been generous, or nice, but no one's looked at me like

Beatriz is right now, like seeing me have a hard time makes her want to help instead of mock me.

"Meg is sleeping with John."

Beatriz's mouth falls open. "Yeah, that's panic attack–worthy."

I snort.

"How did you find out?"

I tell her about the text exchange.

"And if Meg's not talking to me, *and* she's doing drugs, *and* she's sleeping with John… I'd drive home at two in the morning the night before an exam if she needed me to, but if she's with John, I'm worried he'll convince her not to ask."

Beatriz picks up the water bottle and refills it. "You mean to take her to the ER?"

"Yeah."

"Is part of what freaked you out so much the thought that you would have to take John to the ER too? I mean, I know he's not your fave, but—"

"No."

Beatriz looks surprised. I panic. She must think I'm—"Sorry, I mean—"

"Don't apologize." Beatriz hands me the water bottle. I drink half of it. "I'm just surprised. Meg told me a while ago that you're a worrier, even about people you don't like, and since John's your brother…"

I put the bottle down. "He's barely my brother."

"Have things always been like this between you guys?"

I nod.

"That sucks," she says. "To have a brother who's *always* been a dick."

"I mean…there was this one time."

"Do you feel like telling me about it?"

When I hesitate, she rubs my back. I don't know what I did to deserve her. I close my eyes and rest my head on hers.

"It was right before I left for boarding school—" I pause, wondering if Beatriz will scoff at the fact that I went to boarding school, but she doesn't "—and my parents were micromanaging *everything*. Like, to the point where my mom literally threw out all my clothes without telling me, and then bought me an entire new wardrobe that she deemed 'more appropriate' for 'the kinds of contacts I'd be making.' And then she packed everything without even letting me see what she'd gotten, and she hid the suitcase so I couldn't go into it and take stuff out after she'd gone to bed."

"Jesus fucking Christ," Beatriz says quietly.

"Yeah, and my dad took all of my favorite books out of my room because he knew I'd want to take them, and he didn't want my classmates to 'get the wrong impression' of me. So I just came home from hanging out with Meg one day and all my Percy Jacksons had been replaced with Dickens, and Hemingway and Orwell and shit—"

Beatriz kisses my shoulder.

"So anyway, the night before I was supposed to go to school, my parents were away for the weekend, and John had a bunch of friends over," I say, my chest getting tighter. "And they were drinking and doing drugs and shit, and I was holed up in my room...crying." I try to get the last word out quickly, but Beatriz doesn't look like she cares. "And all of a sudden, the door to my room flies open, and John is standing there. And he just stares at me as I'm covered in snot and tears, and my face is red as fuck, and one of his friends calls from the den asking if he's found me yet because I need to learn how to play beer pong before going to boarding school."

I feel Beatriz tense.

"And John just fucking *stares* at me. And I'm bracing myself for him to tell them to come watch me cry like a pussy, or just look at me like I'm a fucking alien for having feelings, but instead John just said—" Christ, this is hard to talk about.

"Yeah?" Beatriz prompted gently.

"John said, 'Nah, Ben blacked out, let him sleep it off,' and he closed the door. None of them came looking for me again."

"Wow," says Beatriz. "I mean, that's not a lot, but for John, *holy fuck* it is."

I just nod. My chest has constricted too much for me to tell Beatriz the last part of the story—how I'd opened my bedroom door hours later to find a box of tissues sitting on top of all five Percy Jackson and the Olympians, with His Dark Materials and a bunch of other middle grade series stacked beside it. For that one moment, John wanted to make my life better.

I kiss her, nudging her nose with mine when we break apart. "Thanks," I say, kissing it.

"For what?"

"Being amazing."

Beatriz grins so widely her eyes look closed. "Any time, Benjamin."

Oh boy. "That's actually not my name."

Beatriz sits up so fast she almost hits my head. "What the fuck else is 'Ben' short for?"

"It's so embarrassing."

"Oh my god, tell me!"

"Ugh, fine." I look at her with exaggerated significance. "It's short for Benedick."

"Benedict?"

"Nope, I wish. Benedi*ck*."

Beatriz just stares at me.

"I know, right?" I shake my head. "It's a stupid family name. I honestly have no idea why *I* got it because they usually give family names to the firstborn, but anyway. That is one rich people thing that I would happily do away with."

Beatriz laughs. "Family names?"

I nod.

"Yeah, Hero got sacked with a family name."

"Right, I remember Meg asked about it your first night at my house."

Beatriz nods. "It suits her. She…she doesn't look it, but she's kind of a badass."

"How so?"

Beatriz hesitates. "It involves my mom. And I…don't talk about her very often."

"You don't have to. But, like, if you feel comfortable, I'm listening."

"Okay," Beatriz says. "My mom…"

"Is a drug addict?"

Beatriz nods. "She struggles with drug addiction. I mean, she's definitely got some mental health stuff she hasn't dealt with, but honestly that's probably why she does drugs. She… well, she just made me feel scared all the time. Like, she never hit me or anything, but in a way that kind of made it worse. I didn't have anything to point to, to explain why I felt so fucking terrified when all I was doing was eating microwavable chicken potpies alone in my room because I was too scared to sit at the table with her, and because she refused to make me food if I ate by myself. And she was constantly yelling at me that I was stupid—"

My arms stiffen as they fold around Beatriz. I can't think of a crueler thing to say to someone with a learning disability.

"—for, like, no reason, except that she felt like yelling at me," Beatriz continues. I can feel her heartbeat increasing. "I just never knew what she wanted from me because it changed every day, and if I didn't know what she wanted, she would just… Anyway. Starting when I was, like, nine, I would call Uncle Leo all the time and ask him to come get me, and he never would."

I still. "What?"

"I mean, his motivations were good," says Beatriz defensively. "He didn't want to make things harder with my mom."

"Yeah, but you were *nine*. That must have been terrifying."

"It was." Beatriz rests her head on my chest. "Eventually, Hero just called the police."

"Wait, what? Wasn't she also nine?"

Beatriz nods. "And it was actually pretty good timing, because my mom was high when the cops showed up, and they took me to Leo's."

"Christ."

"So, yeah," says Beatriz. "Hero's the reason I got out. She might seem pretty docile, but if you fuck with something she loves, she will come for you."

"I'm really glad you have Hero." I pull Beatriz closer and kiss every part of her I can see.

She nuzzles into me and says, barely audibly, "I'm really glad I have you."

BEATRIZ

"How about here?" Hero asks as our train pulls into Kendall/MIT.

"Sure."

We stand as the T slows to a stop and get out. Since Hero and I are from Western Mass, when we started at Harvard we decided it would be fun to get to know the city by hopping on the T and just riding until we felt like getting off. It's been moderately successful—stops like Porter Square and

Park Street were really fun trips, but taking the T all the way to Braintree was a huge letdown.

So I'm surprised when Hero calls a Lyft the second we leave the station.

"Um—what?" I say, climbing in after Hero because what the fuck else am I gonna do?

"I wanna go somewhere."

The driver asks me something in Spanish but I'm too surprised to answer. Hero glances at me, then answers the driver's question. He looks shocked that someone who looks like Hero speaks like someone who looks like me.

"I thought this was our last T trip before graduation." I know it's dumb, but I'm a little stung. This has been a tradition of ours. And now Hero's hijacked the last one we'll ever have.

She doesn't answer. We ride in silence until we pull up in front of Macy's.

"Seriously?" I say as Hero thanks the driver. I hate clothes shopping. I've lost count of how many grumpy trips to the mall Leo chaperoned in middle school where Hero would fit into the smallest size, and I was too big for the largest.

Hero doesn't say anything so I follow her blindly through the store. My phone buzzes.

Ben: This might be weird but last night was actually really nice.

My fingers start to shake. I feel the same way, but I don't know if I can tell him. Last night was the first time Ben and I slept naked together without having sex. Which felt weirdly more intimate and I don't know why. But how safe and wanted and loved it made me feel is freaking me out.

I spent all of college bitching about how partnership makes no sense because there's no way people can evolve at the same pace as another person for the rest of their lives. And while my feelings for Ben aren't making me reevaluate that, they're making me want to.

But what freaks me out most is that none of this makes me want to break up with Ben. If anything, it makes me want to pull him closer.

I blink and realize we're in the formal dress section.

"What the hell?" I say as Hero walks toward me, three dresses that are fancier than what she wore to prom slung over her shoulder.

"I need a dress for graduation." She doesn't meet my eye.

"We'll be wearing gowns."

"We have to wear something under the gowns."

"Yeah, so just wear jeans."

Hero rolls her eyes. "No one is gonna be wearing jeans."

"I am."

Hero doesn't respond but heads toward a dressing room. I sit on the bench in the hall.

"So, anything new with you?" Hero asks. She tosses her blouse over the stall door as my phone goes off.

Ben: I didn't know I could feel this way about someone else but I really like you, Beatriz.

Beatriz: i really like u too ♥

"Trizita?" Hero opens the door, a gorgeous pink dress draped around her. I stand and zip it up. "So, is anything new?"

This is it. The perfect moment to tell her about Ben. I open my mouth, but my stomach flips so aggressively I'm worried I'll fall over. "No, not really."

"You've been out of our room a lot," Hero says, checking herself in the three-way mirror.

"I mean, that's nothing new," I say. "Anyway, how would you know, you're always with Claudio."

"Yeah, but whenever Claudio comes to our room, you never seem to mind." I unzip Hero before she disappears back into the stall. I look up as she hangs something over the door. White lace lingerie. And Hero has only ever worn cotton hipsters.

I snatch it off the door, and Hero yelps, "Hey!" It's a white lace boudoir robe and chemise set. They're made of frilly lace and spell out in rhinestones the words, *I do*.

"Hero," I say, my voice quavering. "Why are you trying on bridal lingerie?"

Deafening silence. For a long moment, all I can hear is the store music playing in the ceiling speakers.

Eventually, Hero opens the door looking like a goddamn bridesmaid. She mumbles something but all I can make out is, "ppz."

"What?"

Hero sighs. "After graduation, Claudio's going to propose."

My jaw drops. "WHAT—" someone out in the store gasps in alarm but I don't care "—the *fuck*?" Hero won't look up. "How long have you known about this?"

She doesn't look at me. "A month."

"A *month*? And you didn't tell me? Is that what was too important to tell me over text?" I ask, thinking back to our exchange the last night of spring break. And how the next day Hero acted like it hadn't happened.

And then Hero glares at me, tears in her eyes, and seethes, "*You* didn't tell me you're dating the guy you've hated since sophomore year!"

My chest freezes. "W-what?"

"If you wanted it to be a secret, you should have told Ben."

Hero's breathing hard. "He told Claudio you guys got together weeks ago."

Shit. "I'm sorry."

Hero huffs as she pulls her skirt back on. "It's okay."

"You're not mad?"

"I mean, I am a bit—I don't get why you'd feel like you have to keep your novio a secret from me—but I know sometimes feelings are hard for you."

I sigh. "I don't know why I didn't tell you either," I say, scuffing my toe on the floor.

"Guess we were both sitting on knowledge."

I frown. "Okay, to be fair, 'I have a boyfriend' is *really* different from 'I'm getting married.' Why did he tell you he was going to propose anyway? Isn't it supposed to be a surprise?"

"Well, first he asked me if I even *wanted* to get married," Hero says. "Because he's not gonna spring that on me like our life is a poorly written rom-com."

The phrase "our life" makes me flinch.

"And what do *you* want?" I manage to ask.

Hero's quiet for a minute. Then she says, "Him."

I can't believe this. "We're twenty-two!" I burst out so loudly that Hero puts a hand on my arm. "I—you—but—why *now*? Why not wait five or ten years?"

"Because Claudio's visa is up a year after he graduates."

My stomach drops. "Seriously? A fucking *green-card* marriage?"

"It's not *the* reason, but it's a factor." Hero's eyes are approaching Cruella De Vil territory. "We know we're going to be together forever, so why wait? And if I can avoid figuring out some long-distance shit with him in Italy, then why the hell not?"

"Because you're *twenty-fucking-two*."

"Why aren't you happy for me?" Hero snaps, turning to

face me. "I just told you the love of my life wants to marry me and this is all you have to say? That I'm too young in your opinion?"

I open my mouth but nothing comes out. Why *aren't* I happy for Hero? She's always wanted to get married; she's had sketchbooks full of color schemes and venue ideas since we were twelve. I knew this would happen. But I never imagined that, come May, I'd lose my cousin to marriage instead of her career.

Oh my god. In a little over a month, Hero will be engaged. Ben will move to Boston. I will have no job, no prima, and given Ben's sex drive, who knows if he'll still want to be with me when we live hours instead of minutes apart.

For the first time since I was nine, I'll be completely alone.

"I am happy for you," I say, turning away from Hero and blinking back tears. "I'm just—surprised."

I see Hero nod in the mirror. "That's fair. I did just spring this on you. But it's kind of perfect that you and Ben are together now." She gives me a consoling smile.

"Why's that?"

"The maid of honor will already be sleeping with the best man."

I do grounding exercises all the way home, until Hero opens the door to our room and sets a bulging bag on the floor. She hums as I pull out my phone.

Ben didn't respond after I told him how I felt. But maybe that's for the best. If we have an expiration date, what's the point in telling him that—that I think I might—

A sound comes out of Hero that makes me almost drop my phone.

"What?"

Hero's mouth and eyes are wide with shock. She doesn't say anything but holds her phone out to me.

BEN AND BEATRIZ

Hero: I got some options ☺ Can I come show you later

Claudio: no, actually

Hero: Why? is everything okay

Claudio: no. we're over.

Claudio: i can't have a whore for a wife

12

BEN

Hero cheated on Claudio. I can't believe it. I remember that conversation we had at my house about deal breakers. And how I assured Claudio that Hero was incapable of cheating. I feel like it's my fault, somehow—like if I hadn't said that, Claudio wouldn't have let his guard down.

Claudio showed me the video John sent him with the message, sorry bro. The video of Hero on top of John in his bed, John saying her name over and over like it's a prayer.

I guess John wasn't asking about Hero because he wanted "fresh meat." But because he wanted her back.

Claudio bolted from our room. I have no idea where he went. Maybe to break up with her.

Someone hammers on my door. I open it to see Beatriz standing there, her eyes a forest fire.

"WHERE IS YOUR FUCKING PIECE OF SHIT ROOMMATE?" she yells, barging past me.

Is she serious right now?

"I take it you saw the video?" I say, closing the door.

"Yeah, the video of your dickhead brother framing my cousin?" Beatriz glares around the room, like Claudio's hiding somewhere. He was so upset when he got that text. And I could tell because he didn't sound upset at all.

"John's not smart enough to frame someone," I snap. "And anyway, Hero was nice to him."

"She's nice to everyone!" Beatriz yells. "She's Jane fucking Bennet!"

The fact that she would use *Pride and Prejudice* to try and support a flimsy argument makes me stew. "Well, she asked Claudio for John's number a few weeks ago."

"Because she left something at your house!"

"Why didn't she ask Claudio to get it for her?"

"Because she's a considerate person who didn't want to add to his heavy workload!"

"Come on, Beatriz," I scoff, turning around because I'm getting really mad now. And I don't have any pencils.

"What the fuck is that supposed to mean?" Beatriz's voice is dangerously low.

"You're not seriously going to claim that's not Hero."

"It's not."

"Jesus fucking Christ."

"What?" Beatriz grips my shoulder and thrusts me around so I'm facing her. Under different circumstances, this would have driven me insane—but not in this situation. Not today.

"You're a smart person, Beatriz," I say. "I know you're close with Hero, but I can't believe you're actually going to deny something with video evidence." My breathing isn't even anymore. "What, are you only smart about books and politics, but not people?"

Beatriz steps away from me. My stomach falls. I went too far.

"It. Wasn't. Her."

I'm too wound up to apologize. "Wow, you're loyal to a fault. Guess it's good to know that if I ever murder someone, you'll be around to take the fall."

Beatriz's face slips. I know I'm being an asshole, but I don't know how to turn it off. This is the only way I know how to defend someone.

But the person I'm attacking has never been someone else I love. And my brain doesn't know how to do both.

"Why are you being like this?" Beatriz's voice is soft.

"Like what?" But I know exactly "like what."

"Mean."

"Are we five?"

"You're acting like you're five!"

"By defending my best friend?"

"I thought Meg was your best friend!"

"What, you worried I'm fucking her again?"

"Ben."

I look at her. She's hurt. I suck.

She steps toward me. "Why don't you believe me?"

"Because you're clearly wrong." I look away from her. "Your cousin is fucking my brother in that video, and you show up here with the audacity to say she isn't, *and* to act like Claudio is the bad guy for questioning a relationship with someone who cheats on him!"

"He's not just questioning it! He broke up with her over *fucking text*."

"Good."

"Why are you being like this?" Her voice cracks.

"What, realistic?"

"No. You just keep spewing your opinions like they're going to change mine, and you're not listening to *any* evidence that might contradict what you think. I thought you trusted me."

"I do. You're just wrong."

"How do you fucking figure?"

"Well, for starters, John is *saying* Hero's name—"

Beatriz scoffs derisively. "That's really not much, coming from one of you."

"Oh sorry, is it some dirty capitalist thing now to say the wrong name during sex?"

Beatriz looks away, but not before I see something lingering behind her eyes. "No, it's a Montgomery thing."

"What are you even talking about?" In the last two months, I've never called her anything but her name and some other choice words that I'm embarrassed to say out loud. I think once when we were drunk I even called her "love."

"Nothing."

"No, no, no." I step toward her. "You don't get to do that. Not again. You did this at my house that night we first fucked—you clearly have a beef with something I did, and you're mad, and you're not telling me why, and you don't get to *do* that anymore, Beatriz. You owe it to me to tell me."

"I don't owe you shit!" she yells.

"Then tell me because you care about me!" I yell back. "If I matter to you at all, Beatriz, then tell me why you're so mad at m—"

"BECAUSE THE FIRST TIME WE HAD SEX, YOU CALLED ME SOMEBODY ELSE'S NAME."

My chest forms into ice.

That can't be true.

Beatriz is shaking. Soon she'll be crying, and it will be entirely my fault. She looks like my mom that time I was six, when Dad yelled at her until she was crying in the bathroom. Pre-asshole John stopped me from following her and said, "Just go to your room, bud."

Oh my god. Meg was right. I've become the person I pretend to be.

"And then after we hooked up," Beatriz continues. "I called you on it and you said—" she closes her eyes "—you said, 'Does it matter? We had fun.'" Beatriz backs away from me. The fact that she remembers this amount of detail three years later kills me. "Half the time you called me some random, obviously white name, and the rest of the time you just kept calling me 'you.'"

And then I remember.

Not the night she's talking about, but the night we first hooked up at my house—when Beatriz got so livid over seemingly nothing, when she looked crestfallen after Hero complimented my cooking and I stupidly said, "Thanks, uh, you."

"Why—why didn't you say anything?"

"I shouldn't have to, asshole."

She hasn't called me "asshole" in so long—not like this, not like she means it.

"Is that why Hero only warmed up to me when we started to be a thing?" I ask.

"Hero didn't know," Beatriz mumbles. Then she says something that shoves a cinder block through my chest. "I only told her we were together today."

I stare. "You—you didn't tell her we're a—"

She shakes her head.

"Why?" A new anger is rushing through. An anger that feels laced with something corrosive, eating away at me. "Why didn't you tell her?" I yell. "She's practically your sister, are you that ashamed to be with me?"

"It's you who's ashamed to be with me!" she yells back, tears forming in her eyes.

"How can you think that? I'm the one who asked you out!"

"I know."

"Clearly I want you, then."

"I know you do." But Beatriz is backing away like this doesn't matter.

"Then why didn't you tell her?" My voice cracks. Beatriz being embarrassed by me brings back all the times girls laughed at me when I told them I liked them in middle school, why I obsessively work out now, that time Beatriz claimed she wanted me for more than how I look. Was she lying?

"I didn't tell anyone because eventually you'll leave!" Tears burst from her eyes. Beatriz shoves her palms across her face. "I don't *belong* with you, Ben," she says, tears flooding down her face. "This isn't going to last. Someday you're going to wake up and realize you can't introduce your Trump-supporter parents to your brown girlfriend, and you've made it *very* clear that your family is more important than anything else in your life. You won't be able to take me to fucking investment banker cocktail parties without one of your colleagues asking me to get them a drink, you won't be respected in the world you someday want to run if I'm by your side."

I want to kiss away the tears on her face, but I'm so ashamed I can't move.

"I know I'm worthy," she says. "I know I don't deserve to be a skeleton in the closet of your life, but—"

She looks up.

"I'm in love with you," she chokes. "And love made me dumb."

My heart is beating so fast I'm worried it'll fall out. I need to tell her I love her too. That I've loved her for longer than I knew love was real, that I'll probably love her till I die, but—

She's right. I can't bring her home to meet my parents, but not for the reason she thinks. I know how they'd treat her. They'd make her feel like a gold digger, or like someone I'm fucking around with until I grow up and find a "real relationship." They wouldn't treat her like the love of my life.

And telling her that she is right before I push her away would be cruel.

"I can't do this anymore," Beatriz croaks.

I can hear us breaking.

"Okay."

She looks hurt. Maybe this is a mistake.

"Wait, maybe we can—"

But Beatriz leaves before I finish. For a second, I feel nothing. Then the hurricane hits.

Punch after punch after punch annihilates my heart as I realize what I've just done.

BEATRIZ

I should go to my room and cry. That's what Lorna would tell me to do. But I pull out my phone and text someone who tried to get with me last semester. They respond immediately, and I'm turning around before I've even left the building.

I book it to the room number they sent and don't bother with niceties when they open the door. I rip their shirt off and put their hands on me to forget about what just happened.

For eight minutes, I'm not heartbroken.

But at the last second, my hand instinctively flies up to their chest—and when I don't feel the goose bumps that flood Ben's every time he comes, I start to cry. Again.

"Shit, was it that bad?" they ask, when they look down and see me uncontrollably sobbing. "Fuck—uh—are you okay?"

I nod. How could I have let this happen? I mumble that I'm fine and tug my clothes on before going out the door.

I'm walking down the hall, tears silently flowing down my face, when a door to my right opens and I hear a sharp intake of breath.

Ben.

Ben is standing in his doorway. I inhale sharply as I realize that I'd been so caught up in escaping my feelings, I didn't realize the person I just slept with *lives* on Ben's floor.

Fuck.

Ben's nose and eyes are red—which shocks me because when I told him it was over, he didn't seem to care. He glances up and down my body, horror sinking into his eyes. I look down to realize it couldn't be more obvious I just had frantic, hurried sex. My shirt is on backward, my shorts are buttoned but the fly is down, and as I look up at my ex-boyfriend, I watch his eyes linger on the flush of my cheeks that always appears afterward.

"Beatr—"

I leave. Hearing my whole name might make me stupid enough to forgive him.

Hero's in running clothes when I burst into our room. She's at my side before the door's even shut. "What's wrong?"

"Nothing."

"Bullshit."

"I'm fine."

"You're not."

"It's nothing compared to what you're going through."

"I don't care."

"Please," I beg, walking toward my bed. "I just wanna lie down."

Hero doesn't say anything as I climb the ladder and burrow under the covers. But she passes me my backpack when I ask for it, and, when she asks if I want to get dinner and I'm too depressed to respond, she goes to get us food from the dining hall.

It's a ritual we haven't had to go through for a long time. It happened *all* the time in high school before I found Lorna, but apparently, I'm so broken, not even the world's best therapist can fix me.

"Want me to text Lorna?" Hero asks when I haven't moved for five hours. I nod. Hero picks up my phone and types a message.

"She's going to squeeze you in at noon tomorrow."

I nod. Knowing I might sleep through it but too exhausted to point this out.

The next day, Hero shakes me awake at 11:30. "You have Lorna in half an hour," she says, pushing some clothes onto my bed.

"Don't you have class?" I mumble sleepily.

"This is more important."

Gratitude for Hero floods through me, and I start to cry. Hero climbs into bed with me and holds me until my phone starts ringing, and she leaves the room as Lorna's voice says, "What happened?"

13

BEN

A knife slices through my chest when we start discussing *Emma* in class, and no one suggests a reading of Emma and Harriet as lovers. Every second I'm not working, I'm at the gym. But it doesn't help.

I've never felt this way before.

I can't read Jane Austen. I turn in a paper late for the first time ever.

I can't read shit Trump tweeted without wondering what she'd say.

I can't even have sex. I tried the day after we broke up and faked an orgasm for the first time in my life.

I just…can't.

MAY 2017

14

BEN

Three weeks later, she texts me.

Beatriz: do u still have my annotated Pride and Prejudice?

Damn. I was hoping she'd forgotten. I've gotten in the habit of reading it every night after Claudio goes to sleep, looking for creases she left in the pages, getting tearstains in the margins. It was the first part of Beatriz she shared with me—my first inkling into who she was beyond the box I'd put her in.

Ben: Yes.

Beatriz: i want it back

Ben: Okay. Want to come now?

Beatriz: just leave it outside. if i see claudio im going to kill him, and no way in hell am i going to b alone with u

Ben: Why?

Beatriz: fucking figure it out

I know seeing her again would hurt monumentally. And sleeping with her would make it worse in the long run, but—

Ben: Do you still want me?

Beatriz: ben, come on

Ben: Do you?

Beatriz: of course i do, i was in love with you pendejo. but right now i just want my fucking book

Ben: You still love me?

Beatriz doesn't respond. It eats away at me that while I can casually mention that Beatriz loved me, she still doesn't know I loved her. That I still do.

Beatriz: hero is coming by since claudio has class.

Ben: Okay. I'll leave it outside.

Beatriz: ok

I put the well-worn book on the floor outside my room and quickly shut the door. I've just finished changing into my gym clothes when there's a knock.

When I open it, I'm shocked to see Hero standing in front of me.

"Um…I left the book there," I say, nodding to the ground.

"I know." Hero looks different. She's standing squarely in front of me, her eyes no longer shy, like she's a hunter and I'm a dumbass fox.

"C-Claudio's not here," I stammer.

"I know. I wanted to check something with you. Did you and Bea break up?"

Oh my god. Hearing it out loud is so much worse than hearing it in my head. I lean against the door frame, my bones suddenly heavy. "Yeah," I say quietly.

"Okay." Hero picks up the book and starts to leave.

"Hey, wait." I step into the hall after her.

She turns around. "What."

"Is she—tell her that—how is she?"

"Stay the *fuck* away from her."

As Hero steps toward me, I frantically move back. She looks like she's about to whack me over the head with the book.

She stops in front of me, her eyes ice.

"I'm serious," she hisses. "Nobody fucks with her, *especially* not pendejo pretty boys who take her heart and break it back into the pieces she's worked so hard to put back together. If you come near her again, I will end you, you misogynist asshole."

After Hero leaves, I stand there shaking.

Beatriz once told me that if anyone fucked with something Hero loved, she would come for them. I just never imagined that someone would be me.

I'm studying for my first exam when Claudio opens the door to our room.

"We're done!" he says, dropping his backpack and throwing his hands in the air.

"I mean, we still have finals," I say, without looking up from my notes. I have to hold them directly in front of my face because hunching over my desk exacerbates how sore my abs are.

"Yeah, but we've got a week to chill." Claudio pats me on the back before collapsing onto the couch.

Claudio and I have been unexpectedly single for almost a month, yet he hasn't acted like anything's changed. It's weird. I've seen Claudio notice the fact that there's a new Kleenex box by my bed every week, so maybe he knows I fall apart whenever he's not here, but Claudio seems…robotically fine. He's acting like Hero never existed, like he's wiped her memory from the hard drive of his life.

And while I still can't have sex without losing it, Claudio is sticking his dick everywhere. Every time I've come back from the gym or library, Claudio's written our code of three asterisks on the white board, and I have to sit on the floor until whoever he's seeing stumbles out to be on their merry way.

"Hey, can you find somewhere else to sleep tonight?" Claudio says without looking up from his phone. This is another development that pisses me off—he's *never* off his phone. He used to be that weirdo who insisted on not bringing his phone to dinner so we could actually have a conversation, but ever since he dumped Hero, I've seen the back of Claudio's phone more than his actual face.

And I didn't realize how much I need him right now. Meg still hasn't reached out to me, I've been freaking out multiple times a week, I can't talk to Beatriz, so Claudio's kind of the only person I have right now. And I don't even have him.

"Seriously, man?" I say, putting my notes down. "Why can't you go somewhere else?"

Claudio sighs. "Do you know how often you kicked me out before you started dating that bitch?"

"Don't call her that," I say, clenching my jaw.

"This is how you get over her," Claudio says. "Get under someone else."

With a jolt, I realize Claudio is becoming the person I always pretended to be—like it's a skin I shed that Claudio picked up and is wearing like a jacket.

"That's not really how I work," I say, picking up my notes again. "I'll find another place to sleep. Just don't talk about her like that."

"Still whipped, man."

"Suck a dick, dude!" I say, dropping my notes and turning to face him. "Just because my girlfriend didn't cheat on me doesn't mean losing her sucked any less!"

Claudio's face darkens, like it always does if I mention anything remotely close to Hero.

"Screw them. They're bitches, man," he says, putting his phone down.

"They're not," I say, standing up. "You shouldn't call them that. There's a systemic history of men using that word to oppress women, and it's not going to get better unless we—"

"Oh, shut up." Claudio stands too. "I. Did. Not. Sign. Up. For. This. Lecture," he says in the rhythm of a clapback.

"Fuck you."

"Right back at you." Claudio shoves his phone into his pocket and heads for the door. "I've got work to do."

"You need your backpack for that."

"Get off my dick!" Claudio yells before slamming the door, leaving me alone.

BEATRIZ

Last class of the semester. Thank *god*.

I pull out my beat-up copy of *Ulysses* while everyone else files in. This class—Modernism in Modern Times—has been dope. It was the class that introduced me to James Joyce, and since I knew *Ulysses* would be a nightmare to get through, I read the whole thing last summer to prepare. And didn't expect to love it nearly as much as I did.

Especially since it could not be more obvious that all the pretentious white guys who think they're the millennial James Joyce have never actually cracked the book open. And they assume that, since I'm a brown woman and *Ulysses* is one of the most difficult novels written in the English language, they automatically know more than me.

Speaking of—Ethan Cartwright (the guy I most frequently fantasize about castrating) slides in next to me. "Sup, Beatriz," he says. I just nod.

Today, we're reviewing the *Ulysses* chapter "Circe"—a two-hundred-page play in the middle of the book (I wasn't kidding when I said this book was wack) that explores sexuality, repression and gender identity. And this book was published in *1922*. I stand by my statement that James Joyce was a prick, but I can't deny that he had an insight into human nature that the rest of us didn't catch on to until, like, 2010.

"Were there any parts of the text that you disagreed with?" the professor asks when we've moved on to general review of the book.

"Yeah," Ethan says, looking up from his lap where he's been texting for the whole class. "'Circe' is the chapter where Joyce fell short. It's in conflict with the rest of the novel. The rest of the novel is realism—Leopold Bloom goes about a normal day where normal things happen in 1904—then all of a sudden we're in a fantasy play. It doesn't make sense."

I restrain myself from rolling my eyes. We literally had a reading in which a Joyce scholar asserted that the purpose of "Circe" was that it cannibalized the previous narrative structure. And that *bizarre* things happen in "Circe"—like the main character turning into a woman, and a pig at two separate times—because Joyce utilizes the dream state to process events or emotions too difficult to do so while awake.

"Did you not do the reading in which Declan Kiberd states that 'Circe' is a dream play?" I ask, pulling out the textbook *Ulysses and Us* and flipping to my purple annotation. "'This episode takes the form of a dream play,'" I read, "'in the course of which—according to the form's pioneer, August Strindberg—"the characters are split, doubled, multiplied; they evaporate and are condensed; are diffused and concentrated; but a single consciousness holds sway over them—that is the dreamer."'" I close my book. "It's not a question of Joyce being an inconsistent writer, it's a question of him utilizing different narrative forms to further strengthen the story."

Ethan scoffs. "It's in conflict with everything the book's done so far."

Oh. My. God.

"Yeah, it's modernism," I say, like Ethan is an idiot because, let's be honest, he is. "Modernists weren't about decorum," I say, restraining from adding "Have you not learned *anything* from this class?" Instead, I say, "*Ulysses* as a work of literature is a metaphor for the modernist movement as a whole. Surrealists like Joyce, Picasso and Virginia Woolf broke all the previously established art rules in an attempt to explore facets of humanity that were limited by the constraints of traditional art forms," I say. "Each chapter of *Ulysses* explores a different aspect of humanity. And since no two facets of humanity are the same, it makes sense that no two chapters are the same either. 'Circe' is the chapter where Joyce is exploring the idea of consciousness, and challenging what the human mind is capable of."

"Yeah, okay," Ethan says dismissively. He turns back to the professor.

And the degree to which he doesn't take me seriously is the cherry on top of a shitty-ass month.

"I had respect for Bloom until he turned into a woman," Ethan continues. "Like, even if this is a dream, that's such an embarrassing thing to dream about. You're only a man if you reject femininity. In that time, I mean," Ethan amends, like he remembers that it's no longer cool to be misogynistic.

And he sounds so much like John Montgomery that I can't keep quiet.

"Bloom is able to 'be a man' by the end of the chapter *because* he embraces his femininity," I say. "That's what Joyce is getting at—repression hinders humanity, which is why 'Circe' is structured the way it is. If the whole book is a metaphor for life, then Bloom is different at the end of this chapter because he opened up a section of his mind that was previously closed. He utilized 'soft skills' to find inner strength."

"Oh please." Ethan rolls his eyes. "No one takes a company public by talking about their *feelings*. 'Soft skills,' or whatever you call them, are only useful to kindergarten teachers and therapists. You're just trying to legitimize the fact that you go to therapy."

I stare at him. And it's like *years* of bottled up anger and resentment have finally reached the tipping point.

"You're right, therapists do use soft skills," I say, closing my books and shoving them in my backpack. "And I'll be sure to use them when you come into my office crying one day about burnout and your failed marriage."

"Whoa now," the professor says. "Beatriz, what are you doing?" she asks as I shove my binder into my bag next.

I don't answer but look Ethan dead in the eyes. "*Fuck* you."

He turns to the professor like a child running to his mother because someone called him a mean name. I turn to the professor too. "And fuck you for letting him talk to me like that."

I shoulder my backpack and walk out of class.

★ ★ ★

"Vamos," Hero says, shaking me awake. "We're going home."

"What?" I slowly open my eyes to see Hero climbing down the ladder from my bed.

"Classes are over, we've got a week until exams start, and we need to get the hell out of here. Dad's picking us up later."

I don't say anything as Hero pulls my suitcase out and starts packing it. This is how Hero's been dealing with her breakup—obsessively taking care of me. Usually it would piss me off, and it still kind of does, but I don't have energy to ask her to stop. The burst of adrenaline I had when I went off at Ethan yesterday zapped me even more completely than I was before.

I didn't tell Hero that Ben and I broke up—she just seemed to know, which is a relief because even though it's been a month, I haven't been able to say it out loud. Like when I told Lorna, I texted it to her during one of our calls.

I've been having two sessions a week with Lorna since Ben and I broke up.

It would be embarrassing if I didn't understand why it was happening, if I was in denial that I've been rejected by people I love my whole life (first my grandmother, then my mother). But I'm not. I get that the only psychological response to Ben failing me is utter annihilation. People who say it's pathetic for girls to be depressed for weeks and not get out of bed over a guy clearly don't understand how trauma works—it's not about the guy, it's about the past failed relationships, and how you hoped this one was different.

"When did you decide that?" I ask, climbing down and tugging on the undergarments, shirt and pants Hero laid out for me.

"Yesterday while you were in class."

I nod. Ever since I told Ethan and my professor to fuck off,

I've felt a little lighter. I didn't realize how exhausting it's been to keep the wakes of discomfort within myself so the pools white people swim in will stay calm. And even though letting it out earned me a reprimand from the administration, it's worth it to stop feeling muzzled.

"We need to go home," Hero said, as she zips up my suitcase. "This year sucked. And you need to see Lorna in person."

I nod, throwing schoolbooks into my backpack. "So when's Leo getting here?" I ask.

Hero checks her phone. "In a couple hours," she says. "Hey, why don't we go to BerryLine while we wait? A classes-are-over celebration."

I hesitate. Hero rolls her eyes. "Dude, just because white girls like something doesn't mean you can't."

BerryLine is this frozen yogurt place on Arrow Street that I've been obsessed with since freshman year. When we discovered it, I was ecstatic to find a place that takes fro-yo seriously because ice cream has always been too rich for my stomach.

Then white girls decided that frozen yogurt was the new chai latte and I started going less and less.

"Fine," I mumble, tugging my shoes on. "What's the weather been like?" I ask, suddenly realizing I've barely left the dorm all week. Jeez. Maybe I do need some fro-yo.

"A little chilly, but you'll probably be fine in that," Hero says, nodding at my relaxed-fit T that features six different authors reimagined as punk rockers.

We don't say much as we make our way off campus and into Harvard Square. Once the little shack that is BerryLine comes into view, I feel a stab in my stomach. I'd wanted to bring Ben here.

I glance up to see Hero looking concerned. "What?" I ask. She shrugs. "You."

"I'm fine."

The line is out the door, so we join the end of the queue on the sidewalk.

"You excited for your apprenticeship?" I ask as we shuffle forward.

Hero's eyes light up for the first time in weeks. "Yeah. I've been emailing with the person I'll be shadowing, and it sounds *amazing*. I honestly feel so lucky to have this opportunity seeing as I didn't go to art school."

Guilt stabs through me.

"How's the job front for you?" Hero asks hesitantly.

"The same," I say, trying to push the anxiety from my mind. "Meaning none."

"Do you…want help or something?" Hero asks as the entrance to BerryLine comes into view. "Like…what about it is stressing you out? Want me to fill out some applications for you?"

I raise my eyebrows at her. "So I can pretend to be you?"

"No, like, you would tell me what you want to say and I'd write it down."

"How would that be helpful?"

"I don't know!" Hero throws up her arms and I'm surprised how frustrated she sounds. "I thought maybe it was the application interface that freaked you out."

"It's not," I say quietly, as we move into the shack.

"Then what is it?" Hero's voice is gentle enough that I look up. Her eyes are big and I see the familiar determination to help mixed with the frustration that she doesn't know how.

"I—"

"Hey, what can I get you?"

I look up to realize we're next. Hero quickly orders a plain fro-yo and adds berries. I go for blueberry-lemon and add mochi.

All the seats are taken, so Hero and I wander back outside. The brick sidewalk is divided by an enclosure filled with trees, their blossoms swaying in the spring breeze. Hero and I sit on the enclosure's concrete curb.

I think about what Hero said as I pop a mochi into my mouth. "I just…don't know what I want," I say quietly. She nods, waving her spoon for me to go on. "Like, my plan before the election was to take a year off, work, and hopefully earn enough money to supplement going to grad school."

Hero nods. "Yeah, you've been a professor since we were, like, nine."

I smile. "I know. But every time I try to research if Amherst Books is hiring, or if I could work as an assistant to someone at UMass…I just get overwhelmed with the fear that it's not what I should be doing. And that fear is doubled because I have no idea what I *want* to be doing."

"That makes sense." Hero digs her spoon down to find a raspberry stuck at the bottom of her cup.

"I always thought I'd work in academia," I say. "But the election is making me feel like maybe that's not enough."

Hero frowns. "What do you mean? You're always saying education is the only path out of ignorance."

"I know," I say. "I'm not trying to say that being a teacher isn't productive. I'm just not sure it's the way *I* can be most productive."

"Can you elaborate?"

I think about the confrontation I had with Ethan. He and I received the exact same education. And while I felt like reading *Ulysses* gave me a roadmap to understand my humanity in a way *nothing* else had, Ethan couldn't even define what modernism was.

Seeing how deep the fissure is in the country right now has made me wonder if academia is the most effective way to initiate change. It's one way, but now I'm questioning whether or not it's mine. The state of the world has made me reevaluate what change even is, and how one goes about making it.

Like, maybe I could make a bigger difference working one-on-one with people who have actively chosen to work on themselves. Instead of standing in front of a room of students, some of whom will never take me seriously.

Ethan made it clear that some people refuse to apply the same critical thinking they would to school on their own emotions. And that means they keep going through life repeating the same toxic patterns, never knowing it's possible to live any other way.

And I'm realizing that the people who possess emotional literacy are few and far between. And if I'm one of them, maybe academia isn't my calling. Maybe there's a way to use my skills of analyzing literature and human behavior beyond getting a master's degree. Maybe what I said about therapizing future-Ethan is more significant than I thought.

"Mijas!" Leo cries when he picks us up at the Johnston Gate. He pulls Hero and me into a hug.

With his arms around me, and his familiar smell taking me in, I feel safe for the first time since Ben and I broke up.

"Let me take those!" Uncle Leo lets go, picks up our suitcases and tosses them haphazardly into the car. "Oh shit," he says as they bounce from the aggression of his toss. "You guys didn't have any breakables in there, did you?"

"Yeah, I packed a bunch of glass vases to bring home and you destroyed them all."

Leo laughs and pulls me in for another hug. "I missed you, Trizita."

I bury my face in his Pinewoods T-shirt and mumble, "I missed you too."

Oh my god, I missed my own shower.

The first thing I do when we get home is take a long, hot shower in a not-school bathroom before throwing on some sweats and wandering onto the screened-in porch. Uncle Leo's sitting on the wicker couch, opera blaring from the turntable in the corner, working on a crossword puzzle.

It's clear where I get my nerdiness from.

"Oh good," he says when he looks up and sees me. "I've been stuck on this one for days."

I sit next to him. Crossword puzzles have always been our thing. Uncle Leo loves trivia, and I love words, although I have no patience for puzzles of any kind. He always asks for my help on the clues that involve puns or wordplay. He's even texted me for help a few times, which was one of the few things I enjoyed doing over the past month.

Leo shows me the newspaper—yeah, he still buys newspapers—and points to a clue that reads "How a yogi overstays their welcome."

I think for a second. "Namaste."

"Yes!" Uncle Leo kisses my head and hands me the pencil so I can fill it in. "I have a whole stack of puzzles I've been stuck on. We can go through them later if you want."

"Sounds good," I say, leaning my head on his shoulder.

I close my eyes and don't realize I've dozed off until I hear Hero say, "Dad, can I look at your sword tattoo again?"

I jerk awake and see Hero tucked into the wicker chair across from me, her sketchbook on her lap.

"Of course!" Uncle Leo puts the newspaper down and pushes the sleeve of his T-shirt up as Hero leans forward to get a better look at his sword in the stone tattoo.

"Thanks," Hero says, leaning back and looking at her sketchbook.

"You redesigning mine?" I ask sleepily as Uncle Leo rubs my back.

"Sort of. I mean, not your nightmare ones, but it has to do with you."

I sit up. "Really?"

Hero nods. "But I don't know if you'll want to see it."

"Why?"

Hero hesitates, then holds her sketchbook up. She's drawn separate caricatures of Ben and Claudio being decapitated.

I burst out laughing. "Oh my god, I love you."

Hero smiles for the first time in weeks. "I would never actually tattoo them, but I need *some* sort of outlet."

"Yeah, no kidding." I lean back against the couch.

"I take it those are the shitheads?" Uncle Leo asks, crossing his arms protectively.

Hero nods. I haven't told him anything, but Hero keeps him up to date, so I assume he knows that Hero and I both fell in love only to have our hearts stomped on.

I pull out my phone and have a great deal of difficulty not pulling up Ben's Instagram to stalk him. I looked at it every day right after we first broke up, but I've been doing it less and less as time goes by. He mostly posts videos of him at the gym and I lost count of how many times I masturbated to them, moaning his name into my pillow as I remembered how that body curled around me.

So I don't pull up Ben's account, but Meg's. Maybe Ben'll be home for the reading week, like Hero and me.

Most of the pictures Meg's posted are of her and John. My stomach tenses, and for the first time in a month, I want to text Ben. To see how he's doing. To ask him if his panic attacks have continued. To tell him I love him, even though he doesn't love me back.

I shove my phone back in my pocket.

"Antonio's for dinner?" Uncle Leo asks.

I sit up eagerly. "Please."

Uncle Leo smiles and pulls up the menu of our favorite

pizza place on his phone. He calls in an order, and I go with him to pick it up while Hero stays home and sketches.

"So how much do you want to talk about it?" he says as we pull out of the driveway.

"I don't know."

"Fair enough."

We turn onto the main road. He smiles at me but doesn't press.

"I just…it sucks," I say as we stop at a red light. Talking to him away from Hero is easier. I don't know why.

"That is accurate," he says. "My first breakup was a nightmare."

"I never expected to go through a breakup," I say quietly. "I never thought I'd fall in love."

"Oh, Trizita." Uncle Leo looks at me as the light turns green. "What happened?"

I can't tell him everything. If I do, I will probably have a panic attack. But there *is* a succinct way to tell him why Ben and I aren't together.

"His parents voted for Trump."

His eyes go blank. "Motherfucker," he says so menacingly that I see where Hero gets it.

"*He's* not like that," I say as Leo stops a little too abruptly at a stop sign. "But…I don't know. His family are like the WASPiest people you can imagine—"

"Oh god."

"—and I just knew that I'd never fit in his world."

"Motherfucker," Leo says again, more loudly. "It's people like that who make me understand why a supernatural being would send a flood to wipe out humanity."

"Yeah."

"This is the guy whose house you all stayed at, right?"

Uncle Leo asks, pulling up in front of Antonio's. But he doesn't turn off the car.

I nod.

"Did you feel safe there?" he asks quietly, looking at me. "I would have picked you up if you hadn't, sweetie."

I open my mouth to say, "Kind of," but instead what bursts out is, "I did with him."

And then I'm crying.

Uncle Leo unbuckles his seat belt and pulls me into his arms.

"I miss him so much," I choke, finally putting words to the feelings that have been pressing into my chest for weeks. "I don't know why, we weren't together that long, but—"

"You don't always have to know someone for a while to get them," Uncle Leo says softly, rubbing my back. Just like he did when he found me crying in Grandma's bathroom when I was four.

I just nod, still sobbing. "He didn't love me," I say finally, wiping my tears.

"Then I will personally send a flood to kill him."

I snort. "Thanks."

"Just because he didn't love you doesn't mean no one will," he says when I pull away. "You know that, right?"

I shrug. "Honestly, the idea of giving love another go sounds terrible. Like, why would anyone do this to themselves?"

He shrugs too, looking out the windshield. I remember that he hasn't really dated anyone since Hero's mom died. And for the first time, I wonder if I'm not the only one in the family apprehensive about romance.

"Love's tricky," he finally says. "It's amazing at the beginning, then it's scary, and if it doesn't go well, it feels like you've discovered a pain no one else has ever experienced in their life."

I nod. Right after Ben and I broke up, part of me did wonder if I should call a scientific journal because I felt like my pain was a new frontier of human knowledge. "So why do people do it?"

"I don't know," he says. I feel like this is the first time he's talking to me like an equal instead of his child. "Honestly… some people don't do it. Some people experience heartbreak like it's food poisoning and go the rest of their life avoiding that mode of sustenance."

"Then what should I do?"

Leo's eyes soften and he takes my hand. "Whatever you feel comfortable doing. And if that's never dating again, that's your prerogative, sweetheart."

"I don't know if that's what I want," I say honestly, because while the idea of setting myself up for heartbreak again is awful, enough time has passed that I remember how incredible I felt with Ben when it was good.

"You don't have to," Leo says, squeezing my hand. "That's what life is for."

Ben texts me at midnight.

My phone goes off and when I check the screen, it takes me a while to figure out I'm not dreaming.

It's a photo. Holy shit, is it a nude? Which would be totally inappropriate, and I'd call him on it, but…I'd definitely put it to good use.

It's a picture of all six annotated Jane Austens. I vaguely remember that he ordered them before we broke up.

I wait for the stab of pain that accompanies every thought of Ben. But it doesn't come. Instead what comes is something meeker, still laced with heartbreak, but with something else too. Something like…regret? Or a what-if?

My thumb lingers over the keyboard as I try to figure out what to do.

I haven't talked to Ben in a month. And given that we were only in each other's lives the month before that, I feel like I shouldn't miss him as much as I do.

But we got really, *really* close. Waking up in the morning and knowing I can't text him feels like Lyra leaving Pantalaimon on the shores of the Land of the Dead. A searing pain I never thought I'd have to feel but it's too acute to ignore.

So now that I've had time without Ben in my life, I'm wondering if it actually would be worse to have him in it. Yeah, it might be painful to be friends with him again—but it doesn't sound any worse than what I'm going through now. Either way sucks—I might as well pick the path that includes him.

I type a response.

15

BEN

My phone lights up as Beatriz texts back. I almost fall out of bed in my haste to get it. I really didn't think she would.

Claudio's not sleeping here tonight. I had an edible a few hours ago, and the high made it seem like not the worst idea to send Beatriz a picture of my annotated Jane Austens. She turned me on to them, so it seemed fitting.

And I've been desperate to text her since the last time she was in my room.

Beatriz: u know u have to open them carefully like every 20 pages so as not to break the spine right?

My heart starts beating so fast, I jump a little. It hasn't beat faster than a snail's pace in so long I forgot how it felt to actually feel it in my body.

Ben: No?

Beatriz: with really thick books its a good idea. before u start reading them, just thumb through it every twenty pages to ease the spine open. otherwise youll be in the middle and the spine will just crack in half and youll have that really annoying spot it always falls open to

Ben: How did I not know this?

Beatriz: i mean, u dont have a lot of nerd friends because ur a weirdo

I smile. It hurts.

Ben: Ha ha.

Beatriz doesn't respond right away. I wrack my brain for anything else I could say because I don't want her to go. A few minutes go by and I start to panic, but then a new message comes through.

Beatriz: so...how r u

Ben: I mean...do you really want to know?

Beatriz: yes. no? im not sure. i know we're broken up but...its weird not talking to u

Ben: Yeah, it's been weeks since anyone's given me an incorrect reading of Emma.

Beatriz: fuck u

She's typing something else.

Beatriz: would u wanna try being friends?

Ben: Yes.

Beatriz: okay

I know she doesn't mean friends with benefits, but my body gets hot at the thought of seeing her in person again.

Ben: Want to get that proto-feminist lit Fight Club going?

Beatriz: im not on campus

Ben: Oh. Where are you?

Beatriz: home

Ben: I just realized that I don't actually know where you live.

Beatriz: Amherst, MA.

I wish she was here.

Ben: Oh, cool. Amherst College was my safety school.

Beatriz: i am rolling my eyes so hard

Beatriz: we could try playing that nerdy card game if you want

Oh god. That is the single sexiest request she has ever made of me. I showed her how to play Magic when we were together (after she asked what "deck building" was because apparently, I talk about it in my sleep). Suddenly, I'm so overcome with everything I miss about Beatriz that I feel like I might throw up.

It's not until I've deep-breathed for fifteen minutes that the fog in my head clears enough for me to respond.

Ben: Sure

I sign on to the digital version of Magic and wait for Beatriz to make an account. She texts me a minute into our first game.

Beatriz: its not letting me play two water cards

It's really cute when she gets the terminology wrong.

Ben: Those are called lands. And you can only play one per turn.

Beatriz: i thought lands were the sun ones

Ben: The water ones, sun ones, tree ones, mountain ones, and skull ones are all different kinds of lands that correlate to the kind of deck you're playing. For example, a deck with only water lands is a blue deck, plain lands is yellow, etc. Also, another word for lands is mana.

Beatriz: ur almost as annoying as you are informed

Ben: I can't tell if you're making fun of me or just stating a fact.

Beatriz: both

Ben: Hey–

I type "sweetheart" but stop myself just before hitting Send.

Ben: Hey, dude

Beatriz: what?

Ben: It's still your turn.

Beatriz: oh fuck

Beatriz plays a land but doesn't immediately attack me with one of her creatures.

Ben: Are you sure you don't want to hit me?

Beatriz: dude, r u really trying to help me when im playing AGAINST u?

Ben: Yeah. I mean, you're still new at this, it wouldn't really be fair if I lay down the entire wrath of my MTG nerddom on you and sent you crying off to your room.

Beatriz: yeah ive been doing enough of that recently

My heart lurches.

Ben: Me too

Beatriz: wait really? i was only kind of serious

Oops. Shit.

Ben: Oh yeah, me too

Beatriz: …really

Ben: Well, have YOU really not cried at all?

Beatriz: ben, i dont wanna do this

Ben: You're the one who brought it up.

Beatriz: no, i made an innocuous comment that YOU read into

Ben: That's bullshit; there's no fucking way that was innocuous, what else would you be crying about?

Beatriz: none of ur business, asshole

Oh my god, I'm horny. Fighting with her awakened something dormant.

Ben: Okay fine. Do you want to keep going?

Beatriz: yeah i guess

Ben: Dude, you don't have to.

Beatriz: I KNOW I DONT HAVE TO

I'm getting hard.

Ben: Okay. It's still your turn.

Beatriz: oh shit thats right

We stay up until one, playing Magic and talking—occasionally sniping at each other, but that just makes me hornier.

I spend the next day studying and trying not to think about the fact that Beatriz popping into my life again made me have my first wet dream since I was thirteen. But losing myself in academics is difficult because my classes are super boring.

Why have I never noticed that finance is mind-numbingly tedious?

Claudio doesn't spend the night in the room again. After I'm done studying, I try rereading *The Son of Neptune* so I don't obsess over how much I want to play Magic with Beatriz again. I feel like I should wait for her to ask me.

And at 10:30, she does.

She's getting better; my phone doesn't go off until halfway through the game. But when I look down at her text, it's not about Magic.

Beatriz: so...r u seeing anyone

I inhale sharply. Is this her way of leading up to telling me *she's* with someone? I don't want that. I know I can't be with her, and I know it's shitty to not want her with anyone else, but—the idea makes me nauseous.

Ben: I mean, I wasn't really 'seeing people' before you.

Beatriz: i know

Ben: Then why'd you ask?

Beatriz: curious i guess

Ben: Why?

Beatriz: to see if i was a fluke or something

Ben: Oh.

We sign off after a few games. I shut off the light and crawl into bed, feeling a little lighter than I did last night. I'm almost asleep when my phone goes off. I reach out to put it on Do Not Disturb but freeze when I see the text.

Beatriz: god damn u Ben, now im awake

She's texting me. Randomly. I unplug my phone.

Ben: Are you usually asleep before 12:30?

Beatriz: yeah, normally i go to bed at like 11

Ben: You didn't the entire time we were together.

Beatriz: yeah well, why do u think that was

Ben: I would have gone to bed earlier if you wanted.

Beatriz: maybe i didnt want to

Ben: Oh, yeah?

Beatriz: yeah

I hesitate. But my heart is a thunderstorm, and my pelvis is aching.

Ben: And now

Beatriz: now i wish i was exhausted enough to stop talking to u

Ben: But you're not?

Beatriz: no

Ben: why

Beatriz: cause i really miss u

Oh my god.

Ben: What do you miss

Beatriz: everything

Ben: I miss how you smell

Beatriz: i miss how u taste

Ben: I miss fucking you

Beatriz: i miss begging u to

Ben: Should we be doing this

Beatriz: no. but thats how it started

Ben: Can I call you

Beatriz: yes

"Ben." Her voice sounds breathy. It destroys me.

"Hey."

"I want you."

"Fuck." My hand is under my boxers and I know Beatriz is doing the same thing. "I came in my sleep thinking about you." I groan, and Beatriz makes that noise that tells me she needs more. "You were wearing my clothes and I was eating you out—"

"Ben," she says again, her voice thin. "Do more."

"I miss touching your body," I say, going faster. "I miss watching your stomach quiver as you ride me—"

"How are you so good at this?"

"I only am with you."

"Call me 'love.'"

"Oh god—"

She tells me things she shouldn't; I tell her everything I've wanted since we broke up, and when Beatriz orgasms, I'm silent because I need to hear it. Hear my name tumbling off her lips, her voice cracking as it rises, and I come all over my hand.

We hang up, and I change my sheets.

I figure it's a one-time thing—she was horny, and I was there. But the next night, she texts me again, sorry about last night.

This feels like a crossroad. I could do the right thing and say something like, it's fine, or whatever. Or I could tell her how I feel. And what else do I have to lose?

Ben: I'm not.

Beatriz: really?

Ben: Yes.

Beatriz: why?

Ben: Because it was the best I've felt in weeks.

Beatriz: then call me

I do. We're naked and I'm desperate and as Beatriz describes what she's doing, I can't believe it took me three years to fall in love with her. It should have taken days.

"We're so stupid," she hisses when she's done.

"I mean, we're not, we have 4.0s at Harvard."

She laughs. "Nice to see you're still an asshole."

"Nice to see you still comment on it."

I open my mouth to say something, but she hangs up.

I say it anyway: "I love you."

BEATRIZ

Well, trying to be friends with Ben resulted in the hottest phone sex of my life. Twice.

I don't tell Hero. There really shouldn't *be* anything to not tell Hero because I should not be virtually hooking up with my ex-boyfriend.

But I can't stop talking to him, and he can't stop letting me.

We play Magic three nights in a row. On the third night, I don't really need his help anymore, and I get nervous because that was the excuse I had to text him. I wonder if I should pretend to forget something when my phone buzzes.

Ben: So how was your day?

Beatriz: fine, studying and shit

Ben: Hey, I've started using your note-taking technique ☺

Beatriz: and?

Ben: Is there anything higher than a 4.0? Because I will have it.

Beatriz: ur the worst

Ben: I know, right?

I try to go to sleep after we play Magic, but Ben burns through my mind and I can't stop myself from calling him.

"I was afraid you wouldn't," he says after the second ring.

"You know me better than that."

I hang up when we're done, sufficiently sweaty. A few minutes later, my phone buzzes.

Ben: You know…we don't have to do this.

Yes, we do.

Beatriz: what do u mean?

Ben: Like…I know we broke up, we can go back to not doing this if you want. If that would be better.

Beatriz: it would be better but its not what i want

Ben: Yeah. That's kind of where I am too. It's never been like this before.

Beatriz: meaning?

Ben: You just made sex limitless. And now I can't really go back to sex that's limited.

I feel like Ben and I are inevitable. Like we could not see each other for ten years, both move on, and then run into each other at a bookstore and start having an affair without either of us realizing what we're doing.

But as long as Ben puts Trump money first, I can't be in a relationship with him. And as long as he believes Hero is someone she isn't, I can't have him in my life.

But I can still talk to him…right?

Beatriz: hey, hows meg doing?

Ben: God, I have no idea.

Beatriz: wait really?

Ben: Yeah. I thought about texting her again, but the idea of John responding was so awful that I threw up.

He's not serious, right?

Beatriz: r u being hyperbolic?

Ben: No, I started thinking about it and then my stomach started to really fucking hurt and I barely had time to make it to the bathroom to vomit. Sorry if that's too much info.

Beatriz: dude…thats not normal

Ben: I mean, for me it's not NOT normal.

Beatriz: wait seriously? how did i not know this?

Ben: Well…when we were together, I was kind of too happy to let it get to me or whatever, so you wouldn't have noticed.

Beatriz: oh. have u ever thought about seeing someone for your anxiety?

Ben: What do you mean? I don't have anxiety.

Beatriz: wow

Ben: What! I don't. People who have anxiety, like, hate social gatherings and can't leave their room.

Beatriz: theyre BOTH anxiety, they just require different kinds of help

Ben: I'm fine.

I almost type "baby" and then remember I can't.

Beatriz: r u though?

Ben: I mean

He's typing then stops. Then starts again, then stops.

Ben: Please don't tell anyone.

Beatriz: dude I havent even told anyone we're talking again

Ben: I know, I've just never talked about this before. I don't even know if I've put words to it before.

My heart tries to leap out of my chest, into the phone and over to Ben, but I shove it back.

Beatriz: i wont tell anyone

Ben: Okay. Well…"help" isn't really something we do in my family.

Beatriz: like therapy?

Ben: Like ANYTHING. You know why John dropped out of high school?

Beatriz: hes lazy?

Ben: He has a learning disability and my parents were too ashamed to get him help for it, which just made John so ashamed that he refused to admit he needed help. That's why he hates me so much.

Beatriz: because ur good at school?

Ben: Because I skipped a grade when he was flunking out. And my dad stopped taking him to all the bank meetings and stopped prepping him to take over the family assets, and instead put it all on me because I knew "how to work hard."

Oh my god. Ben makes more sense now. Everything he's talking about is still outdated bullshit, but if Ben shoulders all the responsibility of carrying on what's important to his family, I get why he couldn't choose us over them. I know how much it sucks to not have parents. I see why Ben wouldn't want to do anything to make them blacklist him the way they have John.

Beatriz: so thats y u prefer to vomit while having panic attacks as opposed to seeing a therapist?

Ben: Yeah. I know therapy isn't bad, and I know how much Lorna's helped you, but the idea of going makes me… I don't know if I can say it.

Beatriz: try?

Ben: Makes me feel like I couldn't go home. Like my parents wouldn't want to see me.

This time I can't stop myself.

Beatriz: Baby ♥

Ben: I know, I'm pathetic.

Beatriz: no. i just hate that the people who r supposed to love u dont see how fucking brave u are, and would make u feel bad for trying to make yourself happier

Ben: I could say the same for you.

Beatriz: yeah i guess

Ben: Anyway. Thanks for going all therapy on my ass. It feels good to say all that.

Beatriz: thanks for letting me. i liked it

And as Ben types a response—I realize how deeply that's true. The most at peace I've ever felt has been in my sessions with Lorna, when we're identifying and solving complex emotional problems. There are no words for the satisfaction I feel when I talk to someone who thinks they'll always be down, and watch them realize it's possible to reach up.

And there's the fact that when Ethan came for therapy during class, my gut response was to tell him I'd see him in *my* office.

Huh. Interesting.

Hero pulls into a parking space and I unzip my seat belt. We're meeting some high school friends at the Hangar for dinner. And by that I mean, I'm tagging along with Hero and her art friends because some things don't change.

The Hangar is this really sick wings place in Amherst. It's this huge sports bar with TVs showing every sport imaginable, but it also has this arcade at the front. Hero and I had countless birthday parties here when we were growing up. We keep coming back because the food is incredible, and they also have a wall of beer taps where you can build your own flight.

It's pretty mobbed when Hero and I walk in, so she gives our name to the hostess and we head to the arcade.

"Air hockey?" Hero asks, putting the glowing square the hostess gave her on the side of the air hockey table.

"Sure."

Hero's friends show up after a few rounds.

"Superhero!" One of them squeals, enveloping Hero in a hug. There are five of them total, and they all look…well, very Amherst. No one's hair is its natural color, the two guys have topknots, and the style of the three girls could be described as either millennial hippie or bohemian chic.

I stand off to the side while they greet each other because they're not really *my* friends. I didn't have a lot of friends in high school. Honestly, the only reason I came is because the alternative was sitting alone in my room trying not to think about Ben.

"Hey, Beatriz." A girl with a nose ring, purple hair and a floor-length skirt gives me a hug once she releases Hero. I think her name's Juniper.

"Hey," I say, awkwardly hugging her back. "How are you?"

"Oh, you know," she says, waving her hand. "Almost done with fucking college! Although I'm sure you have much more interesting stories. I'm not rubbing shoulders with Malia Obama."

Malia actually won't be starting until after we've graduated, but I just nod. Hero and one of the guys start another air hockey game. I sit on a chair and scroll through (not Ben's) Instagram until our buzzer lights up, and we're led to a table.

"So how's Claudio?" Juniper asks Hero after we've put in our order. "Do we finally get to meet him?"

I freeze and Hero goes white. "Um," she starts. "Well—"

"He couldn't get a visa," I blurt out. "So he's going back to Italy right after school ends," I say, hoping that none of them will know how student visas work.

"Aww, too bad!" Juniper says, putting a hand on Hero's shoulder. "Maybe another time."

Hero just nods and I ask about graduation parties. Juniper starts babbling about an epic party that's supposed to go down in a few days, and Hero mouths, *Thank you*, across the table at me. I mouth, *I got you*.

The food comes, and I actually start to feel better for the first time in a while. I didn't realize that I've seen pretty much no one except Hero for weeks, and the change of pace is nice.

I've just ordered my second beer when my phone goes off.

Ben: Hey, are you busy right now?

My thumb freezes, hovering over the message. I glance at Hero, but she's too busy filling Juniper in on her apprenticeship.

Beatriz: depends. definitely cant do phone sex

Ben: Ha ha, no, I wasn't thinking that.

Beatriz: im with some friends atm

Ben: Oh, okay. It can wait.

Beatriz: i mean, theyre Heros friends and ive been on my phone for the last half hour anyway. so they wont exactly notice

Ben: Okay.

Ben types for a *long* time.

Ben: Um, well...talking to you has made me think a lot. I mean, it always does, that's not unusual, I'm not trying to imply you don't make me think. Our talk last night just got me thinking about emotions and shit, and I just...I'm really sorry for what I said to you when, uh...shit was going down.

I choke on my beer. Hero looks up.

"Down the wrong pipe," I say, coughing. Juniper thumps me on the back before asking Hero when she'll be able to actually work on people.

Beatriz: oh

Ben: Sorry, I totally freaked you out.

Beatriz: no, its ok

Ben: Is it?

Beatriz: i just...didnt expect that

Beatriz: ur talking about when we were breaking up right?

Ben: Yeah.

Ben: I realized I treated you like my family has always treated me. And that's not something I ever want to inflict on anyone. And I'm so fucking sorry that the person I inflicted it on was you. When we were together, all I wanted to do was keep you safe and make you happy, and I just don't understand how past me failed so abysmally.

Jeez. This is the first time someone who has hurt me has actually apologized. My mom never even came close, and I know whenever Leo tries to get my grandmother to atone for what she did, she just tells Leo that I'm overreacting.

Beatriz: ok

Ben: You still seem off?

Beatriz: u just...hurt me. a lot. i actually trusted u and i dont really do that

Ben: I know.

Beatriz: then whyd u do it?

Ben types for a while. I glance up. Hero is looking at me. I shrug and mouth, *bored*, hoping she'll buy it. She mouths, *Arcade?* and I shake my head, mouthing, *Tired*. She furrows her brow and my phone goes off.

Ben: I was just so mad about Claudio. And when I get mad I tend to get REALLY mad, and I didn't have anything around to calm me down. I'm not trying to make excuses, I just don't know how else to put it.

Hero is still looking at me. But my mind is so consumed by this conversation with Ben, I don't have energy to put her off the scent. So I start typing.

Beatriz: i get being loyal, but i dont understand how u went from defending ur friend to attacking me. u said really shitty things

Ben: I know. I don't really get it either.

Beatriz: how helpful

Ben: I just...no one ever made me examine my actions before. And I'm starting to realize it's something I should have been doing a long time ago. But I wanted to tell you that I know I fucked up, and I'm sorry ♥ I hate that I lost you but what sucks even more is that I hurt you in the process.

My heart is fucking racing.

Beatriz: u hate that u lost me?

Ben: Of course.

Beatriz: then why didnt u do anything about it

Ben doesn't respond right away. My stomach drops when I finally see the three dots.

Ben: Do you wish I had?

I thought I knew the answer. Now I'm not sure.

Beatriz: it doesnt matter

Ben: Okay.

Beatriz: its just...when we broke up, i felt like u didnt care

Ben doesn't respond—he calls me. I panic, hitting Decline and glancing up to make sure no one's noticed. He doesn't text me again.

I try to hide my panic for the rest of dinner. Why did he call me? And why didn't he text back when I didn't answer?

It's not until Hero and I get home that I realize Ben left me a voice mail.

It's five seconds: "Of course I care."

It's different after that. We don't talk about that conversation again, but neither of us question hooking up again. Ben just calls me every night at ten o'clock, the sex is so good I can't believe it's virtual, then we hang up and text until two in the morning. Sometimes we talk about nothing—about Jane Austen, and Magic, and how Trump should be banned from Twitter—but sometimes it gets deeper. And I tell him things I haven't told anyone else.

Ben: I know you haven't seen your mom in a while, but do you ever see your dad?

Beatriz: ive never met him

Ben: Sorry ♥

Beatriz: its fine

Ben: Is it?

Beatriz: i mean no, it sucks but i dont really know what else to say

Ben: I'm sorry.

Ben: I want to go back in time and shake all the people who've ever been shitty to you. You're so special and shouldn't have had to fight so hard to be okay.

Beatriz: are we talking about me or u?

Hero nearly caught us once. She knocked on the door when I was on the phone with Ben, saying she heard my bed moving around and she wanted to make sure I wasn't having a nightmare.

And a few days later, she does catch us—just not the way I expected. We're studying on the porch when a phone goes off. "Yours," Hero says, reaching for the coffee table where both our phones are charging.

"Thanks."

Hero glances down as she passes my phone to me. And doesn't let go when I try to take it.

"What?"

I look down, and my stomach drops.

Ben: I want your legs wrapped around me while I'm thrusting so deep inside you that our bodies stop being separate and we can't tell where I end and you begin.

That's hot. Also *fuck*.

"What the hell?" Hero says, her eyes zeroing in on me.

"It's nothing," I say quickly, tugging my phone from her. And cursing myself for switching out "horny cis asshole" for Ben's actual name.

"What the *fuck* are you doing." Hero sounds like she's going to kill me.

"I just told you."

"And you're lying out of your ass."

"Whatever," I start to reply but Hero grabs the phone from my hand and starts scrolling up.

"Hero!"

"Oh god!" Hero shuts her eyes and drops my phone, which is how I know she's gotten to the part where I explicitly told Ben how I'd deep-throat him if we were together. Thinking about it sends sparks up and down my body. "You guys are back together?" She crosses her arms.

"No."

She raises her eyebrows at me. "Certainly seems that way."

"We're not."

"Then why are you sexting in the middle of the day?"

"Because." I don't even try to elaborate because I don't know how I could. We aren't back together, but I don't know if I can say that we're still broken up. We're in that no-man's-land between together and not, and I know it's just going to wind up hurting me more.

But I can't control myself when Ben talks to me. And if I'm going to crash and burn either way, I'd rather take the road that will involve some highs instead of low after low.

"Do you *like* being heartbroken?"

"Oh, fuck off."

"That's not how this works, Beatriz!" Hero says, jabbing at my phone.

"What, since you can't be friends with your ex, I can't be friends with mine?"

"That's not being friends!" Hero jumps to her feet, towering over me. "That's letting a horny asshole take advantage of you."

"That's not what he's doing," I say. Nearly every time Ben and I have started something, I'm the one who's instigated it. If anything, I'm the horny asshole taking advantage of him.

"Stop defending him! He's not your boyfriend anymore. And the fact that you didn't even *tell* me he was until just before you broke up doesn't exactly make him look good."

I get up. "I'm leaving."

"I know you still love him." That stops me. "I know you, Trizita. You're not going to fall hard for someone and get over it that fast."

"That's not what I—"

"You can't be friends this quickly without holding on to some piece of the relationship—" she nods at my phone angrily "—*clearly*. And I don't understand why you're trying to get back any part of a relationship that so completely wrecked you."

I don't say anything, and Hero takes that as fodder to keep yelling.

"You've just been shit on by so many people, Trizita, and it makes me so fucking mad that you're walking into a situation where it's going to happen again!"

"Shut *up*, Hero!" I say. "Don't fucking use my past to defend you trying to live my life for me. I can make my own decisions!"

"Well, maybe you shouldn't!"

"Too bad it's not up to you."

"It fucking should be!"

"You fuck up too," I say through gritted teeth. It's a good thing Leo's at work because he hates when we fight.

Hero scoffs. "Hardly."

That does it. "What about that time you mocked Juniper for sleeping with two guys at the same party?"

"I didn't know what slut-shaming was yet! And that wouldn't have even happened if I wasn't picking your drunk ass up from—"

"Oh, so it's my fault you were a—"

"It wouldn't be anyone's fault if you hadn't—"

And now I understand why Lorna was always encouraging me to talk things through with Hero. Because it's like a flip has switched and everything we've been repressing for years *pours* out. It stops being about me and Ben and becomes about Hero and me. She's yelling at me about the time I called her "basically white" in front of her art friends; I'm yelling at her about how she always corrects my Spanish grammar and makes me feel dumb; she's screaming about how I let Meg get me a new room at Ben's house, as if Hero's help wasn't good enough.

"IF IT WASN'T FOR ME, YOU'D STILL BE WITH YOUR MOM," Hero screams and I stop cold. "I fucking got you out, Beatriz, and I feel like if I don't keep an eye on you, you'll get into a situation where I'll need to again!"

My eyes prick. "Why are you being so—"

"Because I will *not* lose you!" Hero is shaking. "Why do you think I'm at Harvard instead of art school?"

I freeze.

"Who's going to calm your nightmares?" Hero yells, her voice cracking. "Who's going to bring you food when you're too bummed to get out of bed? I've been scared of losing you since we were four and I watched Grandma treat you different for a reason I didn't understand!"

"Hero, I—"

"I saw your face when you pushed your blocks down!" Hero yells. "And the look you had every time you walked past mine, and ever since then, I've *sworn* that I will never let anyone hurt you again."

"But—" I'm worried Hero's voice will break because it's never been this loud for so long.

"Why do you think I called the cops that night? I will *not* lose you, Beatriz, I don't want you to die!"

And then Hero's sobbing. "I will not find you on the bathroom floor again," she weeps, and my stomach grows nauseous. I know what she's talking about.

The week before I started seeing Lorna, the night before I spent a week in a psychiatric ward—the only time my mom's ever contacted me. The night I chugged a bunch of pills and alcohol before passing out in the bathroom only for Hero to find me and call 9-1-1.

"I'm doing better now," I say quietly, taking her in my arms. "I haven't been suicidal in years."

"I know," Hero weeps. "But…I'm just so scared. When you and Ben broke up you were so upset, I hadn't seen you that upset since… I'm just scared it's going to happen again."

"It's not. I have support now, I know what my triggers are. And I don't want to die."

I'm shocked by how deeply I mean this.

Hero just nods. I pull her close.

"I'm so sorry I put you through that," I say, my voice cracking. "I'm sorry I'm so fucking messed up, I—"

"You're not messed up," Hero says, turning her head so she's crying into my neck as my arms hug her tighter. "You're my sister."

Hero's quiet for a moment. Then she whispers, "Trizita?"

"Yeah?"

"I'm sorry I look white."

"Wait, what?" I look down at her. "Where did that come from?"

"I know you have a hard time with it," says Hero, wiping her eyes. "I just wish there wasn't anything dividing us. I hate that there are things about me you resent that I can't change."

I pause. "I hate it too," I say quietly. "But until we live in a world where we're not treated differently, we have to accept that there are advantages you have that I don't. And I'll be angry about them, but they won't change how much I love you."

Hero's quiet for a moment. But then she nods. "Okay. I love you too."

16

BEN

Two days before exams, I'm studying for a final when my phone rings. Claudio's in the room for once, and he glances up as I look down at a number I don't recognize. It has a Cape Cod area code. Could it be Meg?

"Hello?"

"Yo, Ben?"

It's not Meg. In fact, I have to cast around for a while before I realize it's Meg's brother. "Peter?"

"Yeah."

Peter has never called me before. I'm honestly surprised he even has my number. "Uh…what's up?"

"Look, man," Peter says, his voice a slow drawl. "I…know it's weird for me to be calling and shit…but I gotta tell you somethin'."

"Okay…"

"You, uh—you know that video John sent Claudio?"

"Wait, what?" I sit up. "Yeah—but how do *you* know about it?"

"It wasn't Hero in that video. It was Meg."

I almost drop my phone. "Wh-what? How do you— *What?*"

"Yeah, I know. It's fucked up, man. I don't know all the details. Meg's pretty upset. She just told me."

"But—John was saying—I mean, he was calling her—" I feel sick. I know my brother is twisted, but this is a new level of malevolence that I never imagined him capable of. It's beyond cruel, it's—

"But why did Meg let him—" I say, but Peter interrupts.

"I don't know, man. Haven't gotten that out of her yet. She's, uh…well, she's not great."

"What do you mean?"

"She's kind of in the hospital."

"WHAT?"

Claudio jumps at the volume of my voice.

"Why didn't you lead with that?" I ask, feverishly picking at a hangnail on my thumb.

"I promised Meg I'd tell you the other bit first. She knows it probably messed shit up for everybody. She's humiliated as fuck, but she wanted you to know."

"Okay…okay…" I'm still trying to wrap my head around what Peter's saying. "So you said she's in the hospital."

"Yeah."

"Did she—did she o—"

"Not that kind of hospital," Peter mumbles, sounding almost embarrassed. "She's, uh, in the psychiatric wing for a bit."

No.

"I think all of this shit just like…hit her all at once, and she just…it was bad. Dad and I took her to the ER, and she's

gonna be in some inpatient care for a bit. You can visit her if
you want. I have the address."

"Yeah, okay." I scramble around my desk for a piece of
paper before remembering there's a Notes app on my phone.
"What's the address?"

I put Peter on speaker as he reads it to me.

"Alright. Peter...thanks, man," I say, taking him back off
speaker. "I—I know John's your friend, and—"

"Not anymore," Peter says harshly. "Nobody fucks with
my sister." And he hangs up.

I just stand there, still clutching my phone, not realizing I'm
frozen until Claudio says, "The hell did Peter call you for?"

I turn around slowly. Claudio's eyes, which have been looking at me darkly since we yelled at each other the other day,
soften a little. "You alright, mate?"

"We fucked up."

"Huh?"

"Hero didn't cheat on you."

Saying it out loud makes it hit all over again. I remember
Beatriz desperately assuring me that Hero did nothing. That
the only other evidence I came up with was that Hero was
nice to John, and how at the time that seemed like enough.
But now that I *really* think about it, Hero wouldn't have time
to have had sex with John, because every second of break she
was with either Beatriz or Claudio.

"The fuck are you on about?" Claudio mutters, his eyes
becoming cold again.

"It wasn't her in the video. It was Meg. That's what Peter
called to tell me."

Claudio goes white. "What—that makes no sense."

"I know."

"She looked *just* like Hero."

"I know."

"Why would Meg agree to that? Why would John do that?"

"I don't know—"

Wait. Yes, I do.

I crossed John after he warned me not to. I stole all his drug stuff, I called him a freeloading junkie, I made it clear that Meg would be better off being with a sack of garbage than him.

John has spent most of my life trying to keep me down, and lately, I've been feeling strong enough to fight back. He'll stop at nothing to get back at me for being everything he's not—I just didn't realize John knew the only way to undo me is to break the people I love.

Destroying my relationship with Beatriz in the cross fire.

And yet Beatriz *still* picks up the phone when I call her every night; she doesn't hate me even though she has every reason to. Instead, she murmurs sweet nothings in that voice she only uses for me, she listens without judgment when I tell her about my freak-outs, and she loves me despite everything I've stood for, because she knows that's not really me.

Beatriz told me she loved *me*, and due to fear of my family I let her go.

"John did it to fuck with me, but that doesn't matter," I say to Claudio, feeling blood on my thumb from picking the hangnail. "You need to apologize to Hero."

Claudio's face shuts like a door. "Nah, man."

Is he serious?

"Do you have any idea how much pain you've caused, how much pain we've *both* caused?" I say, my voice rising. "You love Hero, you idiot—you told me that months ago, and I know it hasn't changed, and if you love someone and hurt them, you try to fucking fix it—"

"Then why are you here?" Claudio shoots back. "Beatriz looks like a zombie every time I see her in Philosophy. *You* apologize, you fucking hypocrite!"

"I will," I say because I can't deny there's one more thing I need to apologize for. Probably the most important thing of all. "I'm going to. I just need to figure out how."

Claudio snorts. "The only way Ben Montgomery knows how to apologize is by finding a way to make it end in sex."

My hands start to shake. "You're being a real fucking asshole right now."

"Takes one to know one," Claudio says, standing up.

I stand too. "You saying it's my fault you fucked up with your girlfriend?"

"If it wasn't for me, you never would have even *had* a girlfriend."

"Doesn't fucking matter now, does it?" I say, my voice rising. "What's wrong with you? Man enough to break someone's heart but not put it back together?"

"Fuck you, Ben!" Claudio yells, getting in my face.

"Fuck you, Claudio!" I step forward, bumping into him. Claudio stumbles. We look at each other. Then I push Claudio just as he makes toward me. He comes at me again, his eyes dark, trying to punch me but years in the gym means I'm more agile than he is. I duck and run at him, grabbing his stomach and we both tumble to the ground. I punch him in the face and he pushes me off, shoving pent-up anger at each other until we're both winded and red-faced.

"I can't live with you anymore," I breathe, wiping my nose as I stand up. "Not if you can't apologize to someone who did nothing wrong."

"Fine." Claudio gets up, rubbing his side. "I'll be back for my stuff later."

And he's gone.

I stand there, wheezing. I pull out my phone and open my text chain with Beatriz. I scroll up, my thumb stopping on an exchange from a few days ago.

BEN AND BEATRIZ

Ben: I want to go back in time and shake all the people who've ever been shitty to you. You're so special and shouldn't have had to fight so hard to be okay.

Beatriz: are we talking about me or u?

Ben: ???

Ben: You, obviously.

Beatriz: but i could say the exact same about u. ur smart, and caring, and gorgeous, even without killing yourself at the gym. and the people who knew u at ur most vulnerable tried to beat that out of u. theres no one like u, Ben. and i just want u to b happy

I pull out some notebook paper and start to write—pausing every few sentences because I've never poured so much of my heart out before, and it's overwhelming. Like I'm drowning in emotions I didn't know I could feel.

When I'm done, I open *that* document on my laptop. The one I spent hours agonizing over after I ditched Claudio in the middle of Magic because Beatriz was consuming my mind. The day she told me her mom struggled with drug addiction and I saw her for the first time.

The day I fell in love with her.

Thank god there's a printer in my room because no fucking way am I printing this out in the library.

I fold both pieces of paper together, write Beatriz's name on it and slip it under her door on my way to pick up a Zipcar to drive home and see Meg.

I have no idea what to expect when I pull up to the address Peter gave me. All I really knew about mental illness before Beatriz opened up to me were the cracks my dad and John made about how psychiatric diagnoses are excuses for people being lazy.

The complex looks…normal. Just a redbrick building with a welcoming lobby. I leave my name at the receptionist desk and tell them I want to see Meg Xie. I'm led to a small room that looks like it doubles as a cafeteria—round tables and chairs evenly spaced around the room, a counter sporting a fruit bowl and a few jugs of juice and water, and a window that looks into a small kitchen.

There's another patient visiting with their parents as I sit down at an empty table across the room. I wish I could text Meg that I'm here, but Peter told me no one's allowed phones once they're admitted.

I pick at my thumbs until Meg appears in the doorway. She looks thin, her skin more scabbed than it was in March—but her face looks calmer than I've seen it in a long time.

"Hey," I say, standing up as she walks over. When I tentatively reach out, Meg falls into my arms. I let out a sigh of relief to find her breathing and shaking and *alive*.

"Hi, Benny."

She sits across from me, tugging at one of the few pink strands left in her hair. "So…Peter filled you in?"

I nod.

"I guess you have questions?"

"I mean…only if you feel like talking," I say.

"I can't believe you still want to talk to me. After—after everything…" Meg trails off before meeting my eyes and sighing. "So what are your questions?"

"You sure?"

She nods.

"Alright. Well—I'm sorry if this is douche-y, but how—how did you end up here?"

Meg takes a deep breath. "I…sort of tried to kill myself."

She pushes up her sleeves to show me her forearms, which are covered in frantic, deep, red gashes, still pink around the edges.

"Jesus." My voice cracks. "Meg—"

"Yeah, yeah, it was dumb," she says, pulling her sleeves back down. "I honestly don't even know why I did it. You know how much I hate blood. And, like, the second I realized I was bleeding everywhere, I started screaming for Peter. He took me to the ER, and here we are."

"Holy shit."

"So…yeah. Now I'm here."

My stomach buckles. For a second, I'm worried I'm going to freak out—or maybe I should just admit that they're panic attacks—but I stop myself. The turmoil in my body has to go somewhere, so my hands start shaking.

"It's my fault," I say, swallowing the sudden lump in my throat. "I stopped being around for a month, and you almost die—"

"No *way* is it your fault," Meg says with gusto that surprises me. "I was an idiot. You were just living your life, for maybe the first time since we were fourteen. It's not your fault I'm a nutcase."

"Meg, you're not—"

"It's okay, I say it with love," she says, waving her hand.

"I'm sor—"

"Don't be sorry," Meg says, raising a finger like I'm a toddler she's chastising.

"Okay," I mumble, pushing my hair back just to have something to do. "But like…how did I not know any of this? I mean, I know we haven't been talking recently, but…I just feel like I should have sensed it was this bad in March."

"I kind of kept it from you."

"But why?"

Meg sighs. "I should probably start at the beginning."

I tentatively reach out and Meg takes my hand.

"This is going to majorly gross you out, but...I've kind of had a thing for John since we were kids."

"What?" How is *that* the beginning?

"Yeah," says Meg, looking dejected. "It started because he was your cute older brother, but then, after you left for Harvard things kind of changed."

"Changed how?"

"I just... I guess I wasn't prepared for how lonely I'd be when you left for school."

My hand tightens around hers, and Meg must sense how guilty I feel because she just raises her eyebrows warningly.

"I'm not smart like you," she continues when my grip eases. "And I didn't think about what life would be like when my best friend was just gone.

"Then the day after you left, Peter took me with him when he picked up stuff from John, but right after we got to your house, he had a work emergency and had to leave. So John and I were hanging out and drinking and one thing led to another and..."

I really don't want her to finish that sentence. "Wait, that was when I first left for school?"

Meg nods. "John and I have been hooking up for four years."

What. The. *Fuck*.

"It started as just sex...but then it wasn't. I told him how I just never seemed to be able to get my shit together enough to go to college like you did, and how depressed that got me—I mean, a Chinese girl who doesn't make it to college? And he started opening up and told me that he felt like his existence was a mistake. Like he was the trial son until you came along and everyone realized that his sole purpose had been to, like, walk so you could run or something."

Oh my god.

"And John just…got me. In a way no one else did. He didn't try to stop me from feeling like a failure because he felt like one too. And I felt really close to him."

"So…was he your boyfriend?" I make myself ask.

Meg winces. "He didn't want to label it," she mumbles, and I *know* my asshole brother strung her along so he could fuck other people.

Just like Claudio did to Hero for two whole years.

"And I was so psyched that you were coming home for spring break, and then when you did come home, I was trying to get you to figure out that you were into Beatriz. It was obvious from the second she walked into the kitchen."

"Really?"

Meg nods, her eyes bugging out. "Dude, you literally couldn't stop staring at her. And when she'd look at you, I could practically see you shove your armor back on, which you don't do with most girls."

"I don't?"

Meg shakes her head. "I've never seen you care what someone else thinks," she says. "And I've never seen someone stare with so much, like, yearning. It was clear you didn't just want her body, you wanted *her*."

"I know," I mumble.

"Wait, are you guys a thing now?" Meg's mouth drops open.

"Can we get through this part first?" I say quickly.

Meg nods. "Right, sorry. I guess…it just didn't occur to me that you realizing how you felt about her would mean *I* wouldn't see as much of you. I mean, I took my one week of vacation per year during *your* spring break for the sole purpose of hanging out with you."

My gut feels like I just ate a bunch of rotten fish.

"Stop feeling guilty, bro," Meg says.

"Sorry."

"But when you came home in March, John got different. Darker, I guess. And he made me start to resent you. Like, he spun it so that I started to believe you'd moved on from our friendship, and that you never came home for weekends because you had this amazing life and I was just…here. Stuck. And I was going to be stuck forever, working at McDonald's and watching everyone become a real adult. So…that's why I was kind of distant."

I clench my fists under the table. "And what about the whole…Hero thing?"

Meg's face crumples. I reach out and take her hand again.

"I didn't know John was filming. Ow!"

I didn't realize I was squeezing her hand so hard. "Fuck, sorry." I ease up.

"He told me Chinese girls in blond wigs had always been a fantasy of his, and then like halfway through, he started calling me—well, you saw it." Meg is bright red. "And I just— I don't know, I guess I tried to forget about it, but we were really drunk a few nights ago, and I asked him why he'd called me that…"

Meg hunches over, convulsing a little, and I look around, wondering if I should ask someone for help.

"And he told me that since he couldn't have Hero, me in a wig was the next best thing."

Meg is fully crying now, and I have never wanted to kill my brother more. She cries and cries and cries until I get up from my side of the table, sit down beside her and take her in my arms.

"I fucked everything up," she weeps.

I just hold her. The relief of finally understanding what had been going on with Meg floods my body and grapples with unadulterated loathing for John, all of it tied up with the guilt of letting it happen.

When Meg stops crying, she squeezes me once before pulling a Kleenex pack out of her pocket and blowing her nose.

"So, enough about my sob story of a life," she says, shoving her tears away and smiling at me. "Tell me about Beatriz. Glad my meddling paid off."

"Wait, what?"

"Did she not tell you?" Meg looks surprised. "I told her you liked her."

"What! Meg!"

"Sorry, dude, but you're helpless!" Meg holds her hands up in surrender. "I know I shouldn't have, I just…you guys are both so stubborn, and were clearly so into each other, I felt like the only way you'd get over yourselves is if someone shoved you off the cliff. And…I just want you to be happy, Benny."

"Okay…" I swallow my irritation. Meg's right. I wasn't going to do anything about being desperately in love with Beatriz. And even though losing her sucked, I'm still glad I had her at all.

"Um—well—we were sort of together," I say. "And now… we're not."

Meg's eyes widen. "Because of—"

I nod. "I was an idiot and didn't believe her when she said Hero didn't sleep with John, and I said some dumb shit, and she broke up with me. But Meg, I don't want you to think it's your—"

Meg puts her head in her hands. "That's it," she says, sitting up, looking more determined than I've ever seen her. "I'm fucking done with this."

"With what?"

"Drinking, drugs, everything." Her eyes are fierce as they meet mine. "When I'm discharged, I'm going to rehab. I'll give community college another try. I don't care if I fuck up my own life, but it's gone too far now that I've fucked up yours."

"I want you to care if you fuck up yours," I say softly. I didn't realize until now how exhausting it's been being the only one who takes Meg's life seriously. Including herself.

Meg must see this in my face because she softens. "Maybe I'll learn to," she says, hugging me. "I know it doesn't make anything better, but I'm really fucking sorry, Benny."

I squeeze her hand. It's not okay, but I'm going to forgive her. Because Meg is my sister in a way John has never been my brother, and there's no way I couldn't.

"I love you," I say, kissing her head.

"I love you too."

BEATRIZ

Uncle Leo drops us off at school the day before exams start. I felt uneasy the entire ride—Ben didn't call me last night. And I have no idea why.

"I'll be back in a week!" Uncle Leo says, waving through the window.

"Bye, Dad," Hero calls. I wave.

It's so much easier to be on campus after a week at home. I just needed to be in my own bed in my own house with

Uncle Leo's amazing cooking, even if time away hasn't really made the whole Ben situation any clearer.

Hero's eyes are on her phone as we walk, but I keep mine up. Knowing my luck, I'll collide with Ben if my eyes are on my phone, even though Harvard's a huge campus.

I don't see Ben—but I do see Claudio. He's sitting on a bench in the grass near the Johnston Gate, and he looks up as we pass.

Hero's head stays down, and I alter my pace so that even if Hero looks up, she won't see him.

But I'm not prepared for the look on Claudio's face when he sees us. His color drains as he takes in Hero's fishtail braid (which took me thirty minutes), a few blond wisps trailing along her face. He looks like he's been sucker punched. He opens his mouth, but before he can say anything, I shoot him such a malevolent look that he quickly looks away as we walk by.

That shithead doesn't deserve the privilege of speaking to Hero.

When Hero opens the door to our room, something crinkles under the wheels of her bag. "What the hell?"

I follow her gaze, and my heart stops. There's a letter addressed to me on the floor—in Ben's handwriting.

"Oh my god," I say, my breath increasing until it sounds like I'm hyperventilating. I wasn't prepared to see his handwriting—to see any facet of Ben beyond typed words or a disembodied voice on my phone. I wasn't prepared for my stomach to buckle and make it clear that I'm not as chill about this as I thought.

"What?" Hero bends down and picks it up. "Jeez, this is taped on like four sides."

I take a step back as Hero holds it out to me. "I can't."

"Why?" Hero asks as I fumble with the door handle. "Trizita!"

I'm out the door, down the hall and locked in a bathroom stall.

Before I can do more than kneel, the bathroom door opens, and Hero says, "Bea?"

"No."

Hero sighs, and I hear her footsteps approaching. "Given that you just bolted like I have the plague, I assume this is from Ben?"

"Uh, maybe."

"Do you want me to open it?"

I hesitate before saying, "Sure."

I hear Hero rip open the tape and unfurl multiple pieces of paper. *What* could Ben possibly have to say that requires two pieces of paper? Is it a love letter? No way, that's a fucking pipe dream. It's probably Ben explaining that he met someone else, and he didn't want to tell me over text when I might be caught off guard while crossing the street or something. He wanted me to read it in the safety of my own room because he's kind and smart and everything I could ever—

"It's not bad," says Hero's voice from the other side of the stall. I hear her fold up the pieces of paper and watch them slide under the door. "I only read the handwritten one because the other one seemed super private. But I think you should read them."

"You do?"

"Yeah. You'll want to."

I pick them up.

"Probably read the handwritten one first," says Hero. I see her feet back against the wall as the rest of her slides down to sit on the linoleum floor. "I can go if you want. But I kind of assumed you'd want me to stay."

"Thanks." My fingers tremble as I open the handwritten letter.

Beatriz—

I know we only just started talking again, so I'm not even sure if this is cool to say, but I wanted you to know: I know Hero didn't do anything. I don't know all the details yet, but when I figure them out, I can fill you in if you want.

I'm not living with Claudio anymore. When I told him about Hero, he didn't believe me, and I realized I'm done putting up with people who mistreat others. I don't expect this to change anything, but it's important to me that you know how much you've shaped me into who I now want to be. I feel like when this started, I was this stupid, lost boy, and now I'm…well, I'm learning what it actually means to be a man.

I know I hurt you, and I will always be sorry for that. I'm enclosing the following letter, because just in case you have any doubt that I cared about you, or for some reason think you didn't change my life irrevocably…this is something I wrote that day you came into my room and told me about your mom. I've loved you since then, Beatriz. And I think it's likely that I'll love you forever.

Ben

Hold up. Did he say he loves me?
I almost rip the second piece of paper in my haste to open it.

Beatriz,
When we fought last night, I felt like the world was ending. It felt worse than every time I've freaked out. And I couldn't sleep until we were okay again because whenever I closed my eyes, I just saw the look on your face. I've hurt people before, and a lot of the time I didn't care. But seeing that I'd hurt you was different because the way I feel about you is different. I guess I feel like we're two halves from Plato's Symposium—like I've been

*walking around half-complete, not understanding why life felt
so inadequate until I realized it was because you weren't in it.*

*And I don't know why I would feel that way if I wasn't
starting to love you.*

*I honestly have no idea because frankly, before we started doing
this I didn't think love was real. But it wasn't until you kissed me
five days ago that I finally understood Jane Austen. That 'you
must allow me to tell you how ardently I admire and love you'
stopped feeling like the ramblings of a thirsty prick and felt like
the words I'd been searching for since you first walked into my life.
I just want you. All of you. Forever, maybe.*

I read and reread the letter, until I'm forced to accept something I never thought could be true.

Ben loves me.

He's been in love with me—longer than I've been in love with him.

I always figured that on the off chance I fell in love, I would be the person to love more, and I would just have to live with the fact that I would always be loved less. But Ben not only loves me as deeply as I love him, he's loved me for longer.

I know it's not important, but it makes a big difference to me that not only am I loved equally, but I was loved first.

And he *still* loves me.

"He—he believes us," I whisper when I finish the second letter.

"I guess so." Hero's voice is flat.

I unlock the stall door and look at my cousin—the fishtail from this morning now completely undone, Hero halfway through two Dutch braids.

"You okay?" I ask quietly.

Hero shrugs, which makes it look like she's trying to crush

her head between her arms since they're curled above her head as she starts the second braid. "Are *you*? This is much more about you than me."

"How?"

"Because you're the one who has the option of getting back with the guy you love," says Hero, her hands dropping into her lap. "If—if that's what you want."

My heartbeat thunders in my ears.

It *is* what I want.

Because Ben has started to prove that the guy who broke my heart isn't the version of himself he wants to be. That he's capable of not just owning his mistakes, but learning from them.

I still don't know where Ben stands with his family—there's a chance that's still a bomb that could wreck anything beautiful he and I build. But his opinion of Hero is what I care about more. And now that he's done being an idiot, I'm willing to see if we can walk through hell only to come out stronger.

I'm willing to be in love.

I stand. Hero sizes me up for a second, then sighs. "Yeah, go."

"What?"

"Look, I never thought Ben was capable of that," Hero says, nodding at the letter in my hand. "I still don't think he's good enough for you, but…well, I at least no longer think he deserves to die."

I nod. "I—I have to go find him."

"Don't forget a condom."

"Who even are you?"

Hero laughs for the first time in weeks. "Just…cuidate," she says warily as I head for the door.

I nod and tear through campus into Ben's building until I'm in front of his room.

17

BEN

There's a knock at my door. I check my phone. Meg said she would try to visit me if she has time between being discharged from the hospital and starting rehab, but I didn't think I'd see her this soon. I open the door and—

Beatriz is in front of me.

"Hi." My voice cracks. "Um—did you get my—"

"So he really did move out," Beatriz says, her eyes blazing as she looks at me.

"Uh, yeah," I say, drinking her in, in case this is the only chance I get. "Didn't I say that in—"

But my words are lost because Beatriz leaps into my arms, her breath hitching as her lips find mine. Shivers travel up and down my spine before spreading through my whole body.

"Beatriz." I kick the door shut, clutching her so tightly, but it's not tightly enough.

"Ben." Her hands are under my shirt, caressing me like I'm the only thing that matters and I raise my arms above my head. God, I missed touching her. Making love to her over the phone was hot, but it's nothing compared to the fire that ignites when our bodies touch.

We break apart and stare at each other. I know my hair is a mess because Beatriz never leaves it any other way when she's near me, and when I look down, I see her nipples harden under her bra.

"I missed you so fucking much," Beatriz says before kissing me deeply, taking my hands and placing them on her ass. I groan.

"I love you," I say sliding my hands up her back and kissing her neck. Something wet falls into my hair and I look up to see that Beatriz is crying. I hold her face in my hands. "I know I said it in my letter, but I need you to know how much I mean it. I'm sorry for everything," I say, thumbing her tears away as I look into her eyes. "But especially—" my chest constricts but I breathe through it "—I'm so fucking sorry I called you someone else's name the first time we had sex."

Beatriz inhales sharply.

"I know that is, like, the least sexy thing to say right now," I say. "But…it just seemed important. I love you. And I know now that that means owning when I fuck up. And making sure you know that it won't happen again."

Beatriz nods. "…Thank you," she says. She leans up to kiss me, but before she can a fresh wave of tears falls down her face as she cries harder.

"Hey," I say, kissing the tears on her cheeks.

"It's just—no one's told me they lo—that that's how they feel about—"

I pull away so I can look at her vulnerable, beautiful face. "Beatriz. I love you." I nibble the tip of her nose and she giggles. "I love you," I say again, something deepening inside me and I kiss her body more urgently. "I am deeply, enduringly, in love with you."

Beatriz gently pulls my face from her neck and our foreheads touch. "I love you too."

When our lips meet, it's frantic. Beatriz pushes us toward the bed, taking her bra off and guiding my hands to her breasts when we lie down. I need her to understand how much I love her, how much this is more than just sex. How it's *always* been more than just sex.

"I love every part of you," I say, kissing the stretch marks that curve around her breasts. She sighs so softly, I don't know why people describe sex as dirty. Nothing before this moment has ever felt so holy, so pure.

When I flick her nipple with my tongue, she moans, "Get me naked."

I do. Her body is so ready that my hips buck in anticipation. I wrench the rest of my clothes off, making Beatriz gasp in alarm and excitement. I reach under my bed for a condom but she stops me.

"We don't have to—I have an IUD, and if you've been safe, we could…*not* if you want." She looks sheepish and my eyes widen.

"You—you're sure?" She's the only person with whom I've had unprotected sex.

She nods. "I wanna be as close to you as possible."

I inhale. The condom falls to the floor.

"Now," she says desperately.

My hips meet hers, her body opening like it craves me. "*Fuck*, Beatriz."

She's wet as she grips me, moaning as I slide further and further. Everything is heightened. She arches into me, her heels digging into my lower back, and I don't know if it's how I can feel all of her—or the fact that this is the first time we're having sex knowing love is mutual—but I don't feel like I'm on earth anymore. I lose sight of everything that's not the rhythm Beatriz and I make together.

Then she's on the edge and so am I. She flips us over, pinning my hands above my head. Then she stops and looks at me. "What?" I say, remembering the fateful night two months ago when she stared at me in the home theater.

"I just—don't want this to end."

I don't know if she means the sex or us. But I know the answer to both.

"It won't." I thrust upward and Beatriz goes limp with pleasure. I gently tilt us so we're face-to-face, one of her legs between my hip and the bed, the other pulling me toward her so every part of our bodies is flush.

"Deeper," she murmurs. "I'm so close."

"Me too." I push until I can't hold off any longer, and when Beatriz comes apart, I lose myself inside her. Goose bumps flood my body, and I can't believe I've done anything in my life to deserve feeling this good. We breathe heavily, my arms winding around Beatriz as her hands tangle into my hair.

I don't know how long we lie like that.

I know I'm fine on my own—but with Beatriz, I'm infinite.

"You're the love of my life," I whisper, not realizing until I say it how true it is. This woman taught me how to love. How can she *not* be the love of my life?

"You too," Beatriz says, her voice cracking. "It's so fucking scary."

I nod, my cheek rubbing against her forehead as she nuzzles into my neck. "But I still want it."

"Me too."

I smile and raise my head, kissing the bridge of her nose, and Beatriz grabs the Kleenex box as I gently pull out. Once she's clean, Beatriz pulls me to her and kisses every part of me she can see, making me smile and laugh so relentlessly that my face aches because I haven't been this happy in weeks. Maybe my whole life.

We don't put our clothes back on. Instead, I mold my body to Beatriz's and kiss her until the sun's gone down, then I make love to her again, until I realize I'm hungry.

"What time is it?" I ask groggily, opening my eyes when we're done and surprised to find it's dark.

Beatriz reaches for her shorts and checks her phone. "Like ten."

"Are you hungry?" I ask. "I know some of the dining halls have cereal out all night."

"I am, but putting on clothes sounds like so much effort."

"Do you—" My stomach won't stop squirming around the question I want to ask. "I mean…are you gonna go back to your room before tomorrow?"

"Um, no." Beatriz sounds like I could not have asked a stupider question. I can't stop smiling.

"Want some ramen?"

"Sounds perfect."

Beatriz slides out of bed and pulls my sweatshirt on as I make ramen in the microwave.

"Is there something wrong with *your* shirt?" I say, raising my eyebrows at her.

"I just really missed how you smell," Beatriz says meekly, looking down like I'd find this embarrassing instead of invigorating.

"Then wear that all week, if you want."

Beatriz smiles and wraps her arms around my stomach as I sit next to her, putting the bowls of ramen on the floor. I kiss her forehead before I hand her a bowl.

"Cheers, mate," she says, blowing on the soup.

"Oh…speaking of, like, British stuff," I say after she's taken a few bites. "Um—kind of a lot of shit went down with Meg." She looks up at me, panicked, and I say quickly, "She's alive and well, don't worry. But she might not be your favorite person anymore."

"Why?"

I tell her everything: why Meg started using, the fact she's been in love with John, and the worst part—that it was Meg in the video, unintentionally posing as Hero.

I expected Beatriz to be livid with Meg, to start yelling about how much she hates her the same way she did with Claudio, but she doesn't. Instead, Beatriz's eyes go wide. She puts down her soup, ducks under my arm so I'm holding her, and spreads kisses across my collarbone.

"I'm so sorry," she says, placing one last kiss on my chin before meeting my eyes. "You must feel fucking awful."

"Aren't you mad?"

Beatriz sits up and looks confused. "Why would I be mad?"

"Because it's Meg's fault that Hero had to go through all that."

"Um, no it's not," says Beatriz. "It's *Claudio's* fault. He's the one who broke her heart without hearing her side of it. And it's not Meg's fault she fell into a manipulative relationship with the world's biggest cunt, who took advantage of how depressed she was. None of this is Meg's fault—like, at all."

A tide of relief rushes through me. I was worried this would drive us apart again, that Beatriz would be angry that another person I love had hurt someone she loved.

"I'm so relieved," I say, my voice breaking. "I—I was scared I'd lose you again."

Beatriz shakes her head. "I don't have it in me to lose you again."

★ ★ ★

The next day, I'm reading on my bed while I wait for Claudio to come by for the rest of his stuff. He texted me earlier telling me when he would—probably so I'd be out of the room—but I have to give him something. Meg wrote him a letter in one of her hospital therapy sessions and wanted me to pass it on.

"In case he has trouble believing it," she'd said.

Claudio looks surprised when he opens the door and sees me lying there. "Uh…hi."

"Hey," I say, sitting up and hopping off the bed.

"I assumed you'd be…not here," says Claudio, putting down the empty boxes in his arms and shoving clothes inside.

"I had to give you this." I grab Meg's letter from my desk and hand it to him.

"The fuck is it?" Claudio reaches out gingerly, like the letter's going to burn him.

"Meg wanted me to give it to you."

Claudio freezes, his hands on the envelope. I let go and start to leave.

"Hey, wait."

I turn.

"You wanna…hang while I read it?"

"Okay." I'll be honest, I'm dying to see Claudio's reaction to Meg's confession. Maybe we could be friends again. But if he acts like it changes nothing, I'll know for sure that Claudio's become someone I can't have in my life.

Claudio sits down on what used to be his bed as I collapse onto mine. He opens the letter and starts reading, growing paler and paler every second.

"No," he says, his voice cracking. "Christ—fuck—WHAT—no!"

"Yeah, my brother's one impressive shit," I say. I have no

idea what the letter says, but I assumed Meg outlined everything that had happened.

"What did I do, what did I do, what did I *do*," Claudio says frantically, jumping to his feet and pacing. *This* was the reaction I'd been expecting when I got off the phone with Peter. It's just too late.

"You fucked up."

Claudio looks at me, panic-stricken. "So…none of it was real?"

"I mean, John really was fucking someone who looked like Hero, but apart from that, it was all bullshit," I say. "She didn't cheat on you—like, at all."

"Cazzo! Ammazza!" Claudio yells, punching the wall above his desk and immediately yelping.

I sigh and get up. "Let me see."

Claudio's hand looks fine—no blood or bruises, just red from the impact. I open the small freezer compartment on our mini fridge and hand Claudio an ice pack.

"Thanks," Claudio mutters, taking it from me and putting it on his hand.

I sit on my bed again, watching Claudio. I can practically see the horror churning through his head as he realizes he has no one to blame but himself. It's a horror I recognize because I felt it only days ago.

And maybe that's why I'm able to say, "You alright, man?"

"I mean, no. I—I ditched Hero because—I dunno, because I couldn't see through everything I was feeling, and I let jealousy and betrayal outdo logic or something. I mean, I had a *ring,* for Christ's sake." He opens the drawer to his desk and pulls out a tiny black box. "And now I just—what the fuck do I do?"

"I mean, what do you wanna do?"

"I want her back," says Claudio. "If she really didn't do

anything, then there's no reason we couldn't be together. I still want to marry her."

"Uh—"

"What?"

"Dude, you *hurt* her," I say. "Like—really fucking bad. Have you seen her at all since you guys broke up?"

Claudio doesn't say anything.

"She's not the same," I continue. "Like, she's doing okay because she's a badass, but she's different now. If you deserve to be with her again, you have to acknowledge that and make sure she knows you won't do it again."

Claudio looks at me. "When did *you* become the therapist?"

I shrug. "A lot of shit's gone down that's made me reevaluate, just…everything. I don't know, I guess I have more clarity."

"Are you back with Beatriz?"

When I nod, Claudio's eyes go wide.

We officially got back together after our ramen, when we were tangled up in my bed again. It was a hard conversation because we had to talk about…a lot of tricky shit. Like the fact that in a few days, I'll start a job that makes her uncomfortable and move into an apartment hours away from where she lives. And that even though we want to be in a relationship, Beatriz doesn't feel safe coming to my house anymore, not with John or my parents there.

And while it sucks and my instinct is to be mad, I get it. The world I come from values money over her human rights, and my brother traumatized her cousin in a way that also broke us up.

Frankly, I'm not sure *I* want to go ahead with the life I always planned.

But if the last two months have taught me anything, it's how to recognize love that's conditional. My dad values me *if* I make him proud. But Beatriz just values me. Even after I hurt her, she loved me enough to work through it and take me back. And I'd be the biggest idiot in the world to prioritize the former after having the latter.

"Fuck," Claudio says, putting his head in his hands. "Just… fuck."

I pat his shoulder and start to leave.

"Wait." I turn as Claudio gets up. "I'm—sorry," he mumbles.

"For what?"

Claudio closes his eyes like he can't believe I'm making him say it. "For…being shitty to you. And calling your girlfriend a bitch."

"I mean, you shouldn't not call her that *just* because she's my girlfriend," I say, annoyed.

"I know," Claudio says. "I know…"

"So…what are you gonna do?" I ask. I meant what I said to Beatriz about not putting up with people who mistreat others. And I need to know if Claudio measures up.

"Talk to Hero," he says, running his hand through his hair. "Explain. Apologize. Tell her—I dunno. Tell her something."

I clap him on the shoulder again. "Just…try to make it right."

BEATRIZ

Hero doesn't respond when I tell her the truth about the video, which is how I know she's reeling.

"Wow," she finally says. "That's some creative bullshit he pulled."

I don't know how to respond. I've never seen Hero so down that she copes with dark humor. That's more my thing.

"Are you okay?"

"I...don't know," she says, tugging at her fingers. "It is nice to finally understand what the fuck happened. But... that's kind of it," she says, looking up at me. "Like, I don't want him back."

"I mean, that shouldn't even be on the table unless he apologizes."

Hero nods. "But even if he does—I don't know, Trizita. How do you move on from something like this?" She looks up at me. "Like, I can't really look up 'healthiest way to patch up a relationship that ended because an asshole pretended to shoot porn with you.'"

"Yeah."

"Fuck this," Hero says quietly.

"Fuck...what?" I ask.

"Everything. I thought I had everything figured out—I had the guy, I had the job, and now I just...don't know what to do."

I hug her. "You'll be living at home, right?"

She nods, her face tightening. I'm about to ask why when there's a knock on the door.

I glance at my phone, surprised. Ben said he would come by to hang out after his final, but his final only started forty-five minutes ago. I know he's smart, but—

When I open the door to see Claudio standing there, he looks so ashamed that it's the only reason I don't punch him on sight. "Is, uh—is Hero here?"

I glance over my shoulder to see that Hero's gone white. But she's standing and walking toward the door.

"Hi," she says, her face blank.

"Hi." Claudio's voice shakes. "Can I, uh, talk to you?"

Hero hesitates before nodding slowly.

"I'll, um...go do something," I say, grabbing my phone and

walking out the door. I slide down against the wall next to our room because I really want to hear how the fuck Claudio's going to defend himself or apologize for all the ways he fucked up.

"What are you doing?"

I jump and look up to see Ben grinning down at me. Oh my god, he's so hot, even in sweats.

"You're done already?" I whisper, pulling him down next to me.

"Yeah, I'm a genius," he whispers back. I shove him and he chuckles.

Claudio is in there, I mouth. Ben's eyes go wide. He crawls over to the door and presses his ear against it.

He's my favorite person.

He beckons and I kneel beside him. We must look ridiculous.

"I know I fucked up," I hear Claudio say.

Hero responds, "Well, yeah," and then says something unintelligible.

Claudio's voice wavers as he says, "I can't believe I did that, I don't know what came over me to let it happen—"

Hero interrupts to say, "Is your way of apologizing really to blame it on some otherworldly presence, pendejo?"

Ben and I look at each other in surprise. Hero sounds like *me*.

"I haven't slept in weeks," Claudio says, so desperately I almost feel bad for him.

"That's not my problem."

I grind my teeth when I hear Claudio say, "Isn't it enough that I still love you?"

Hero's voice quakes as she yells back, "No!"

I know she's about to cry, and Claudio's voice cracks as he says, "Just tell me what I can do to make it better."

"Nothing!" yells Hero. "You broke my heart and abandoned me when I tried to tell you I didn't deserve to be in pieces!"

And now Claudio is fully crying as he says, "I'm sorry, I'm so sorry, I really am, I wish I could go back and undo it."

And Hero says, "But you can't, and I don't trust you anymore," and I hear them both sobbing. Then everything is quiet.

Ben shoots me a confused look and presses his ear harder against the door. Then his face falls, and he scoots away as fast as he can. And in a second, I know why—Hero and Claudio are having passionate sex.

"Well, that was…something," Ben says, as we close the hallway door.

"But…Hero's never had sex," I say, trying to wrap my mind around what just happened. I heard Hero moaning, which is the only reason I didn't barge in there out of fear that Claudio was assaulting her.

"What?" Ben's mouth falls open as we step outside. "But—how?"

I laugh. "Not everyone is ready at fifteen, dude."

"I—but—still, that's weird."

"I mean, not really," I say, taking his hand. "Hero likes to be in control of everything, to the point where she doesn't enter situations if she can't see the outcome. I can't think of anything that makes you feel *more* out of control than great sex."

"I guess that's fair."

I don't say anything as we cross campus, until we've made our way to Ben's room.

"You okay?" he asks, putting an arm around my waist and kissing the top of my head.

"You know, I feel like our relationships are kind of inverses of each other," I say as Ben opens the door to his room.

"What do you mean?"

"Like, Hero and Claudio had this perfect beginning where everything fell into place, and you and I…"

"Really fucking didn't?"

I laugh and nod. "And like…everything about them was out of a rom-com, but now—"

"We're really fucking happy and they're kind of a mess?"

"Exactly. I'm worried, though." I pull at my fingers.

"Yeah?" Ben pulls me onto the couch, taking both my hands and kissing every one of my fingers.

I smile, putting my legs across his lap. "I don't want them to get back together."

"It's not really up to us."

"I just don't ever want Hero to get hurt again."

"I know, love. But sometimes hurt can help you grow, right? I mean, look at us."

Hero's hair is freshly washed when I come back from hanging out with Ben. Claudio is gone.

"Hey," I say softly, closing the door behind me. Hero looks up, her face impassive. "Uh—you okay?"

Hero looks at the floor. "I fucked him," she says softly.

My mouth falls open. Hero has only ever referred to sex as "getting cozy" or "hooking up" or "sleeping together."

"Did you want to?"

Hero nods. "I actually really did. It was weird."

"Oka-a-y," I say slowly, sitting at Hero's feet. I glance up at her laptop and see her staring at a document titled "Final Art History Essay," but no words are on the screen. "So… you guys are back together, then?" I try to keep the trepidation from my voice.

Hero's face crumples, and she buries her face in her hands. "No."

"Wait, what? But—but you *slept* with him. And—you're you!"

"I know." Hero's voice breaks. "I'm so stupid, I'm so fucking stupid. He was here, and I was mad, and then it was just happening, and I missed him so much, but when it was done I realized he hasn't changed, and so it's over." She says the last part with ringing finality as she looks at me.

"What do you mean, he hasn't changed?" I ask.

Hero sighs. "Remember when he and I went away for a weekend a few weeks after we got back from spring break?"

I nod, remembering how Ben and I didn't leave his room the entire two days.

"We went home so he could meet Dad," Hero says, not noticing that my eyes bulge. "So Claudio could…ask permission, or whatever."

I grit my teeth. "The fuck did Leo say?"

Hero sighs. "He told him it was my decision. But if it was what I wanted, he'd support us. But while we were there," Hero says, biting her lip, "we…signed a lease on an apartment in Hadley."

My jaw drops. *"What?"*

Hero grimaces. "Yeah…we were gonna move in after graduation to plan the wedding, it just made sense. And that way he could get to know Amherst and Dad, and it just seemed right."

"O-okay," I say trying to keep up.

"And so just now after we had sex," Hero continues, braiding her wet hair, "he asked if I'd thought anymore about what color couch we should get for the living room and I told him we weren't moving in together, and he said…" Hero drops the braid and shuts her eyes. "And he said he assumed we'd just moved up the wedding night."

"WHAT."

"And I told him we *weren't* getting married, and he got

upset, and I told him to never talk to me again. It's really over," she repeats, her voice cracking. "I'm done with him."

Hero starts crying, her body shaking and her voice ringing, and I want to kill Claudio. But that won't make Hero better. What will make Hero better is holding her as she cries and doing everything I can to help her through it.

So I put my arms around my prima until her crying subsides.

"I really am sorry," I say quietly. "I—this is just so—"

Hero waves her hand, saying a little too sharply, "It's fine. This way I can focus on my apprenticeship. And help you figure out what you wanna do," she says, smiling at me with too much enthusiasm.

"Actually, I…think I might know," I say, sitting down at my desk.

Hero's face slips but she quickly rearranges it. "That's great! What is it?"

"I think I want to become a therapist."

I go to Ben's room after my last exam. He just had his first ever therapy appointment. After the hot mess of the past three months, even he couldn't deny he really needed it, and I'm dying to know how it went.

"What's up?" I kiss him as the door opens. "Was therapy alright?"

He nods, but his jaw is tight.

"You okay?"

Ben closes the door and says nothing, just holds out his phone.

Ben: I can't start work Monday.

Dad: Your jokes do not translate over the phone, Benedick.

313

Ben: I'm not joking.

Dad: Well, you're sure as hell not serious.

Ben: I'm sorry.

Dad: Did Meg put you up to this?

Ben: What are you talking about?

Dad: There was an apparent miscommunication between your brother and herself to which she is overreacting. And before you deny it, may I remind you that we must support each other as a family.

Ben: Do you really mean that? About supporting each other?

Dad: This is tiresome, Ben. I have work to do.

Ben: I don't want to work in finance.

Dad: Excuse me?

Ben: Can I call you? There's some stuff I need to say.

Dad: Benedick, if you are serious about throwing your life away there is nothing more to be said. Might I remind you that you have no skills to make a living elsewhere. Your mother and I have worked hard to give you everything you could possibly want and it's still not enough. If I don't see you on Monday, don't bother coming around at all. I didn't raise sons who refuse to be men. You disappoint me once again.

"WHAT?" I stare at the phone in disbelief.

Ben shrugs but his lip is quivering.

"Hey," I say, putting his phone on the desk and my hands on his shoulders. Ben doesn't look at me.

"You know you *are* a man, right?" I say, running my thumb along his twitching cheek. "Like, more than any other guy I've met."

"How?" Ben's voice cracks with restrained tears.

"This," I say, gesturing to his phone. "Could you have said that a few months ago?"

Ben slowly shakes his head.

"You're willing to grow," I say. "*That's* the difference between a boy and a man, and if your dad doesn't know that, it's his fucking problem. Besides, do you know how incredible a cis white guy has to be for me to be like, 'yeah, that's my person'?"

Ben snorts, his face still strained.

"Want me to castrate your dad?" I ask. "He *is* a Trump voter—"

Ben inhales to speak, and it's like his breath hits a dam in the back of his throat. I stand there as he bursts into tears.

"What am I going to do?" He wheezes. I remember how embarrassed he was the first time he broke down in front of me. But now Ben cries unabashedly, his hands flying to his face to wipe away tears, not to hide them from me.

I step toward him, and Ben leans into me as I struggle to get my arms across his broad shoulders. He snorts.

"Need any help?" he asks, smirking through his tears. "Should I get shorter?" He bends his knees, and I playfully shove him, making him laugh. I start to pull away, saying, "Fine, I won't, then," but Ben's arms tighten around me and I hold him close.

"I have nothing," he says quietly after his tears have subsided. "We have to be off campus *tomorrow* and I—I'm not allowed home."

With a jolt, I remember what Ben told me a few days ago—how he'd never tried therapy out of fear he'd be disowned. How that's exactly what just happened—but Ben is still here.

He chose us over his family. No, not just us—he chose himself.

I curl him into my body as his tears fall down my neck.

"I'm just...powerless." He reaches for a tissue and blows his nose. "And that's exactly what they wanted."

I cock my head to one side.

"They always intended for my only choices to be 'do what we say' or 'have no way to live,'" he says, turning to face me. "My dad has a point—I *don't* have any life skills because they never showed me how. I was never shown where the laundry room was in my own house, I've never seen a job application. I was just never taught how to be independent because the continuation of my parents' wealth relies on me being *de*pendent. Dependent on them, on the money, on a community that has always discouraged me from being myself."

I take his hand.

"So when, for the first time, I tell my dad I might want something different, I—I'm told—"

This man is soft in every way that matters and was bullied until he only recognized himself as hard.

"I love you," I blurt. "I—you are so important to me, Ben. I have no idea what to do right now because this whole thing is outrageous, but all I can think about is how proud I am of you, and—just—I'm not going anywhere," I finish, breathing heavily.

Ben is still for a moment. For a second, I'm scared I've made a horrible mistake but then Ben kisses me with so much passion, we fall over, landing on the couch. He grinds down into me and my legs are spreading and there's no piece of him that I don't want.

"I believe you," Ben says, desperately pushing his hands up my thighs.

We shed our clothes. This feels like consummation. This feels like building a new future.

I didn't think it was possible to love Ben because of where he came from, and he felt the same way about me. But that's because we mistook where we're from for who we are.

I hold him when we're done, stroking the back of his neck. Ben snuggles closer.

"Ben?" I whisper. He pulls his head up.

"Yeah?"

"Come home with me."

Ben freezes. "…Seriously?"

I nod. "You need a place to dump your shit so RAs don't yell at you tomorrow. And next week, if you want, I can help you figure something out."

Ben pulls me to him. I kiss his temple.

"You know," Ben says later when I'm helping him sort clothes into boxes. "Claudio mentioned something about having an apartment. Maybe I could ask if he needs a roommate." But his forehead is wrinkled.

"Do you want to live with Claudio?" I ask.

"I'm not sure," Ben says, carefully folding some shirts. "He's…trying."

I frown. "What do you mean?"

"I know he's got some issues, but he's trying to be a better person. We talked before he talked to Hero."

I raise my eyebrows. "Really?"

"Yeah. Meg wrote him a letter in one of her therapy sessions and she wanted him to have it."

"What did it say?"

Ben shrugs. "I didn't read it. But given Claudio's reaction, I'm assuming she broke down everything John did so it was clear Hero did nothing wrong."

"What was Claudio's reaction?"

"Punching a wall."

I laugh. Ben just looks at me.

"Wait, seriously?"

He nods.

"Christ," I say, folding some polos. "Did he say anything?"

"Yeah, he apologized to me for some dumb shit he said after I found out what John did. And he said he'd try to make it right with Hero. I'm just not sure if he actually did or not."

"I mean, she doesn't want to get back together with him. So that kind of answers that."

Ben is silent for a moment. Then he looks at me. "What do you want me to do?"

I inhale. This is it—the moment for me to tell him that I want him to shun Claudio and never talk to him again. To tell him that to do right by me, he can't be friends with Claudio.

"It's up to you, babe," I say, standing on tiptoe to kiss his cheek. "I have my issues with Claudio, that's obvious—but I know he was your best friend. So it's not really my place to tell you what to do."

"I mean, I'm not sure I want to be friends again."

"That's fine too. I just wanted you to know that if you feel okay enough about Claudio to live with him, you and I will be okay. It actually might be convenient for us to have a place to have sex that isn't my childhood bedroom."

Ben laughs. "And I'd get to see you over the summer."

I grin at him. "*And* that gives us time to figure out...us, post-graduation. I mean if—that's something you want."

Ben looks blankly at me. "Of course it's what I want," he

says, incredulous. "I've been in love with you since you told me Jack Kerouac was a twat."

I burst out laughing.

Ben walks over to me. "Look, I—I can't really picture myself getting married. Or passing my genes to the next generation. At least, not yet. But I *really* can't picture a version of my life where you're not my best friend." He engulfs me in his arms. "I want this. I want us."

I wrap my arms around his neck and whisper, "I want us too."

★ ★ ★ ★ ★

AUTHOR NOTE

*Historical note: I took artistic license with two historical details in this novel—1) Greta Thunberg did not rise to global prominence until 2018, and 2) By March 2017, the Oscars had already taken place. If there are any facts that I unintentionally fudged, sorryyyyyyy.

This book is set a few months before the Harvey Weinstein story broke, and #metoo was birthed. It starts a few months after DACA was rescinded, and kids who are American in every way except legality were deported from the country. It begins at the precipice of the worst presidency in American history. And it's how I processed living through everything that happened since 2016.

I wrote the entirety of *Ben and Beatriz* in COVID-19 quarantine. I wasn't working, and I needed to cope with hardship through art. The power of creativity has never been more underrated than during times of crisis—when the world is horrifyingly spinning out of control, and there is *literally* nothing you can do, turning that fraught, frightened energy into something beautiful (or just something that YOU have control over) can be the only way to get through it. Art is how I've lived through things I was sure would kill me. Because creativity is not just a pastime, but a lifeline.

When COVID hit, I had been querying a different novel for six years—a novel that I wrote before, during and after I was diagnosed with PTSD, depression and anxiety, and a story in which I started to grapple with my history of child abuse and trauma. SHOCKINGLY, a tragic novel about super sad shit wasn't enticing in an era where the president was traumatizing people every day. Once I accepted that it wasn't that novel's time, I turned to an idea I'd had a year previous—an idea that hatched while I drunkenly watched my favorite production of *Much Ado About Nothing* starring David Tennant and Catherine Tate. The 80s beach villa set of that *Much Ado* shifted into a spring break sojourn to a mansion of New England WASPs. The "merry war" betwixt Benedick and Beatrice transformed into a forbidden attraction kept at bay by the ingrained prejudices of race and class.

I thought about the racism I had faced at the hands of my own WASP family. The entitled snubs I encountered from the boomer patrons at the bookshop where I worked, in the same town where I attended prep school. The racism that was not just disheartening, but *nauseating*. Nauseating to have boomers recommend books to me because "you're related" to an author I've never heard of who has curly brown hair, brown skin and curves; to have old white men shake their car keys in my face and "jokingly" say to the only POC working in the store, "I don't suppose you have a valet service to fetch my car. What happened to the good old days?" To have my own white relatives make it clear I had to choose between being white and being a person of color, acting as if that request was not only reasonable but possible.

Once I realized that my dream of becoming a published

author would not be accomplished with a book about tragedy in a time when people desperately need comedy, I opened my laptop in April of 2020, and wrote like a demon until a full draft of *Ben and Beatriz* was finished in July. I shocked myself with how the words poured out, with the fact that I was writing steadily for eight to twelve hours a day as I melded fiction with both my own experiences, and a Shakespearean story that I know so well.

By the end of August 2020—after six years of trying and failing with my tragic novel, and five weeks of querying *Ben and Beatriz*—I had signed with a literary agent. I don't tell this story to be all, LOOK AT ME, I'M A WRITING GENIUS, I CAN WRITE A WHOLE BOOK IN EIGHT WEEKS WHEN IT TAKES LESSER MORTALS YEARS! Because HA, that's so far from the truth it's not even funny. I spent eight years working on the tragedy I wrote before *Ben and Beatriz*, and it's still unfinished. Honestly, if/when I go back to it I will probably rewrite the whole thing from scratch. I include this information because the velocity at which I wrote *Ben and Beatriz,* and the speed at which it made its way to you guys, is fucking insane— it is *insane* what can happen when you calm the negative self-talk in your mind telling you you're shit, sit down and *just write*.

Writing saved me. *Art* saved me. *Ben and Beatriz* distracted me during a time I desperately needed it, while also allowing me to process past anger that I needed to sift through. I wrote it to recover from growing up in a world much like Ben's where it was made clear that I would always be second class because of my gender and skin color. At a time when I couldn't see my friends, I could write about other people seeing their friends; about young people living together, falling in love and meandering around Harvard Square with no masks on because in their world, all that mattered was the story.

If you also have an itch to create, listen to it. Fuck your parents for telling you that art can't be a career; fuck the friends who mock you if you're not good at something the first time you try it; and fuck ANYONE who makes you feel bad for something that makes you feel good (unless it's harassment or murder, don't do that). Make things that no one else will see; like the embarrassing time I wrote a third-season-fanfiction of *Fleabag* because Phoebe Waller-Bridge destroyed me to the point where I was getting acne breakouts from stress over how unresolved (but fucking brilliant) the end of that show was. And those breakouts didn't go away until I sat down at my computer and finished the story. No one has ever read the five episodes I wrote (except someone who PWB also destroyed, and my husband because he's funnier than I am and helped with the comedy bits), and I wrote with that intention. I wrote them not for acclaim or production or publication, but because *I* needed to. I needed to finish a story the way Beethoven got off his deathbed to resolve a chord progression someone else played on the piano. I had an itch that made my life worse until I listened to it, and when I did, my life became infinitely better.

If you have that itch too, listen to it. Make something for *yourself*, and fuck what anyone else says. It's an itch that, if scratched, might just save your life. It definitely saved mine.

To quote the great Stephen Sondheim:

"Anything you do,
Let it come from you.
Then it will be new.
Give us more to see…"

All the love I have in the world,

Katalina

ACKNOWLEDGMENTS

I wouldn't be me if something I wrote wasn't twice as long as it needed to be. SO HERE WE GO.

Firstly, thank you to my incredible agent, Larissa Melo Pienkowski, and everyone at Jill Grinberg Literary Management. Larissa, thank you for knowing when to push me and when to tell me to calm the fuck down. You are not only fucking great at the agenting side of your job (which I could never do), but you're also a dream writing partner and truly remarkable human being. I look forward to a long, fruitful partnership. ☺

To my editor, Brittany Lavery, and everyone at Graydon House. Thank you for taking a chance on this book, for believing in the power it could have and making this little nerd's dream come true. To the ridiculously talented Bokiba for so perfectly and specifically capturing the heart of the story in its cover. To Carolina Beltran at WME for not giving up on this story, and for working as hard as you do to get Latinx stories told.

I wouldn't be the amateur Shakespeare scholar I am were it not for the incredible teachers and theatre directors who recognized the kinship I felt with the Bard, and did everything they could to feed it. Thank you to David R. Gammons and Jennie Israel for seeing in me an early hunger for Shakespeare and giving me every possible opportunity to nurture it. To Spiro Veloudos for telling me to never apologize for being smart when sixteen-year-old me felt like knowing too much about Shakespeare's sonnets was shameful. It was the first time anyone told me I was smart. To this day when I start to doubt myself I remember you pulling me aside and saying, "Never apologize for being smart. You're not starting to yet, but just make sure you don't."

To Peter Carey and everyone at Lyric First Stage for casting me as Rosalind in *As You Like It* when I was seventeen, and for making it clear that this was something I was good at when I truly believed I was shit at everything.

To Nick Walton and the Shakespeare Birthplace Trust—I would not love Shakespeare as much as I do, nor would I have come to understood how much I needed him in my life, were it not for you. Thank you for giving me the tools to unlock his words and inhabit his world. I don't think I will ever have the words to say how grateful I am, or articulate how much your education and encouragement shaped me into who I've become.

Thanks to the Royal Shakespeare Company for blowing my teenage mind and showing me that Shakespeare's stories are truly timeless, and that the true joy and excitement of Shakespeare Study comes from conceiving and adapting his stories in ways that seem impossible. AND THAT THE OPTIONS ARE ENDLESS!

To Josie Rourke for directing her inimitable vision of *Much Ado About Nothing,* and David Tennant and Catherine Tate for being my ONLY Beatrice and Benedick (fuck you, Branagh). If any of you nerds are reading these acknowledgments (because I am definitely a nerd who reads all the acknowledgments), go find the Tennant and Tate production of *Much Ado* on Digital Theatre and watch it now. It was the production that inspired this novel.

To the great Sir Jonathan Bate for being my favorite Shakespeare scholar, and for writing the introductions to all the RSC editions of Shakespeare's plays as well as *The Genius of Shakespeare*—an insightful work that blew my mind as to what kind of analysis Shakespeare's work could fodder, but also one that taught me how to structure a boss-ass paragraph.

To Josh Funk for pushing me to keep writing, and for answering my questions about the query process. There were moments when I wanted to give up, but your words of wisdom and insight into the industry were always enough to help me keep going. Many thanks to Abigail Ory for answering my ENDLESS Harvard questions, and to Laura Duncan for critiquing my query and sample pages.

To Tara for being equally as excited as me throughout the *Ben and Beatriz* process, and for being the only other person in my life whose idea of a fun night in is reading *The Origins of Totalitarianism* while drinking blackberry cider. And also for giving incredibly detailed feedback on the manuscript that gave it the last push it needed to be where it is today. Your friendship and intellectual companionship means so much to me. You came back into my life when I needed it most and I can't tell you how glad I am that you did.

To my therapist, for effectively saving my life. I know you would say that you didn't save my life, but instead gave me tools and I saved my own life, and that is true. But I still would not be where I am if I hadn't walked into your office and you told me I had PTSD, sticking by me through the horrendous diagnosis and recovery. Therapists do not come in a more valiant shade than you.

My mother—Mami, thank you for always doing the best you could and for being the only person I could count on throughout my childhood. We were dealt a pretty shitty hand, but we've come out of it closer, healthier and with a firm understanding of how to break the abuse cycle. Thank you for loving me unconditionally, and always supporting me, even when it was hard. I love you.

My stepfather—Julian, thank you for being my number one fan since I was fifteen, and eagerly reading anything I wrote, even when it was homework. Having such an excited fan in the house encouraged me to keep going more than I think I know. I love you.

My family—Andrea, Jeff, Scott and Linda. Thank you for welcoming me into your family and making your home the kind of oasis I never had growing up. The main reason COVID sucked so much was because we couldn't come to Amherst once a month. And Andrea, thanks for asking to read literally every draft of *Ben and Beatriz* upon hearing I'd finished a revision. It really made me feel appreciated and loved.

Tyler—my life partner, my Ben (even though you could not be more different). I could learn every language known to woman and *still* have no words to articulate how much you mean to me. Thank you for all the times you (sometimes literally) picked me up off the floor as I cried that I would never make it; for sticking by me through my trauma recovery, even when we were on different continents; and for coming downstairs in the middle of the night and telling me to go to bed after writing for twelve hours. I love you with so much of my heart that none is left to protest.

And lastly, to the mastermind Billy Shakes himself—I'm pretty sure you were an asshole, but *man* did you get human nature. Thank you for giving me skin to inhabit, and words to understand myself during my darkest times, as well as teaching me that there is no exhilaration more epic than an obsession with words.